He came to me in the ni₁

I stood by the bay w clients left, searching the qu not identify, with a yearning I dared not name. By a cool stir—a velvety smoothness to the darkness, I sensed his ghostly presence. His hunger was crackling energy, my appetite whetted by remembrance, his by what forces of denials endured—for how long, I could not fathom, yet his touch was thistledown—a hand wafted over my shoulder caused my skin to vibrate and tiny down on my arms to lift, as if a storm raged outside, in place of inside me.

Iron bars clamped my body to his, back to chest. He bent his head to my neck with no ceremony or gentleness, his want fueling his kisses, biting my ears, brushing his rasping jaws against my enflamed cheeks as he searched my mouth. *"Don't say no. Don't. I cannot..."*

He left the plea unfinished in a strangled moan as he gripped my hair, thrusting strong fingers through tangled curls and, turning me, held my face in a vise. *"I tried to stay away."*

I could no more resist than stop a gully-washer rushing down a ravine.

I felt myself lifted, floating in unyielding arms as he wafted me to bed.

Praise for Sharon Shipley and…

SARY'S GOLD, which won Pipeline into Motion Pictures' Grand Prize for the script and is also a stand-alone novel, the first, in "Love, Lust, and Peril: Sary's Adventure Series." It also shortlisted as Best Western in The Chanticleer International Book Awards.

Also by Sharon Shipley and published by The Wild Rose Press, Inc. are *SARY'S DIAMONDS*, an African adventure, and *SARY AND THE MAHARAJAH'S EMERALDS*, love and lust in torrid India, and *DANFORTH THE DRAGON*, a children's book.

The Wylder Ghost
and
Blossom Cherry

by

Sharon Shipley

The Wylder West

The Wylder Ghost and Blossom Cherry

Cover Art by *Diana Carlile*

The Wild Rose Press, Inc.
PO Box 708
Adams Basin, NY 14410-0708
Visit us at www.thewildrosepress.com

Publishing History
First Edition, 2022
Trade Paperback ISBN 978-1-5092-4058-6
Digital ISBN 978-1-5092-4059-3

The Wylder West
Published in the United States of America

Dedication

For my other gun-slinging Range Rider, Skip

Prologue

The young girl with tiny breast buds just poking her thin scrap of a dress tumbled off the empty mail car, barely able to stand on Wylder station's splintery gray platform, hot under her bare feet. Frail from deprivation during the month it took her to arrive, still her dirty face held a nascent loveliness of the beauty she was to become—luminous green eyes wary and enormous in the thin, grimy face that had begun the journey with the plumpness of youth—pointy chin, slightly pug nose, and a too-full mouth were framed in a tangled wilderness of red-gold hair.

She looked across and beheld the faded sign… *Longhorn Saloon…*

Chapter One

Six Years Later

I reckon I fell in love with every John, Dick, and Harry…

Sorry.

Madame Solange doesn't like me to call 'em that. Customer, guest, gentleman caller—*that's a hoot*—client, or john. I've heard them all. Yet we're just a bunch of like-minded gals who work above the Longhorn Saloon, tossed here like tumbleweed by the fickle winds of bad fortune. Howsomever, I've always been hot as a biscuit in *that* department anyhow, so it suits me well.

I like to call them—lovers. For while they're with me, they think they're in love, though I have no illusions. Personally, I think some men suppose squeaking bedsprings *is* a love song, and they don't never want it to quit.

Madame Solange—her real name's Sadie Bloomer, no relation to the other Bloomers in Wylder—likes to call us a "brothel" and aspires someday to be as highfalutin as the Wylder County Social Club acrost town. I suspect she used to be a soiled dove herself. She's from New Orleans and has airs, but this is new territory, and she can call herself Queen Victoria or Annie Oakley—or anything she warrants—for all anyone cares in Wylder, Wyoming, the year of 1884.

Mr. Levi Gruenvald, Longhorn's owner, turns a blind eye, still not sure he wants a whorehouse upstairs, but he sure cottons to the extra traffic, and we girls look sweet and tempting as hot cherry pie to a starving man—if I do say so myself.

No. I'm not pretty. *Interesting*, I think I heard tell once. Nose too pug, eyes too big, chin too pointy, and I have a big mouth. Put them all together and shake them up, I guess I am passable. Besides, the first farm girl who hailed from Podunk, Iowa or *Anywhere,* Indiana, plain as a mud fence in a rainstorm or pretty as a portrait of Lillian Russell—if she's the marryin' kind, and yearns to be a miner's or a trapper's wife—well! If she ain't hitched or stolen within the first week gone by, there is something wrong with the universe.

Least here in Wylder.

However, back to the fellas who pass hot-blooded and fleetingly through my "boudoir"—ofttimes too fleetingly, Little Mae and Big Bertha snicker. "Boudoir"…I like "boudoir," as they say in Paris, France. Sounds more elegant than "crib"—specially when my clients are lonesome, or haven't seen a female for a year and a half down in the hell of a copper mine or lost in snowdrifts rounding up cattle from the lightning-quick blizzards, or they look at me with big cow eyes and tell me their wife died two years ago, and they're just getting over it, and one look at me was all it took and they will be forever grateful…

And this really gets me goin'—when they say it's their first time. Blushing all the way up from their big feet they've yet to grow into, up past sweet-pink-fanny cheeks, reddening their upright soldiers, and all the way up to scrubbed freckled noses. They always want to marry me right afterwards, but I tell them to go home to their ma for a few years, that I'll wait for them.

I always give *them* a special event.

Well, it should be! No wham-bam, forgot-your-name-ma'am, but a real humdinger, lollapalooza, slap up, go to hell, Fourth of July, firecracker-explodin' *screwing!*

Sometimes, my clients ask for extra things. A strip tease, or if they can watch me take a bath. Yesterday, in front of God and everybody, Biskits, a sweet ranch hand cook, lingered, twisting his old felt hat in his hands. "Miss Blossom?" he sez, with a yearning glint, sly and shy, all mixed up.

I braced myself.

"I'm kinda small."

I thought he meant—*you know what.*

"Fiddlesticks! You do the job!" I winked to set him at ease.

"No, Miss Blossom," he said stubborn-like and looking at me slanchways.

Oh, oh, this must be bad.

His gaze took on a covetous yearning toward my wardrobe. "Always wanted to see how them there silky things felt like, you reckon, next to your ski-yun?"

I squinted at him.

"Like maybe your spare bloomers. And maybe…" Biskits blushed, turning his grizzled cheeks cherry red. "Lace me all up real tight in one a them there corsets? Don't have to be one a yore frilly 'uns."

His eyes belied *that* request.

"An old one," he corrected, anxious. "I ain't so very big, or perticular," he repeated.

4

I was flummoxed, though I eyed him kindly nevertheless—he *was* on the small side, barely taller than me.

"Why not?" I grinned. "Might be fun." Besides, I was bored and uneasy.

Truth be told, there was an *odd feeling* about my room, making me not want to be alone much. A notion as if someone was always here, watching me, and if I turned my head real quick-like, or slanted my eyes sideways, I'd catch a body lurking. Fanciful, I ken, yet the sensation of someone lingering, listening, and seeing all I did—it would not go away without a fight. Ofttimes, I needed to take laudanum to sleep because the peculiar sensation was as strong as burnt coffee on the back of the stove.

Back to Biskits. For the next hour, paying me handsomely solely by his obvious pleasure, plus a tin of cornbread with chili peppers, Biskits strutted up and down admiring himself in my triple pier glass, pirouetting as best a bowlegged barrel-chested cook *can* strut in my best shimmy, with his gray curly chest hair peeking out, my second-best bloomers, garters, and… I drew the line at my lisle hosiery!

Howsomever, his feet fit fine, to my alarm, in my second-best satin slippers with the bows. From there, he graduated to an old gown with a ripped seam, and my parasol. I even smudged his eyes with lamp black and rouged his cheeks. I'd seen a gambler wearing eyeshadow and lip rouge once, so it wasn't so peculiar.

I paused, my hand hovering over his jaw as I daubed on a bit more rouge.

I could *swear* I heard laughter—nay, *chortles*, the kind with tears running down one's face—coming from the corner under the eaves by the big ugly red chair.

I darted a knife-blade glance in that direction, expecting someone had snuck in and was watching the show Biskits and I put on, which I'm certain sure Madame wouldn't cotton to.

I made a face. The laughter must be coming from the Longhorn below us.

Like I said, not my first belief that some varmint was hovering, watching everything I did. I started, hand in the air with a brushful of burnt cork. My mouth dropped open.

I swear on a stack of Quaker Bibles I detected a dim shape in my looking glass, the shape of someone standing behind me, and I heard a mocking chuckle. The notion dropped like a hot rock when I caught Biskits reaching stealthily for my expensive lip pomade, and I put a stop to his parading about like Missus Astor's pet horse when he fondled my green velvet gown that matched my eyes, with stars in his *own* eyes. Adamant, I stood guard before my chifforobe. Finally, Biskits divested himself, put on his long johns, and giving me a shy beatific smile, backed out the door.

I gently suggested that perhaps next time he might take his trade to the Wylder Social Club, as they had ever so many more dresses. I put the spooky spell behind me.

Then there's the chaps that want me to flail away at them with a riding crop! Sorely tempted sometimes. "I don't want to hurt you none, darlin'." I always back away from these requests and let Big Bertha down the hall perform that strange task. Life is hard and ugly enough at times without asking for extra pain.

Last, there are others who simply want to talk about their favorite dog, or an older brother who was in the northern army and never came back, or a little sister who got lame falling from a pony, or tell about a sweetheart who went to her reward from consumption but who will always remain pretty and untouched in their minds.

I never tell those fellas that they stayed a little extra time. They needed it.

Chapter Two
Looking for Love in All the Wrong Places

Of course, I never meant to fall in love.

But danged if I didn't.

Take this cowboy. I've liked boys since I was twelve or thirteen and *loved them*—if you cotton to what I mean, since I was fourteen or thereabouts, but I never got my head in a noose over any man.

I spied Flint from the top of the stairs, looking up as if he saw a heavenly angel, and *he* was all *I* clapped eyes on. Not the overflowing spittoon or bar slick with spilt rye whiskey. I didn't hear the tinny tinkle of the out-of-tune piano pounded out by Mr. ByJingo, Longhorn's black piano player, or dustups over hidden aces, or the slap of greasy cards on splintery wood tables.

Not a bit of it. Only Flint.

Rosy light, from a scorching dusty day through the saloon's one stained-glass window, shone all round him as if he just came from the Franklin Mint, all shiny and new.

Oh, my sweet Lord.

Tree-top tall. Shoulders broad as a yoke of oxen. Eyes, blue as robin's eggs, and he smelt sun-washed. Did I say he owned a smile, white and pearly as the picket fence around the new Baptist church?

A gentleman, I figured. Not just a cowhand.

At least at first. That came way too late.

But they say, when you kiss a robber, count your teeth!

Yes, he was special. 'Specially after that cowboy *doffed*—a fancy word for *took off*—his hat and sailed it across the room, and not so much tackled me as damn near swallowed me whole.

I would have loved him special too, giving him an extra show…but he shucked his clothes and waltzed me onto the bed in record time, before I had a chance to admire his twin sets of hard-packaged tanned muscle and broad golden-furzed chest. Reveling in his heavy weight, I felt his swelling manhood press my tender bits too. He seemed not to care how big he was and small I was. I didn't let on. Sometimes too big is good too— just lay there gazing up at the face of Gabriel, in a dreamlike haze, till he bent and used his teeth to pull down my shimmy and nuzzled my little rosebuds. Usually, clients maul my sweet little bumps like I was their pet hound dog, but this range rider was gentle, giving me much pleasure, till I thought I'd swoon from sheer bliss at his featherlike tonguings. Then his grazing grew fiercer until my bubbies bloomed like cabbage roses in place of the modest rosebuds they are accustomed to be.

I never felt that het up in a *loooong* time as this perfect specimen of a male worked his way down my flat belly, all the time bussing me with talented workable lips, experienced from rolling cigarillos, and gently bruising my soft white flesh, well practiced on white, brown, or blackberry, I was guessing. He knew his way around.

When he reached my private parts…just aching for

it by now—it was usually the other way around…that might not be new to me, but most gals don't talk about it—I launched myself to the ceiling and floated there, while he pleasured me with that talented tongue. If he meant to seduce me with his Frenchified ways, he succeeded, and if this be shame or sin, lead me on and send me straight to the cookfires of hell. I moaned as he ground his hand against that proud bone protecting my secret parts, until I squirmed, stuffing my knuckles in my mouth, 'cause Madame Solange would come storming in with her broom handle, or what was handy, if she suspicioned my gentlemen clients were taking too much advantage of her easygoing rules—and more important, her detailed pay schedule.

No hitting where it showed, no split lips, wash first is mandatory, and no longer than forty-five minutes, and nothing special, only straight God-fearing missionary positions 'less they pay premium up front for "French" or what she calls "Oriental."

Something stopped me, however, from completely joining in this cowpoke's pleasure, testified by his breathing like a horse galloping in a race with the devil for the finish line that I was apparently giving him.

I couldn't put my finger on it, but something wasn't right.

Damnation. Someone is here! Watching us! Dang it!

The air felt heavy, smelling of copper like right before a storm, though the sky was sunbonnet blue. The room was brooding and angry, and if I turned real quick, I'd see a varmint from the corner of my eye.

Like I said, not the first time I sensed this weird feeling making me look over my shoulder, or imagined a hand on my arm, and my neck would prickle, or searched the dark before turning down the lamp wick, or imagined someone behind me in my looking glass, and would have swapped the room with Little Mae if it weren't the best, with the bay windows above the Longhorn Saloon, across from the Wells Fargo Line.

The room had a disapproving, sad air. Lord kens there were plenty of shenanigans going on, now and in the past. Perhaps I fancied a lingering air. Nevertheless, though uneasy, I rippled and groaned, throbbing where it counted in delicious, never-ending waves after my body took over my mind—it usually had its own sweet way—until I feared I would not survive the bliss, for *this* cowboy never tired. Flint was that stallion on a mad gallop right off a cliff, till I too didn't want to end this extravagance of bodily delights, and though my flesh felt flushed and used, I was galloping right off that same cliff, alongside Flint.

Moreover, when Madame Solange—her name sounds like So-Long, but the "g" is soft—pounded on the door, I told myself I only wanted Flint to get his money's worth, but that wasn't true. I would have paid *him*, but Madame could take the shine off an Indian Head penny. To be fair, she paid for our rooms, inspected the clientele, and gave Little Mae, Big Bertha, Flora, and me our cut.

"Never mind her," I inhaled. "We'll ride to the finish line…"

Then…I heard the voice as clear as window glass. "*Are you certain this is what you want? He's not worth warm spit, you know.*"

The voice was as if from another room—*or in my head.* I froze.

Flint frowned down at me.

"What, sugar?" I asked to cover my confusion.

Flint threw me a *What are you on about?* kind of look, shrugged, and muttered, cross, "Didn't say nuthin'." His mood after that was like I tossed water on him from the rain barrel, and he commenced pulling on his Levi's as if already thinking on somewhere else.

"Guess I didn't either." I slid down, pulling the quilt to my chin and feeling a shiver of unease.

Chapter Three
The Unwanted Tenant

I soon forgot about Flint's odd mood. He'd be back, I told myself, self-satisfied. As I lay drowsing and musing in blissful surrender and playing with the ribbons of my *peignoir*—that's another Frenchy word, for robe—I sighed, coming back to the here and now with a *thunk.*

As most of the girls, except for Lilly Pearl, who ran off with the Chinese launderer last year, I had no real hold on this cowboy, other than that of a featherbed. All a female can do in my position is give them hot cindery looks, from between half-closed eyelids, or say things like, "Sure hope you're in town a while, sugar," or maybe, "Sure like to finish what we started, honey."

And then give them my, "Go-to-hell-on-a-hot-poker" look.

That's when thoughts of New Orleans flew out the window and I dreamt of sweet little ranches with a certain cowboy.

"*You can do better than a mezquino tinhorn, a cheap four-flusher…*"

I stiffened and quit fiddling with my ribbons.

"What?" Scooching up, I pressed my mouth to keep from screaming and scowled at the corner. If I'd had my hand on the Bible, I'd a been compelled to say the voice came by that big ugly red chair. It was empty, of course. I was purely heated up, that was all.

Still, as I sponged my face and arms and private bits, I kept peering at that red velvet chair in the corner under the slant. It had been there since Moses was a baby, by the looks of it. And rarely used. Shivering in my all-together, I *swore* I discerned a shape lounging there. *A man shape…*like a shadow on the wall. I checked my kerosene lamp. Flame flickered in a draft from the ill-fitting bay windows. I was being giddy. Besides, sometimes my circular coat rack with my straw hat seemed just like a person stood there, giving me a fright more times than once, or even my wig stand sitting on the dresser.

A mocking chuckle floated through the air.

"*What is wrong? Did my bullet strike the target?*"

"I didn't hear that!" I told the room, muttering, "Stupid wig stand!"

A full-throated guffaw ripped the air ragged.

I started, suddenly conscious of my unclothed state, as if I strutted naked as a jaybird in the Longhorn saloon or right down the middle of the streets of Wylder, Wyoming instead of shivering in my empty room.

"*Now, Miss Blossom—I doubt that is your real moniker, by the way—I've been called numerous things over the years, but never a wig stand…*" The chuckles sounded muffled in thick fog.

I scrambled into my dressing gown, collapsing on my vanity stool. Staring wide-eyed, I dug out my flask, taking a shaky pull of the snake venom they serve in the Longhorn. I keep it squirreled away for when my monthly visit from Auntie Scarlet comes.

I could see that red chair right through a hazy man-shape that sat with one leg thrown over the arm. The shade flipped a revolver in the air and burned holes in me, it appeared. At least his head seemed turned in my direction. I took another pull, never taking my eyes off that chair. The form strengthened, taking on faint color.

Leather hat, almost a sombrero but flat on top, an arrowhead on a thong around his neck. Was that a leather vest? Yes. Glints of silver medallions and fringe, like vaqueros or buckaroos up from Mexico wear, dully gleamed in the flicker from the kerosene lamp. Not daring to move for fear the apparition would move also, or disappear altogether. I wasn't sure which I wanted. I peered closer. It looked like there was a large dark glistening red stain on the vest… The trousers were tight leather, as if as painted on with molten tar…

I took another long pull of snake venom and corked the jug. The face—what I imagined *was* a face—was yet in shadow of the overhanging eave.

I wasn't scared—yet.

Honest.

Cross my heart.

I began chuckling—more like whistling past a graveyard—and stood, slowly revolving with the jug in my hand, ready to do damage.

"Who—who *are* you?" I croaked. My voice, which I pride myself on, was rough as a cat's tongue. Silence.

I laughed, letting the jug droop. Those glints. Surely, sunlight bouncing off the porcelain wash pitcher with the lily of the valley trim. *Of course.* Late sun was in my eyes too, for Flint had been an afternoon client. '*But what about the voices?*' The devil in me snickered.

Oh, Lordy. And my jug was empty. I wouldn't look at the corner. Well, maybe a little. I needed sarsaparilla right quick, with a tot of whiskey. I could get *that* past Madame Solange's quivering nose, and called for the daft scrub gal that fetched and carried, poor little mite. *The manager was good, giving her a job. Young ones should stay away from horse's hooves.*

When the scrub girl returned, I was still shooting such ferocious glances at that dim corner they could have set a fire to the red chair. I eyed her close to see if she spied or *sensed* something too and guessed why I really called for her.

She just sloshed a half pail of warm ginger beer down, looked at me dully, wiped her nose on her sleeve, and conveyed, "Missy So-*lange* says they outa sarsaparilla and 'sides, you ain't paid your last bill."

So much for that. When I looked again, the light had shifted, and I made out the red chair, not even scorched, and empty of occupants real or imaginary.

****

With a sour smile plastered on my face, thinking wicked thoughts about Madame Solange, I brooded at my vanity and commenced undergoing the evening's toilette. Arsenic whitener, almond cream, Dr. Mysterium's hair tonic—still feeling Flint's hands, his lips, dreamily caught in the sticky net of memories of the past few hours. Quirking a grin of reproach at myself, I dumped the odd episode into the midden heap behind the stables where it belonged, vowing to stop indulging in Longhorn's spirits. At least for a day or two. I really had to lay off that rot gut, if the spirits had gone to my head. Good enough for cowboys but not my complexion. Levi Gruenwald, Longhorn's owner, distilled it himself from raisins or potato peelings.

****

Madame arranged to have us all on display every now and then, like a parade of pet ponies. It had been a long, profitable evening. I gazed languidly in my looking glass smugly admiring my reflection. Boisterous lovemaking does that to you—the full lips and flushed cheeks—brushing my long, crinkly hair till it resembled waves of golden red silk, like pine shavings, in preparation of rolling it up in rag curlers.

"*Not worth it, you know. He's a two timing cabrón. And his eyes are a little close together, if I may say so.*"

I halted mid-brush. "You again!" I began to sputter. My eyes narrowed. The brush bounced on the floor. Hard. My face grew ashen in the cloudy mirror under the mask of Dr. Magneto's arsenic unguent.

I whipped my head 'round, ready to lambast any varmint who had snuck in, hiding like a craven polecat spying on me.

And me with arsenic cream on my face!

"Show yourself, you sneaking cowardly sidewinder!"

The room remained unresponsive… *Empty.* I put my head in my hands, afraid to look in the corner. *Just tired, that's all.*

As I reluctantly returned to my beauty ritual, came that mocking, irritating chuckle again.

"*I sincerely wish I could, ma'am—show myself, that is.*"

My brush lifted off the floor, floating before my eyes as serene as a paper boat on a pond—wobbling up and down on its way to me, from whence I flung it, until landing gently on my dresser with a faint *click.*

I grabbed it before it could take off once more.

That deep chuckle sounded again. "*Do you like

what you do? Your ah—generosity with your evident favors? I do say you put your whole self into your, ah—work. No offense. I am not on the side of the angels myself."

I shook my head, pressed my temples, and clamped my teeth, gritting out, "*No-no-no-no-no!*" And jumped up, looking wildly about, grabbing my hefty curling tongs, regretting the sweet little derringer was in my bedside table across the room.

"Come out, you gutless bastard! Peeping Tom! I have a gun!"

"*Ho-ho...! That little pea shooter? Now, I regret that, chica, but you are a few decades late...*" And the varmint nearly choked himself laughing.

I ran for the derringer—*the voice still came from over by my red armchair*—yanked the drawer, grabbed it, and backed to my dressing table, waving my sweet little pistol in wide arcs and darting looks at the door for escape. "This *peashooter* can still make daylight in you! Show yourself, you mangy flea-bitten dog! And then get the hell out!"

I stamped my foot and pointed at the door. "Damnation! Just go!"

I heard mild cussing in return, as if someone mumbled to himself in consternation. I recognized Spanish, and a language sounding distantly Indian...

What was worse, the voice came from behind me. "*I am afraid I already have too many holes in me. I am beginning to look like a panner's sieve.*"

I darted a look, angry and fearful, in my looking glass. My skin prickled. I witnessed no one. I spun round in a circle, holding my lady pistol tight to my chest.

"I'll shoot! I'll shoot you right in the gizzard, but I am not such a crack shot, they tell me, so it might be a tad lower. You! Behind that chair over there!"

I wasn't brave enough to approach the big ugly chair. A leftover monster of a chair. Heavy carved arms, faded red velvet upholstery like a Spanish grandee might own, left here Lord kens when. Afraid I'd find nothing. *Or something.*

I scanned my long pink velvet drapes. No boots showed beneath.

"*Oh, none of that nonsense. Do grow up!*" That sardonic chuckle again. "*Haven't you ever seen a ghost?*"

I backed, hitting the door with a thud.

The voice seemed by my bed now. I spun. A long depression formed in the feather comforter, as if someone lay there. My pistol drooped in my hand, forgotten. I fumbled for the doorknob behind me.

"*Not exactly Sarah Bernhardt, are you? I don't think you have the mettle anyway.*"

My finger tightened. I fired. A hole appeared in my feather comforter. Feathers exploded, dusting the air. Too late I recalled Little Mae was on the other side of the wall, yet the noise below, I hoped, masked the sound.

"*A tad overacting, don't you think? But with those histrionics—*"

"Sarah? Who?" I could not help asking. I wrinkled my brow, instantly regretting it. In my profession I needed no furrows in my face. "What histrionics?" Wasn't sure what that word meant either, but it didn't sound anything flattering, and I still waved the pistol.

"*Careful, damn it. You'll shoot someone!*"

The depression in the bed lifted.

"That's the general idea."

"*If you aren't careful, you will come up short a few toes. Such pretty little toes, too. A shame. They could always call you hopalong.*"

I opened the door. Had to be Little Mae or Big Bertha—leaving sweet little Flora out of such doings— who put some cowpoke up to mischief.

Nothing but empty hallway. No scampering feet. No giggles in the dark. Slamming the door, I stomped in place. After a few tetchy moments, I scanned my room with narrowed cat's eyes to catch the scoundrel creeping out from under the bed or wherever.

"*You truly do belong on the circuit,*" the voice drawled, amused. "*I hear tell a whole troupe of actors come through even this insignificant hell hole.*"

"Insignificant! Why Wylder is—"

The voice continued its bored fashion. "*Place isn't big enough to pluck a chicken without getting feathers in your teeth...*"

I witnessed, to my horror, prints—boot prints— marching across the thick pile carpet. The footprints headed toward me. I edged away. Sensing a breeze on my face, I detected a faint odor of aromatic tobacco and musky leather. I felt my cheek touched. I sucked in a breath, but after halting, the boot prints marched past me, stopping at the chair. The chair shifted. I heard it *scruff* the carpet. The seat depressed slightly.

"You bastard!" I swung my sweet little derringer at the chair.

"*I could be. A bastard,*" the voice continued reasonably. "*Yet ma was... Never mind that now.*"

The sigh seemed impatient. Bored even.

"*I'll leave you to your clod-hoppers, cow hands, and hog-sloppers…and please don't slam the door. It hurts the ears.*"

"Get out!" My voice was as raw as my nerves.

"*Now, that's problematic…much as I'd love to honor your request. Believe me! I want to be here in this Godforsaken room no more than you want me. I don't cotton to being jailed with an hysterical shrew, prone to putting bullets in a man's gizzard…or anywhere else.*" The voice faded in bitterness.

When I put a quality to imaginary voices, I kenned I was on the road to the lunatic asylum in Cheyenne. *But those footprints?* I glanced at my kerosene lamp flickering in a draft. *How silly.* Of course! Light playing with shadows. And I was hearing a row with one of Little Mae's johns, though it was awful late for that, and hadn't I heard her snore through the thin walls? Regrettably, my shout had summoned Big Bertha, foretold by her thumping, waddling gait charging down the hall. I could see her, rolling sleeves of a voluminous flannel nighty with the primroses, even on the hottest nights, over ham-hock arms, and doubling meaty fists.

Bertha came barreling in, blood in her eye. Brawling, bloodying noses, and tossing reprobates out on their ear and into the alley out back was the best sport, and she scarce missed an opportunity.

"Where is he? Where is the horse's arse?"

Wish I knew… "Sorry, Bertha, for—for spoiling your beauty sleep. Not that lucky tonight."

She looked closely. *Not sure about the beauty sleep remark, either.*

"Suffered the most terrible headache." I smiled my most winsome. "Took some laudanum. Maybe too

21

much. Reckon I had a nightmare," I vowed, trying hard not to stare at the red chair.

Bertha nodded wisely. "Laudanum's good taken with a pinch of peyote," and she launched into her own medical herbal lore. Some of which might not actually kill you.

The second I was rid of her by shoving her out the door, similar to moving an ox from a holding pen into the slaughterhouse, and feeling a right rattlebrain, I turned that boudoir upside down and sideways, swatting through wardrobe flounces—furbelows, ruffles, and lacy unmentionables that you couldn't hide a two-year-old child behind. Even peeked under my bed skirts, and lastly, hesitantly, behind the big red chair in the corner.

Something touched my hair. Like a cobweb. Brushed my sleeve. A hand circled my waist. The merest brushing sensation on my lips occurred as I scrambled up—a *cold* sensation. I was near that state between crying and laughing when one feels the mind crumbling like day-old cornbread.

"This is your last chance." My voice wavered like a child's on the verge of tears as I backed.

"S-show yourself! Damn you."

"*I thought you conveyed the idea you did not wish to see me. That is a relative term, of course.*" The voice was in my ear, scarce an inch away.

I jumped from the chair, like a scalded cat. "Oh, why don't you stop!" I shoved at the chair, then spied the scrolled vent in the floor behind it. My hiccupping laughter won out over hysteria. *That was it.* Voices from the Longhorn! But just as quickly, I disavowed the notion.

"*Believe me, chica, I don't mean to disturb*

you…but loco as it seems, I have been—" The voice paused as if searching for the right word. "*—nailed to this consarn chair far too long. Why, earlier, I actually ventured to the middle of the room.*" The voice held such gleeful awe at this dubious accomplishment I almost trusted it.

"Oh! I—I think I *saw* you." I flapped my arms. "I'm talking to phantoms, now!"

"*Apparitions, haints, spirits, phantoms, specters, ghosts, spooks…*" I heard the bitter laugh again like footsteps on gravel. "*Take your pick. Now leave me. I need to rest. It takes energy….*"

"*Me*, leave *you*?"

The growling chuckle faded as before as into a thick muffling fog or mist. I waited, tense, fearing the touch, the brush on my lips and faint scent of tobacco and leather, far into the night, before tumbling into troubled sleep.

****

"What's botherin' you, little darlin'? Ain't 'zactly with me."

Chester Flatts was my favorite…*one* of my favorite customers. Easygoing as a buggy ride at sunset, undemanding, unhurried, lazily stroking my thigh until I wriggled around in invitation, conscious of the time, but a worried pucker pinched Chester's sandy brows. He halted. His honest face, prairie-burnt from breaking mustangs all day down at the corral, raked the room with concern.

"You always bother me, Chess, darlin'," I flirted back. Hoping to hurry him along. *I'm just going mad, is all.* I hopped on board, straddling his thighs—muscled as ironwood from clamping a horse all day—bracing both hands on his ropy upper arms. "Now, what would be worrying me, when I imagine I gotta ride home on this fine untamed mustang?"

They like talk like that.

I began to gallop up and down on a man's favorite hobby-horse. The frown was replaced with a look of holy delight. However, Chester had an unholy *gleam* too, as he flipped me over, under his long cowboy bowlegs, and we bucked all the way home and back again. Ofttimes, Chester and I lie there in bed and talk afterwards, like now, if there's a minute or two.

"What's with you, little darlin'? You ain't yourself. Is someone worryin' you?"

"What, Chess?" I answered vaguely. Chester felt my mood, and that wasn't good.

"I'll lasso 'im, who-some-ever he may be."

I choked a laugh.

"Won't tangle with none of your gal friends, though." Chester snorted with a gap-toothed grin. "Or Madame So-lange. She'd scare a bobcat plumb out of a tree."

Actually, I wasn't listening. I *was,* but not to him.

I was listening for a *footfall,* or a sound too high to hear…

"Dunno, Chess." I hung my head so tumbled curls fell like curtains around my face, and I mumbled, embarrassed, "It's like—I'm being watched—all the time."

Even then, when I heard an amused snort from the corner by the red chair, I clenched my fists to keep from looking over.

Chester's sunny eyes grew stormy.

"Just let some scabby lowdown coyote try it. Heard

of them pre-verts spyin' on females in their bath and outhouse and such…"

I didn't let him finish, for didn't I delight in men *looking* at me, admiring my rounded hips, smooth thighs, tiny waist, and high bosom? I made a face over my own conceit.

His coppery eyes flicked the room, squinting at doors and windows. "Reckon somebody's peerin' at us right now?"

"I don't know!" I was miserably sorry I'd said anything. "Just goosey, I reckon, Chess, honey."

I feel a breeze like somebody stands close.

I see things out of the corner of my eye.

I turn slowly in the middle of the room like a great ninny to spy out whoever's there…

Someone is here all the time.

Watching me. *Wanting me…*

"Maybe ya need to get away—from all this," Chester vowed earnestly, reddening. Chess'd like to think of himself as my feller, ignoring what I really do. "A few days, like."

"Just thick-headed, Chess, honey." I shrugged, pondering that. We girls had no real holiday. Though I could scarce wait for Sunday.

Every Sunday we four, Big Bertha, Little Mae, and Flora and me, have our own little hootenanny after church. Madame Solange provides free drinks that ain't watered down, 'cept for Big Bertha, who can imbibe with the best of us and sorta goes over-limit by a hogshead or two, and brings her own besides. Sometimes, Madame hires a buggy for a Sunday drive, out to a little watering hole half-mooned by rocks. A time for frolicking, washing hair in spring water, swimming naked and free, splashing and dunking each other…and if a few natives, miners, or cowpokes, happen to wander by and perch on the rocks, they appreciate us enough to leave us be. We put on a show anyway, showoffs that we are. Gets the men all fired up for next week, judging by Monday's stampede up the stairs.

Chester had got up and started brushing walls, studying the ceiling, even poked in my wardrobe. I don't know what he thought he would do, naked as a cherub, if some polecat was in there, but I sure liked to watch his bottom, hard as two India rubber balls from bouncing on a saddle all day. "Nothing up there, Chess." I shrugged. The shoulder of my shimmy dropped down. He didn't even glance over.

"Just an old attic," I pouted.

I hated the notion of anyone prowling around overhead, looking down through a crack, though.

After another round of fooling around, I buttoned up his shirt, gave Chester a kiss on the nose, and promised, with a lazy, lip-licking smile, "Next Friday then, Punkin Pie?" Like it was a real date.

****

But Darlin' Chester got me fretting over it like a bad tooth. That night, after Corky, my once-a-month farmer, finally left—he was all about plowin' fields! I took a lamp down the hall past the girls' rooms and through a low door that led up to the attic. Thrusting the lantern through the trap door, I scrambled up, afraid of what I might see, or of what might spring out at me.

The floor, shadowed behind uprights running into darkness the length and breadth of the Longhorn, was thick with chaff—nary a boot print marred the boards

26

as I held the lamp close. Still, I tripped on a plank sticking up, falling on my knees and barely holding onto the kerosene lamp, then sprawled flat on my face. "*Oooof*!" Rising, I stomped about some, to shake out the soreness, then, feeling foolish for getting my nighty dirty, stomped back to the trap door.

I'm at the front—or rather, my room is—with the big bay windows overlooking the train station and the Wells Fargo. "To my right, nothing but alley. To the left, the hall I'm standing in and the staircase down to the saloon. So there's only one wall 'tween me and anybody," I brooded. The room next to me was queened over by Little Mae.

She's three hundred pounds of little, but the men joke, overmuch to my mind, that they "get more for their George Washingtons" or "more bounce to the ounce" and such. Little Mae doesn't mind. I don't think. Anyway, she wouldn't be spying, would she?

Then my mind turned dark as a bear cave, with notions taking a wicked turn around a bend. "*Shoot!*" I muttered, once back in my room. "Maybe Little Mae gets extra sport for special customers, peeking through a spy hole, and she don't have to mention it to Madame."

"*Looks like you've been wallowing in a pig sty,*" greeted me, as I returned to my room.

I froze in place, hand over heart, mouth open so wide a fly could fly right in.

I ran my hands over the wallpaper, looking for any spy holes. "Consarn you, Little Mae!" I rapped the wall, ready to rush out and confront her. Then I recalled hearing Little Mae's familiar waddling tread go downstairs some while ago.

"*You were raising old Ned up there. What was all that stomping around? How can a man get any peace?*"

I realized I was near the big red chair and jumped back like my nighty was on fire.

"Oh damnation, wherever you are, please stop! I am not amused! At all!"

"*What you get for wearing your best night-dress in an attic,*" the voice scorned. "*You look like you been rassling with a bear.*" Then, as if deliberately provoking, "*Now, I prefer my women all dainty and sweet-tempered as little china dolls...*"

"Oh!" I whirled about. "And I suppose china dolls do not sass back!" Earned me another wicked laugh. I checked behind the dratted chair, rewarded by a lot of empty space, a missing button, and a pat on my bottom, and scrambled out like I was on fire. *Okay, so not there.* Surely the varmint was skulking on the other side of that dammed wall.

I was bound to poke around Little Mae's room.

Chapter Four
Ruffled Peacock Feathers

Next afternoon, I waited till Little Mae went to the privy after breakfast, then slipped into her room. I checked walls, behind picture frames, and the peacock feathers crossed over her crucifix, that I always coveted. Stroking the pretty colors glittering like isinglass, I dreamt of far-off lands, wondering if I'd never see such sights. Thinking on the time, I peered close and, running my hands along the wallpaper's red-and-gold paisley pattern, and sighed. "Not even a piddly little old pinhole!"

When I started to leave, I ran smack into Little Mae, who shoved me back like she was the prow of a battleship hell-bent for harbor as she bellied and bosomed me like a bit of flotsam to the center of the room. Blocking me against her massive bed, her gaze alighted on her open jewel box.

All right, I peeked inside.

I had even tried on her jet earbobs, though I grumped that they only showed up how beady black her eyes were. She waddled to her wardrobe and yanked it open. A swell of tentlike gowns big enough to cover the Sheik of Araby—and all his wives, too—burst from its confines.

Too wide-eyed, I ventured, "Why, Little Mae, what are you on about? Just came to visit." As I backed to the door, I held out my hands, showing I had filched not a bean.

"Never done that before! Visit!"

That was true. "So then I got a reputation for being right unfriendly. Want to set that to rights."

"That why you were fondlin' my peacock *fans,* tryin' ta yank 'em off the *wall?*"

"Admiring them, Little Mae, that's all. Ain't never seen anything so grand in all Wylder. Can't imagine what kind a birds…" All the while, I was backing out the door.

I stood in the hall, shaking, as the door slammed shut. I had a reputation for being too full of myself and had no real chums, but I was suddenly lonely for girl gossip, late-night rum merrymakings, and smoking cheroots behind the chicken coop. Madame didn't cotton to smoking. I heard Flora's titter and Big Bertha's rumble down the hall, laughing over something, even now.

High time I climbed down from my high horse.

Truth to tell, I felt *beneath* them.

You get that way when your pa was a *pick a number,* like at a roulette wheel and where it stops nobody knows. A man *called* my dad, I found out, died of the consumption when I was five, before Ma took up with someone else. A *lunger*, the undertaker told me cruelly, 'cause he figured Ma had no coin to pay.

I vowed I'd *always* have coin to pay. Even then. Whatever I had to do.

I had no time for girlie chat. I was fighting madness—and maybe for my livelihood, if Madame found out. I pondered if insanity ran in my family. Ma vowed Uncle Joe was crazy as a box of frogs, but Ma seemed all right.

I didn't take laudanum that night but sat bolt upright, armed with my derringer, until my eyes felt like anvils sat on them, and the feed store's cock-crow woke me, unharmed and sane.

That wasn't to last.

"*Good morning, little one. Sleep well after invading your, ah, friend's room?*" the voice said, mock-pleasant.

"I'm not answering you! And no thanks to you, if I didn't!" I folded my arms and lowered my chin.

"*You look no worse for wear. I'm glad you didn't take the opium, though. And I favor you out of those head rags.*"

My hands flew up to my rag hair-winders. "I don't hear you! And I don't take opium!"

"*Now I wonder what do you suppose laudanum is? Mother's milk? Sarsaparilla?*"

I clapped hands over my ears. "I don't!" And I began singing "Seeing Nellie Home" at the top of my lungs, though quickly lowering my caterwauling to a loud hum.

Madame Solange often accused me I had a button missing, always dredging some new clarification for my defects. I could never hint of hearing voices to avoid a heap of new monikers falling on my head. She had many *sobriquets* for me. *Sobriquet*. Another of those French words. Soon, thanks to Madame Solange, I'll have a whole lexi-con of Frenchy words and can set my sights on a crib where the ladies are more stylish. Like New Orleans, where they speak a lot of French.

Every gal must have aspirations.

"*And free of the voice?*" My devil oozed in my ear.

On rumination, with the help of John Barley Corn, I figured it *had* to be some fool whispering through the scrolled vents letting up heat from the Longhorn behind that danged red chair. Whoever the idiot was, I would not let them wind me tight as a rope around an axle.

As if in defiance, I spied a curl of smoke, followed by a sweet whiff of cherry-scented cigarillo. I studied the vent, yet saw no smoke, curling, or otherwise.

"Need to just pack your carpetbag and go, while you still have two wits to rub together," I muttered to myself.

"*And just as I was getting used to the idea of sharing the room with a scratchy, harebrained female...*" came the drawl from nowhere.

I didn't hear that, or stubbornly pretended not to. I looked about my pretty room. It was just the way I wanted it—lacy curtains with red bobbles, and pink velvet drapes from Lulu's old dress. Lulu was a doxy who ran up too big a gambling debt, courtesy of the Longhorn, and scarpered in the night. That still set me back dear. The hated red velvet chair. Wallpaper with the big cabbage roses and lilacs. My vast four-poster, the only one in the whole crib, and my lovely carpet patterned with bluebonnets and ivy.

I tucked John Barley Corn under the mattress.

That wouldn't help.

Besides, how could I leave Flint?

I dug out the bottle again.

After the fifth pull, I allowed the notion to creep in that the sensations of a body watching worsened especially when Flint came by—like a fug of a cheap cigar or stale bay rum on unwashed bodies, if I had to put words to it—a disapproving murk made the room hazy and humid even though dry and clear as fresh laundry outside. Moreover, the air changed back whenever Flint left, like a window was opened on a muggy day and stray breezes wafted in.

Chapter Five
Sharper than a Serpent's Kiss

The feeling came on stronger next time. *Someone observed us.*

Oh, yes, indeed. Flint, my cowboy, returned.

I was determined in accommodatin' him till his boots fell off.

indulgently watching Flint roam my room, I had plans for *this* cowboy extending far beyond four walls. I didn't mind his tour. Some like to stretch and build up if planning another romp.

He was by my dresser.

Only thing on it was my old velvet jewel box, frayed and piebald as it was, holding a cameo, a prized mother-of-pearl wedding brooch, even though set in brass instead of gold, and a worn opal ring some cowhand gave me. Somehow, it made me uneasy. Flint passed by, glanced in the mirror, slicked his hair, and returned with a toothy grin that melted my heart.

Later, after we romped on the bed sideways, top, and bottom, making a right wallow of the sheets, and a bed slat bounded to the floor, Flint pinched his brows, freezing like a deer in the woods, and in the midst of mutual attentions, he sat bolt upright, his knees on either side of me—as if someone goosed him in the fanny. A queer look twisted Flint's rugged face as he frantically swatted, trying to reach his back like a bee stung him.

I looked straight up his broad chest and angel face, laughing. "What happened, sugar?"

I watched, confused, as Flint's forelock suddenly stuck straight up in the air like it was stiffened with Silver Star Starch…or someone yanked it—*hard.*

Flint smacked his head yelping, "*Ow-waw!* What the Sam Hill, Blossom? What was *that*? God *dang* it!" Flint flailed like he was smacking flies.

Then his hay-colored hair flopped limp over his forehead just like always, in that cute cowlick he had. He brushed the hank crossly from his face. "Hunh! What the Billy Blue *hell*?" He smacked my arm a tad harder than was necessary. "Why'd ya do that for?"

"Do what, Flint?" I was still gobsmacked from the way his hair stuck up like a flagpole.

"Keep pinchin', an' hittin' me, and pullin' at my hair?"

I drew up my knees, bucking him off, and acted all innocent, pretending I hadn't seen anything strange, *like Flint's hair standing straight up, stiff as a cardboard collar!* Yet, I had an omen. *A bad one.* Then things happened fast.

A sound, like a *mallet on meat* followed his accusations and the smack on my arm.

Flint's head jerked sharply sideways.

With a startled look, almost comical, Flint rubbed his jaw. Swearing, "Sweet Jesus! What in tarnation?" He leapt buck-naked for his holster, when his head suddenly swung the other way. A red mark bloomed on his cheekbone.

I screamed, yet Flint looked…not shaken—more flummoxed, stalking the room, waving his revolver, and once it looked like he stumbled over nothing but his own big feet, and he finally smacked himself on the ear as if to clear his head, looking like he wanted to blame me too over his odd antics. After prowling, scowling, muttering more curses and, "Sure don't get what funny business is going on here!" Flint returned to my featherbed, distracted but determined to carry on even though he peered, suspicious, all around him. Flint was a little rough as he took it out on me.

I tried to carry on too, but I swore…now standing by the bed was a…tall, rangy-legged, long-haired male…

Hair black as coal tar.

A rough, bronzed, sunburnt face.

A large nose. No, not large, more—hawkish, narrow, curved as a sword blade.

One hand on what looked like a bullwhip looped on one lean hip.

Flexing, rawboned fingers gripped the whip as if itching to use it.

The other hand grasped the butt of an ancient Colt Dragoon revolver.

I could not quite make out his face, yet the shadowy rippling figure by his stance—*oh, my sweet Lord, it was rippling*—was undoubtedly aggressive and spoiling for a fight.

I jerked. "Flint!" I cried, trying to toss him off and warn him all the same. My cowboy tumbled to the floor, cussing a blue streak. "Balls! Dang it, Blossom, what the hell's *wrong* with you? You ain't even tryin'! First yer hittin' me, then knockin' me on the floor!"

I detected a whine in his voice. Had I heard it before?

I scarce took notice, darting looks everywhere, trying to conjure up the image again. I didn't need to look far. There it was at the end of my four-poster!

Someone else is here! I wanted to scream, *We are not alone, Flint!* My gaze was still glued to the man-shape hovering midair—scuffed boots did not *quite* touch the floor or they faded into a kind of swirling mist, or some such spectacle. I could even make out massive silver spurs, like Mexican gauchos favor. I wanted to giggle, or weep, or scream. Instead, I stuffed a corner of sheet in my mouth and pinched my eyes tight.

The most frightening thing, though…I could see the wall on the other side of him.

A riot of pink cabbage roses showed *behind* the apparition wavering in and out of view—almost solid one second, and in the next blink of the eye, the man-form faded into a curl of candle smut. I had a sensation this *specter,* the only way I can name it, observed Flint with bullets for eyes and me with something indescribable in his unwavering gaze, but that I wanted to flinch from.

I blinked, but now 'twas just my long pier glass where my handsome cowpuncher had slung his hat. Jumpin' Josephat! Was I going all peculiar, like the lady who wore two hats, one atop the other, and dressed her cat in doll clothes? I mumbled shakily, "Purely sorry, F-flint darlin'. H-had a hitch in my side. There, that's better." Plastering on my damnedest come-hither look, I sank back and raised my arms in invitation. I had to distract him.

I had to *not* see it.

Still discombobulated, and moping some, Flint

hopped back on, carrying on like a trooper. I stayed fiercely on him, not once watching where an apparition seemed to ripple like a breeze through fog from the corner of my eye, horribly aware frowns still wrinkled Flint's sunburnt brow, with his sandy cowlick bouncing up and down and muddying his sunbonnet blue eyes.

Afterwards, after a disappointingly brief round of pleasure, for Flint, at least, he dressed hastily. Had trouble buttoning his shirt, and hopped about one-legged in the wrong boot, cursing and grunting, getting more vexed by the second.

At the door, he turned and looked everywhere but at me. "Warn't exactly a humdinger," he sulked. "Yer off yer game, girl! Sure, ain't getting *my* money's worth…"

I began to apologize. My heart hurt.

I watched him yank open my door—and run into a brick wall.

Bushwhacked.

Pain knotted Flint's handsome face as he jolted back inside clutching his midriff.

His leather vest dented in like an elbow…no, a fist had punched him. I could see knuckle impressions in the leather. He staggered—checked his big, booted feet. "Con*sarn* it!" Flint's face flushed red as his bandanna. "Musta tripped." Rubbing his chest, Flint glared at me to deny it.

But then, on the floor—we both stared at it.

My mother-of-pearl brooch with the brass filigree bounced on the carpet and lay quiet by Flint's left boot.

His eyes grew cold and gray as his name. Then Flint grinned his lazy, lopsided grin.

"Well, now. How'd that little old gewgaw get

down there?" He said it easy as pie and swooped to pick it up. Or tried to.

My brooch skipped away—even hopping up into thin air once, and plunking down nearer to me. I giggled. My brooch looked like a toad jumping about on my carpet as he tried to catch it.

Flint's face reddened. He scrambled to catch the bauble as it cheekily danced off—when he pitched face first, just like someone booted him, over-catching himself before he went ass over teakettle. Scowling, Flint snatched at the pin like he was indeed trying to catch a hopping toad and hurled it at me.

"Ya oughta get that dang rug fixed and keep yer cheap gimcracks off the floor! Dang near kilt myself!"

I searched the offending rug and found no complaint. Still the same gold carpet entwined with ivy and bluebonnets, like always. "But it wasn't on the floor! It was on my dresser."

"Musta got caught on my sleeve when I mussed with my hair, then." His eyes were innocent blue-gray, daring me to naysay different.

But you were buck-naked as the day you were born, I wanted to answer. But maybe it happened later, when I wasn't looking. *Lord kenned I was seeing things, all right.*

I closed my hand around my brooch and smiled like all was right with the world. My heart felt like an ox cart sat on it, though.

Chapter Six
To Hell in a Handcart All the Way to Cheyenne

"I ken you are here." I was proud how calm I put it. "You can't hide."

I sat in bed, knees hunched under my chin, contemplating the corner, staring hard to see— *something*. I would not say *ghost,* although I could no longer deny it. The peculiar goings-on. The misplaced hairbrush. A pillow shifting on the bed. That hopping brooch. Odd scents and right-before-a-storm-sensations when flesh goosebumped and hair stood on end.

I strived to stitch the ill-fitting fragments together into a whole cloth. The end garment still seemed ragged. Either I was headed to an asylum in a handcart all the way to Cheyenne, or all was not as it seemed betwixt heaven and hell.

I chose the latter.

"What do you really look like?" I grumped. "Wild Bill Hickock, Custer, or the Hunchback of Notre Dame?" I was putting on airs. That was one of the books I read once, and a fine romp it was, too.

"I reckon not!" I answered myself. "Custer and Hickock had fair hair and weren't cowards. Fools maybe, but not cowards."

My ghostly *desperado* had glossy raven hair, that much had been clear.

The air rippled. A forewarning of my irritating

phantom's presence, I learned.

His answering voice came, mellow as warmed honey but with a deeper amber tone more like warm blackstrap molasses. "*I have a somewhat large bulbous nose with a wart on the end and small squinty eyes set rather too close together for true handsomeness, I suppose. My chin, I admit, is a small amount weak. That is why I grew the three-foot-long red beard. Now my teeth. I* do *have some. They just don't* show *much in the front, and…*"

"Don't be silly! And take that for hitting Flint."

I hurled my china dog from my bedside table. It struck something midair between me and the red chair. I heard a satisfying, "*Ooooph!*" The dog fell harmless to the carpet. I had been staring hard at the chair. Now what! I scrambled from bed, waving my arms before me like the blind.

"*Now, now. No fisticuffs. You almost hit me, you know. I must say, you have a swing like John L. Sullivan.*"

"Oh!" I stamped my foot. "Do stop playing the fool. You do plenty of that. And stand still!"

The laughter came from the red chair again. The seat depressed slightly. I heard the scratch of a lucifer, then made out a lavender plume of cigar smoke.

"*What do I look like? Truth, I don't have a notion. Never looked at myself outside of a horse trough. Somewhat ordinary, I conjecture. Own a scar through one eyebrow…other than that? My face is—rough. My nose broke from too many card games and not enough losses.*"

He—it—chuckled.

"*Also, too, I didn't reckon on the lady was married,*

and then there was the time…"

I pretended to be put out, even though usually slavering for any lurid tale to entertain the hours in spells between clients when sorting out my undies drawer, or mooning out the bay windows, or darning a sock.

"Oh, please! Spare me your shadier exploits. I'm sure I am uninterested in your shabby past."

The wretch snorted. *"Lady, you haven't begun to dig that well."*

A long silence. I held my breath, straining to hear more. A bored sigh came from my left. *Too close.* My neck hair fluttered.

"I'm here. Don't have to hold your breath or look so hornswoggled. I'm not going to take advantage of your soft white flesh."

"I'm not! And I *never* look hornswoggled."

I heard *brushing.* Leather rubbed against leather behind me. He—it—circled, then was quiet.

I swiveled, hands out in a blind man's bluff, swatting the air. "Where are you, now? Sneak! Yellow-belly! I know you can show yourself. *Coward*!"

"Are you ready?" A man-figure rose from the red chair, graceful as a gunslinger dismounting a horse. Striding across my room, he seemed to bloom in the growing dusk. *Damnation!* I didn't flinch.

Or back.

I didn't! Even when he was an inch from me.

"I may be a sneak, as you put it. Never a coward. And I admire beautiful women. So does that exonerate me? I promise, I will not take advantage—unless you extend an invitation. I realize you are not exactly exclusive, but I will overlook that, if you promise to

parade about more in your all-together, especially that pink shimmy-thing, when we are alone. I enjoy those little scars on your left buttock, by the way, though I can't read it."

"Oh! How *dare* you!" My hands flew to my backside, cupping my bottom. "Those are—burn scars!"

"*Hmm, yes, I ken it was 'cheeky' of me.*" The figure strangled a laugh.

I would not tell him that I'd backed my bare five-year-old fanny, after a bath in a tin washtub, too close to our little potbellied stove and branded *Hot Blast,* the stove's name, on my tender bottom. I still had the imprint in fading pink on my bottom.

Hot Blast.

I'd almost forgotten, except when some wag brought it up.

I dropped the cupid clock I meant to hurl as the apparition steadied.

No denying it now. I plainly made out a ruffian with long, taut-muscled legs encased in skin-tight black leather chaps over equally tight faded Levi's, showing everything he had, his rangy legs in a gunman's stance. The same bullwhip as before looped at his waist, and a brace of long-barreled Army revolvers in crisscrossed gun-belts were slung low on his slim hips. Hard-knuckled, scarred hands rested on that belt. A black leather vest barely covered a gleaming coppery chest of scarred packed muscle, with a faint line of black silk feathering down to below his silver pant buttons.

"*Forgive my rough handling of your cowpoke friend?*"

"N-not if you were the last m-man in the universe!"

43

The vision chuckled. "*Hardly applies to me. But I will do my utmost to change your mind. I had—certain talents, besides...*" His voice took on a satisfied purr. "*Never mind that now. In time, perhaps. If you are lucky and I'm in the mood.*"

I was too lost, though, to catch his jibe—lost in the emerging face of a square-jawed male.

High, sharp cheekbones one could almost cut paper with, coppery-bronzed as a well-burnished saddle, the color of sumac leaves in the fall. A pale scar sliced one ferocious, black as anthracite, hawkish brow winging across a high forehead. His nose was long, arched, and somehow regal, above a brutal mouth. Hair gleaming as black water on a moonless night, parted in the middle, flowed unheeded from a widow's peak as sharp as a raven's beak. One incongruous plait hung down the side, twined with silver trinkets and feathers. Eyes narrow, long, flat, slightly slanted, and giving away nothing, yet odd in such a dusky face—they were clear blue-green, like sunlight shining through water, or blazing like jewels set in amber.

I flushed, gasping, sensing a familiar heat in my belly. That occurred too rarely with my clients—the throbbing in my tender bits crying out for attention. The apparition, very much male, I noted, strode toward me like wading through fog. I pointed down, the other hand over my mouth to stifle screams. His—*Its*—boots never touched my carpet, vanishing beneath swirling mist.

"*It has been long since I enjoyed the unique pleasures of a woman,*" the voice growled throatily as if unused to speech.

I backed from the specter's hand, thunking against my door, scrabbling for the brown china knob behind me. Looked down in a daze. A shimmer, a disturbance in the air, trailed down my arm.

"*The softness, the warmth…of a female.*" The apparition's voice was the brush of pine needles, the sighing of wind across shingles. "*I forgot this—ache. Until now…*" The voice sounded strangled, as if the apparition held back only with the strongest will.

Shrinking, feeling the wood panels cut into my back, I dared to gaze up. The apparition studied me with perplexity and disturbing hunger in his odd flashing eyes, now the color of sunlit blue-green glass with irises rimmed in darker green. I could only stare, feeling my heart beat like a tom-tom, and an almost unendurable insatiable pressure.

It was embarrassing. Inexplicable. Maddening.

My robe ribbons came unloosed. My body, unguided by me, leaned closer. A hand caressed my breast—a shadowy hand…I could look right through and see my pink nipples, yet it had the warmth of living flesh.

For that glimpse into hell or heaven, the male, at least a foot taller—and I'm five feet seven, barefoot, and tall for a female, I am told—wavered.

I awoke, dazed, on the floor.

A face wearing a perplexed, aggravated expression brooded over me.

"*You are not one of* those, *are you?*" The accusation was clear.

I attempted to roll away. A pressure on my chest pinned me.

"One of what?" I croaked. *Crazy? A woman gone loco?*

"*A wilted violet—all smelling salts, corsets, and*

perfumed lace hankies." The figure snorted and looked off.

"You floated. You disappeared," I accused.

"*Yes, ma'am. Sorry about that. I* can *walk…it's just easier this way. One gets accustomed to being alone…and forgets—civil niceties.*"

From far off, I heard Little Mae, Big Bertha, and Flora twittering away on their way to flapjacks, eggs, and biscuits…human, normal voices. I longed to be with them.

"I don't care either way. As if you kenned a civil nicety if it bit your nose!"

The voice and face faded. "*Have it your way.*" My head thunked on the carpet.

I scrambled up to join the others like the devil chased me.

****

Flint returned, open as a prayer book and just as boyish, as if no bad words kept us apart.

"Plum wore me out yesterday, Miss Blossom!"

He dug the toe of his cowboy boot into my carpet, twisting his hat. My heart felt fit to burst with relief, so glad to see someone solid, smelling of horse flesh, with life's blood pulsing in the crook of his muscled arm and hollow of his neck.

"Yesterday, I felt like I been pulled through a haystack backward. Couldn't rope a cat to save my life. Came back for more, I reckon." He grinned, bashful, as I dragged him in.

I giggled at the notion of him roping a herd of cats. His hay-colored hair did look ruffled in a stack. Later, after he went after me like chasing a herd of stampeding longhorns instead, I lay contemplating a huge spread. A substantial farmhouse with ruffly curtains in the windows and me as at home in leather chaps, rounding up horses, as in starched aprons, baking rhubarb pies.

I put the odd episodes to the farthest corner of my mind and nailed the door shut, vowing to lay off the laudanum.

For now, idly admiring Flint's body until he blushed becomingly and I saw his better self standing at attention like a good little soldier. He caught my gaze, cocked his head, and looked down, grinning.

"Now, ain't that a shameful wicked sight?"

"We must hide it again then," I said in a purr, reaching out for him. "I know a secret place." I licked my lips and cupped my breasts in invitation, though I hardly needed to give Flint encouragement, judging from the way he dove at the bed, plunging deep like a gunslinger sighting a target and hitting it dead center. Kenning well the *hoorah* I was fomenting in Solange's cashbox and ledger sheet, I gave him second helpings.

Madame, with an abacus for a brain, kept office at a table located at the bottom of the stairs in a little alcove by the swing doors. She kept court all afternoon and most of the night, sipping scuppernong wine, playing cards, chatting up customers, and guiding them to the right rooms, and she didn't miss much. Gradually Levi got used to her being there. At end of day, she toted up, giving Levi Gruenvald and Rattlesnake Jake, lord of the bar, and even ByJingo, their under-table cut, and that paid for her own room too.

But I didn't care how long Flint tarried. I'd settle with her later.

I couldn't, however, avoid looking at the corner. Wondering if the blasted phantom would act up. It did seem like a bed pillow was hurled across the room, but I put it down to Flint clearing the field of play as he swooped atop me. I swear the next lovemaking was as scrumptious, like a hot biscuit on Sunday morning, as the first, like two old lovers who want to start a barn-burning, and we burnt up that barn, the outhouse, *and* the stables, until we lay pinked and half-dead with sweet sweat coating our skin…and Sweet Jesus, if he didn't want to do it again…but there was only so much *settling up* I could afford with Madame, so I laughed and told Flint to go rope a calf or something.

Chapter Seven
A Lady Proposes

I tell you all this, Dear Reader, to show how it was with me, and why I was so blinkered.

A poisonous sidewinder curling up by my breast could have been no more deadly than Flint, to my pocketbook and to my self-respect, though I did wonder betimes about his milk-fed appearance and *gosh-all-get-out-ma'am* manners. Ofttimes, I caught an icier glint in those eyes, but then, some blue eyes are always a tad cold, like moonlight on frost.

Sure enough. As I sashayed down to the Longhorn near suppertime before the evening's onslaught, Madame Solange was gunning for me at her usual table.

"I suppose you think I don't *notice* how long you carried on with that range rat?" She stabbed the ledger with her nail.

I held my tongue.

"That extry amount of time gets docked from your pay!"

Though I kenned it would happen, I blinked at that.

"It's not like they are lining up!" I retorted. "And Flint's not a range rat! 'Sides, I was going to square with you."

Damnation. And I had my eye on a fine piece of lace clear from Kansas City, down at Lowery's dress shop, to trim my shimmy. This would set me back some.

Dang. But Flint was worth it, I told myself, after all the pale miners, punchers straight off the back of a horse, and earthy wranglers…rarely farmers. They were too tired and too poor, and most had a thin wife who kept a sharpish eye on them anyway.

"Could be that no-good *range rat*, will carry me right off," I sassed back. I spoke boldly, kenning well I had no such promise of a wedding ring, but I was feeling my oats. I vowed I'd ask him, though I had no claim to do so. Yet the second he came through the door next day with his shy grin, holding a limp Shasta daisy, somehow the time did not seem right.

This occasion was sweet and slow, and if we fell asleep, bodies all entangled and still connected, we woke to start the lazy slide again. Flint left after two or three more insistent raps on the door. I hated it when my cowboy rose from the bed and stood boldly in the doorway buck-naked like over-proud of what he had. However, Madame pretended not to be entertained, though I saw her eyes lower and widen a pinch as Flint dropped silver in her hand.

Flint smirked and winked at me, as her birdcage bustle waddled off, coming back to bed.

"Flint!"

I could wait no longer. Sitting up, I denied him. Tumbling over, I threw my legs across his waist and sat on him. He put his arms behind his head and grinned up, smugly tolerant.

I blurted, "Aren't you tired of punching for somebody else? Wouldn't you…" I lowered my eyes, "like ownin' a nice little spread all to yourself?"

His smile vanished. My heart beat faster, but I hastened on. I had rehearsed what I'd say. "Are you ready to have that ranch?" I would ask, all perky. I could just see sparkly windows and fresh curtains, rag rugs on polished pine floors. Fresh sourdough bread steaming from the cookstove, and me, queen of my own house without ever taking orders from Madame. Not that I did anyway, but still…

I looked at my hands. "I'm not against children," I said, desperate.

When he was quiet a long while, I saw a flicker of annoyance I'd never before beheld in Flint's eyes, usually clear as a still pond under a summer sky. Sludge entered those twin pools. His mouth pressed hard and thin. He sucked a tooth and squinted a look that shriveled me some. Then, Flint wriggled out from under, threw me off, and rummaged for his Levi's.

As he dragged them from under the bed, he grunted, "What the Billy-blue-blazes are you on about, Blossom?" He made it a kind of a jest, but I kenned better. "I'm a cow puncher. I don't settle down. Got a drive this fall…"

I didn't hear the rest. "I thought you loved me!"

"I do, gal! I'll be back. Someday!"

At that instant I kenned he wouldn't. He would tarry in Cheyenne for a month or two and find a new girl to fool with.

Then I made my second mistake.

"I—I have a little nest egg saved up at the bank," I said, over-prideful. I wanted to impress him with my responsibility. I wasn't a flibbertigibbet frittering money on ribbons, clothes, horehound, peppermint drops, and licorice whips. Well, not all.

"Me, who only went to the fourth grade, owning a banking account over at the Wells Fargo? Imagine that!" I preened some. "It wouldn't take much." I meant to put a down payment on a small ranch.

He snorted. His smirk threatened to undo me. I forgot my generous information with his next words.

"An' turn into a shriveled old man nailed like a horseshoe over the barn door afore I'm thirty? With a whole passel of hungry ankle-biters, I s'pose? Hah!"

His eyes took on a blank flat look, like a cold iron on the stove, and I kenned he must have misunderstood. He was just tired. He didn't realize I'd be working right alongside! Flint cast an unreadable look and hastily buckled his chaps and crammed on his hat. I did not like the final feeling.

"Hunh!" He stopped at the door, hanging back, one hand on the transom, and said wonderingly, "So, you got yourself a little old bank account, fancy that!"

"Not so little!" I boasted. "Saved up fifty-three silver dollars, seventy-one coppers, and fourteen half-eagles."

"Glory be, ain't that a wonder!" He cocked his head and gazed in that appealing way he had. "And seventy-one coppers?" He made a jest of it, so I lobbed my pillow at him.

That night I wept secretly in that pillow. Not for the cowboy, but that I was not enough to tie Flint to my corset strings. To make him give up the dangers and excitement on the trail that I myself secretly craved.

Dang Flint. He wanted punching cows, not owning them. I'd grow old and lose the best bedroom in a few years. I was almost twenty-two. Then I really wept, stuffing the sheet in my mouth when I could no longer hold back. The night seemed dark and empty. Even the moon, shining liquid pearls, hid its face

Chapter Eight
When a Robber Kisses You...Count Your Teeth

I felt a presence. Not like when ma stood in the barn doorway looking up and caught me in the hayloft with the next-over farmer's boy, knickers all askew and petticoat half undone. The voice behind me held mockery but also something else. Sadness. The chair was empty.

I looked over at my bed, flinching.

A figure lounged full length upon my scrumpled-up counterpane.

"*By the way, he* did *filch that brooch you're so fond of. The one fell on the floor?*"

"It wasn't like that. He put it back!"

The fiend's loud guffaws choked with mockery.

"Quiet! You're going to wake up Old Ned. Though I have little doubt you already shook hands with the Devil."

"Now that hurt."

"I doubt it."

I swatted, smoothing the spread, trying to lay hands on whatever or wherever the varmint was.

"Don't do this anymore!" I finally wailed. " 'Specially when folks are around. Either show yourself or don't." Which I realized was a contradiction.

A sigh of weariness that seemed to come from a

bottomless pit. "*I don't always have a choice.*" The depression lifted. I fancied footfalls circling the room.

"*Have you opened it?*"

I pretended not to understand. The voice floated from the bay windows now.

"So vexing! Stay in one place, darn you!"

"*Ma'am, I have been indeed performing* that *little act for far too long.*"

I remained mute, jaw clenched, arms folded, a scowl knitting my face. I must have looked very *un*appealing like a shrew, yet I refused to glance at my old jewelry box.

Cheekily, my faded velvet box lifted from the dresser, bobbling across the room before dropping. I darted to catch it before it struck the floor, cradling it in my arms, like a baby.

"Okay!" I said crossly. "You can do annoying tricks! Don't be a child."

"*Very well. I will take it back.*"

There was a small resistance—a disturbance of the air. The box lifted, wrenched from my hands and waggling, just a foot from my face, before wobbling back and thumping down on my dresser.

"Humph! I'm hardly impressed."

"*Well? Aren't you going to open it?*"

"Oh, what's the use?" I stamped my foot. "You probably pawed all over my things."

The lid seemingly lifted of its own accord.

I gaped, appalled, and cried out, "*Ohhh!*" My fingers flew over the compartments. I lifted the small lid to the tray beneath.

Empty.

The velvet box was stripped of all I held dear, of

my past, what I'd managed to cram into my rucksack. Even bits and bobs of no consequence, save for my memories. What was worse, a locket had a tintype of Ma's image, as I'd like to remember her, no matter the genuineness of the faded portrait or veracity of the metal.

"*I'd venture they should pay you for your service. Not the other way round. But what do I know?*" The phantom's words seemed anvil-heavy with satire.

"He didn't! Flint wouldn't!"

"*Regret I showed you. Pure bloody-mindedness on my part. My pardon, madam. You prefer to remain in ignorance.*" The words were stiff as a cardboard collar.

"Don't call me that! And why are you so mean?" I held the box with one hand and swiped tears with the other.

"*One grows bitter, confined in this room, pleasant as the occupant is. Damned sorry for my callous actions.*" I imagined a slight bow by a shifting of the light.

I childishly hurled the empty box in that direction. "Oh, take it and go to Old Scratch!"

"*As you kindly reminded me, I already have...*"

I had a second shock. Lightning bolted to my toes. My mouth locked. I made an *awking* sound, swaying as if a high wind held me upright only by the fiercest opposition.

My phantom, I kenned by a glint of silver medallions—the same roughhewn figure as before, fashioned out of nothing, was different—appearing as if he were in a play...

Dust billowed all about him.
He was running. I saw him.

I had a flash of intuition this happened in the past.

It wasn't my room any more, but a wilderness.

Drab plains, dotted with cactus and distant lavender mountains....

A thud of boots on hard ground and screams. Woman's screams.

Shadowy men with pistols rampaged. Dust boiled up in hot clouds. By their fearsome expressions and ugly open mouths, it appeared they shouted threats or orders and curses. Then, a woman in a fine traveling robe stepped out of the swirling mist, only the mist was formed of dust with golden glints...a small boy behind her held onto her skirts... Hues like washed-out watercolor boldened into more vibrant shades.

A rough hand reached from the golden fog and ripped a pendant watch from her neck. I heard more muffled shrieks—men's cries, the crack of a rifle, horses' whinnies. A man in a long duster, with a red rose blooming on his chest, thudded backwards to the dirt. Another figure fell from a horse, seemingly to my carpet as I jumped back.

My phantom, brandishing two long-barreled colts, withdrew from the swirling ochre-ish fog, the lower half of his face hidden behind a faded black bandanna.

I jerked my head to the right as one bright golden wheel I recognized as belonging to a Wells Fargo stagecoach rolled through the chaotic mist before the entire tableau—action, people, and horses—swirled, dissolving faster than a sugar lump in a cup of scalding tea.

I stared unseeing for long seconds with my mouth open. "What was that?" I croaked.

"I'm...unhappy you had to see that. Sometimes for

my sins…" My phantom gestured. I realized I could see him again. "But what…? Was that you?"

"They trail after me like a bad vapor, when I am…roused. And you, God forbid…" He struggled for words. *"Rouse me. Put it out of your mind! It has nothing to do with you. It is done! In the past. I will try not to let it happen again."* The angry tone made the air vibrate. The man-shape wavered, fighting to remain solid but nevertheless fading like steam on a windowpane. Medallions on his leather vest winked out like faraway stars.

I felt hot, cold, all at the same time, like coming down with the ague. Goosebumps pocked my arms, while sweat trickled between my bosoms.

"By the way, I put all your gewgaws back. He didn't get far."

I refused to look at my jewel box.

Then I found them. The old contents lay on my dresser. All of it. Chill with a dampness, as I touched them, as if they had lain in morning dew.

"Don't thank me."

"But—what I saw! What had that to do with…this?" Gesturing to my baubles, I meant the odd scene.

"Nada, little one. Your cowboy's theft brought back my own wicked deeds. It happens." He hitched a shadowy shoulder. *"Now. Allow me to rest. And I would rather, for the time being, that you do not parade around in that sheer nightdress you love so much, as well as that pink shimmy thing."*

"Goodness! Soon I will have nothing to wear."

The chuckle faded. *"That's the general idea…"*

****

I stomped down for breakfast, still in my flannel nighty, hair tied in rags—I'd show him!—on that Sunday before church. Sunday breakfasts and the outing to church service were a treat, one of the allowances Madame Solange afforded us. The back room was all atwitter, like starlings on a telegraph pole. Starving as usual, I snatched a hot biscuit, lavishly buttered it, and was reaching for watermelon preserves when I heard Flint's name. The biscuit was sawdust in my mouth. I choked it down, taking a hot swallow of Solange's coffee, spitting out the eggshells she always boiled in it, and asked crossly, "What's all the hoorah about?"

"Wasn't he one a your'n?" Little Mae flounced, giving me a milkmaid's simp. She kenned good and well I was sweet as a taffy-pull on Flint.

I shrugged. "What was that name again?" Reaching for another biscuit and thick brown apple butter, I piled my plate, making a teepee of ham, red-eye gravy, three sunny-side-up eggs, hot sage sausages, and cornbread, without thinking. Their eyes grew round, and they started grabbing biscuits before I could take them all.

I stared at my plate. Now I'd have to eat this, or Madame Solange's wrath would clap like thunder around my ears.

"Didn't you'all hear?" Little Mae cooed. "He done run off with Jewel."

I looked quickly to the end of the long table. Jewel's usual place by Big Bertha was indeed empty. She was a sometime girl anyway—whenever one of us was visited by Auntie Scarlett, she could be lured from the Vincent House Hotel on Wylder Street and their restaurant kitchens.

My breakfast sat like an anvil in my tummy. "Poor t-thing," I stammered. "When did all this happen?"

"Poor thing! He was a handsome devil! Late las' night. Looked out my winder, and there they was a gallopin' off, with Jewel and a big old carpetbag hitched to his saddle."

My heart dropped to my toes. He had filched my pathetic baubles for Jewel.

"She'll regret that when she gets saddle burns and…" I began when they burst out tittering to beat the band, making comments like, "Hell's bells, Blossom! We *all* get saddle burns!" I hoped they choked on their biscuits.

I stuffed down eggs, ham, and redeye gravy to smother the pain, without tasting, challenging them with bulging cheeks that I didn't care. How I gobbled it all down, when my neck was choked with grief, I will never ken, but I did. Later, I got rid of it in the privy and went to my room to brood, mutely studying my face in the mirror, consumed with searching for bags, large pores, sagging jaws, or spidery lip-lines like the wife of the Wylder Mercantile who had a mustache.

Satisfied I was not turning into a hag, I twisted before the pier glass to give myself a proper vetting.

High breasts—on the small side, perhaps—with soft pink tips, slim creamy columns of legs, narrow knees, neatly rounded hips, none too wide—*Room to grow?* my inner devil suggested. Plus a tucked-up fanny. And my long white neck was rather elegant, 'specially if I raised my chin. My face was long and thin too, but I had big eyes and a soft wide mouth just made for kissing.

I sighed. Jewel was a golden mulatto, young, with

skin sleek and high-colored as a fresh peach. A wonder every man over the age of twelve wasn't head-over-heels goony over her. Why'd she have to pick *my* cowboy? I hated her. I hated Flint. I'd never get over it. I despised *all* men! Love bit with fangs that sank deep. And so I silently raged as I readied for church.

"*Thank you, little one...that show was most enjoyable. Have you quite gotten over your displeasure?*"

Shutting my ears, I cast a sour glance at the corner from whence the comment floated, grimly ignoring him. I refused to cover myself. The day was already sultry. I determined to trek to the pool with the others after the mercifully short service, eschewing the picnic later, for I pinched an inch of fat at my waist, thanks to the hog's mess stuffed down earlier.

I traipsed about the room, airing myself at the window, showing off my bottom as I leaned on the sill, lifted my arms above my head, making my breasts hike up into two delectable little puddings with cherries on top, hoping to evoke more phantom comments so I could tear into *whoever.*

I heard a low chuckle, then, an unmistakable sound of a snore!

Really!

Huffily, I donned my Sunday-go-to-meeting clothes. Fine sheer muslin. Short puffy sleeves. A modest neckline with no danger of imperiling the pastor's rectitude, *or* the pastor's wife's censure, a matching Battenberg lace parasol, plus new white kid slippers, cheekily leaving off both stockings and bloomers.

They'd only get wet later.

****

Next day, as I readied for the evening—which ofttimes began mid-afternoon, if drovers were in town—I lifted my abundant hair with the right amount of curl to look messily unkempt, like I just got out of bed. Finally satisfied I was not falling apart, I carefully applied beetroot to my cheeks, bee's-waxed and sooted lashes extra thick, and carmined lips with the inexpensive stuff from the hawker who ambled through Wylder with his packhorse once a month and whose arrivals were much anticipated by us four girls.

Tonight, when I descended for my first gentleman of the evening, I wished to slay them like wild Indians on the warpath with my appearance, belying any speculations over the slightest inconsolability over Flint—the cheating, two-timing skunk. Thus, I scarce noticed the female with hair screaming of cheap henna dye palavering with Madame. Must be an out-of-towner, I vaguely supposed. "Like she dunked her head in red ink," I murmured to Big Bertha in passing and forgot her.

After entertaining a traveling card shark, a notorious cattle rustler who was never caught, an out-of-town editor looking for a suitable spot to print a yellow rag newspaper, plus my usual with the deputy sheriff, it was after two when I removed my allurements.

I wasn't alone again. Soon, I'd be crazy as a quilt. If I turned sharpish enough, I'd see the wretch lounging quite comfortably in the red chair in the corner where the roof slants over the eaves.

No one was there…

I wasn't disappointed.

I wasn't!

Yet there was that companionable feeling.

"Am I *that* pathetic?" I threw my slipper at my image.

A curl of smoke ebbed and flowed about my head like a halo from hell. I smelt cigarillos and heard amused laughter. "*Yes, I am rather afraid you are, if you are going to fall for every* tacanyo *thieving saddle humper.*"

I was in a pool of light, courtesy of my oil lamp with the teepees and an Indian maiden painted on the glass reservoir. The rest lay in cozy dimness. I couldn't spy the wretch. "Why torment me?"

"*Come now.*" He laughed. "*Aren't we being a mite overdramatic? I only point out what is plain as that rather large but pretty nose on your face.*"

"My nose is not large! I didn't know he was a thief!"

"*Don't mind me. Ofttimes, I'm a poor judge of character—since I don't have any myself.*"

A headache was trying mightily to scream itself awake. I put my head in my palms. My shoulders tensed as I felt a brush of lips on my nape, sending barbs of excitement prickling my toes. *First time that happened!* I was of two persons, one craving the touch, the other frightened of that desire. I was lost. Doomed to the cook flames of Hell. I never applied to fortune tellers, or attributed stray breezes or suddenly closed doors to haints. The church warned against such. I was practical—hard-headed. Then I thought of Flint. At least in some areas.

I held my breath until dizzy, waiting.

Someone else, not me, arched her neck, dropping

her head back. The sensation of lips on my arms, my breasts, my long neck, my mouth—it roused me. I sat bolt upright. "Please. Don't!"

"*Forgive me. So long since I smelled a woman's sweetness, or perfumed warmth. Her special fragrant musk down there that drives a man loco. Like mountain roses, perhaps lilacs, mixed with pure wildcat.*"

As the phantom murmured between brushing kisses, I watched wisps of curls in my looking-glass float from my neck.

"You—you are quite a poet!" I gasped. "I would not have thought it in—in such as you."

"*I read too—and occasionally take a bath.*"

"I didn't mean…"

"*I know you did not, little one…I mean you no harm…only to ravish you—a little.*"

I sucked in and held it until woozy, inescapably turning my head, sensing a mouth on mine, cool, but growing warmer with desire, like embers combusting. I flinched, terrified. I felt strong hands. My shoulders gripped, my body roughly turned around, drawn up until pressed hard against an unmistakably male body. I kept my eyes closed, fearful of opening them, and I returned the kiss with growing heat, breath shallower, then faster, leaving my heart thumping, aching for more when the deep probing kiss left off. The surrounding air hummed, choked with longing and static vibration. With sorrow too, perhaps, as thick as felt.

I touched my bruised mouth, recalling the sensation of cool insistent lips that kenned what they were about. I never let my johns kiss me. That was private. Only Flint, when he got around to it. But now I had never been bussed so thoroughly, so pleasurably.

Ludicrous!

I caught my white face in the mirror with fiery spots on my cheeks, my eyes wide and haunted. Just mine. Just *my* eyes. I scowled at the image.

"Am I a love-starved maiden-auntie, or a timid spinster whittling away desires with fantasies verging on the sinful? Phantom lovers!" I scoffed. "That's for stick-in-the-muds who read Jane Eyre!" I warred. But was not the urge, simply to be one with someone, bred and born in *both* man and woman, leading to such thoughts, until blissfully, lustily, manifested either side of hell?

Next day, the dream faded somewhat, yet I kenned the happening could not be explained. If this be madness, then I would gladly be a raving lunatic. I craved this phantom, this man who was not man, but more than any I had knowledge of, carnal or otherwise. There was no comparison to the earthly lovers—inventorying the parade of miners, trappers, mercantile owners, and preacher's sons I had known biblically or otherwise—that came paying for my favors.

That night, I touched myself to sooth guilt and the demands of my body, aching with desire for something that could not be. Could never be. Recalling his masculine frame built on brutal big-boned lines, no matter his ranginess, the satiny amber skin. The icy turquoise eyes, glittering bottomless pools, from which one could fall into another world, if venturing too near.

The tightness of his trousers.

I felt myself melt into a feverish blush in the dark. I cupped my breasts, feeling the nips harden into little raspberries and smoothed my belly down to my private place…

Chapter Nine
The Withdrawal

Something clawed at me.

A memory, like a dull mouse stealing a piece of cheese from a clever cat.

I found myself, on my half-day, with my feet marching toward the bank. As I approached the teller's window with an over-bright smile, I told myself I had a mind to buy new dress goods down at the mercantile, fresh off the Wells Fargo stage. That was all.

"How may I help *you?*" The teller with the fresh young face and wispy mustache had a knowing look with a hint of something I did not wish to see. Part smirk. Part puzzle. Part anxiety.

"Why, I just want to withdraw a little old mite from my savings account. I made up my mind to purchase some dress goods." I rattled on to delay the inevitable. I smiled giddily and handed over my made-out slip.

"*We*-ll!" He looked arch, turning the scrap of paper over, as if he had never before beheld one in his born days.

I wasn't too alarmed. Not then. I rarely touched my savings, yet hardly a week went by without socking away at least a penny or two. I was known here. No one could take it out but me. Or so I supposed.

"I can see why you are surprised. I don't usually…" I babbled on. "You see, there's a dress I'm thinking of making, it's got little violets all over, and…" I trailed off at his expression. I could no longer deny his nervousness as he darted distressed looks at the Wells Fargo president.

Flashing a mouth full of teeth, he summoned him. "Best Mr. Blandings handles this. I, ummm, need to see a gent about a horse."

I was meant to believe he had to use the facilities out back and smiled politely, though feeling increasing unease. Approached by the manager's stern visage, my knees unaccountably knocked beneath my flounces; I braced them against the teller window while he looked down through glasses pinched on a fleshy nose.

"Now, little lady. What can I do for you?" He spoke as if cajoling a child from having a tantrum by offering a peppermint.

My mind went blank as a snowdrift. *Why, I want my money. I want you to tell me it is safe. That Flint didn't do away with it. He is not spending it on Jewel. It is not possible! This is a bank!*

Instead, I gritted my teeth to keep from shouting, or lowering my head on his chest and bawling. The old flirtatious instincts kicked in. "Why, Mr. Blandings. I never kenned I merited such personal service from you! I would have made ever so many *more* withdrawals." I batted lashes and curved him a knowing smile. *Please don't say it!*

"We acceded to your wishes a few days ago, Miss, ah, *Cherry*," he said too cold for my liking. "We can hardly fund it to you twice." He unpinched his spectacles and studied me with eyes like boiled eggs.

"Why, whatever do you mean?" I bridled like a southern belle, despising the quake in my voice.

Raising brows high as his pitched voice, he intoned, as if he could not believe my cupidity, "When receiving your note, we acceded to your wishes. Naturally." He was all bristles—a tempest was coming, and he averted it with a brandished umbrella.

"*My* wishes?"

"Of course. When Mr. Corrigan…"

I felt woozy. My face crinkled and blanched while I held on to the teller's window ledge. I felt wood grain beneath my fingers, and cold brass bars on my hot forehead as I leant against them, aware the teller watched with a rapacious gleam. I kenned so little of the man I'd pinned my heart on. *Corrigan.* Flint *Corrigan.* I had not even kenned his last name. I shook my head as if attacked by a pesky fly, listening hard as I turned wearily around and the manager continued. "…said you were, ah—laid up?" I heard.

He made no attempt to lessen the blow. "We emptied your account and made out the cashier's check, as per your missive's request. It's done all the time." He snorted and checked his turnip watch.

"But you can't!" I raised my voice. "It's mine!"

"Obviously a man has a right and proper access to his wife's account," he snorted. Looking down his nose, he stuffed the watch back. "Most females—" Undecided whether to jolly, lecture, or chastise, he went on, "have no head *or* desire to dirty their pretty little hands over financial affairs which they would scarce make heads or tails of at any rate."

We were attracting quite a crowd.

"He wasn't my husband!" I hissed back, panicked. "And I am well able to handle my own affairs!"

"Obviously not! And same as"—he threw me a

knowing leer—"to hear tell. In addition, we had the note with *your* signature. Really, madam, you are causing an incident."

I seemed frozen at the window. Unable to turn, to meet the stares, afraid to let go for fear I would drop right there on the floor, I hung on as he stalked back to his office and returned waving note paper that I recognized as mine. Pale blue, printed with pink ribbons, forget-me-nots, and a large curlicue *B* for Blossom—along with a maroon account book.

"Here 'tis. That day's records. You do see?" He drew a fat finger across a line.

Sure, enough, a reasonable signature was present.

But not mine.

My handwriting is childish and careful, I must confess—a schoolgirl's attempt, with big rounded letters staying within the lines. Easy as child's play to recreate. I crumpled the note and dropped it on the floor, departing without a word, spine stiff, chin up, feeling stares and folks pointing. They weren't, of course. Why would *anyone* care that I lost fifty-three silver dollars, seventy-one coppers, and fourteen half dollars?

Gone.

By hook or crook, I was grimly determined to build it back up and keep it stuffed under my mattress, if I had to take ten johns a night!

I have to laugh.

How prophetic.

Not the johns.

The mattress. The treasure…

****

That night, as I addressed my toilette with a

vengeance, my room changed, again charged with vibrations thrumming my back teeth. "Don't even think of being here!" I snarled.

"*You are—discontented? Or is that just your usual come-hither scowl? And must you show all of yourself tonight? Could you not leave some small portion of your anatomy for later?*"

Recalling Flint salted my rejoinder. "Scarcely your business! And discontented is like saying a hailstorm is a dewdrop!" I savagely yanked my bodice down farther, till near popping out the top.

"*I meant not to pry…gets boring, however, watching your endless parade of…*"

"All right! You are most correct. My judge of horseflesh is pitiable. Every penny. Every cent saved. Gone! Are you satisfied?" The heat of a chili pepper scorched my words. Emboldened, smarting over his revelations regarding Flint's perfidy, I sneered. "Couldn't stay away, huh? I thought you were gone."

Though I had not grown used to it, still, I did not flinch at his sudden appearance. I shot a glance at the massive, worn, red velvet chair. A dim form lounged, idly flicking a bull whip, one leg slung over the arm. I fancied I heard the *snap* and *crack*. As if watching a yellow-bellied racer snake, I remained still wondering which way his words would sting.

"*Gone? I haven't vamoosed anywhere, little dove, as you know well.*"

I raised a brow. "But here—all the while?" I spoke as pointed as a hat pin, venturing closer to the chair, wanting to get a rise out of him. Wanting to hurt him.

The figure wavered as if made from thin silk, wafting in a breeze.

I held myself still. I didn't exhale. Waiting.

Out of the corner's dimness, his hellishly handsome face smiled wickedly back. The same eyes, the lurid green-blue of the sky before a storm, and just as soul-destroying.

Phantom or human, I still refused to wrap my mind around this aggravation like brown butcher's paper about a Christmas gift. Biting my lip, I coldly contemplated him as if he were mud I must scrape from my shoe, determined to make him feel as unsettled as I.

He idly snapped the whip, after a warning glance, ignoring me.

"But—but, I haven't *felt* you!" I goaded. "Do you—do you…watch? Answer me if you have any gentlemanly qualities left in you!"

I curled my lip, waving my arm meaningfully at my bed. "But here? All the while?" Each word, bitten like crunching hard candy, was answered by that infuriating laugh—that scornful look, one brow cocked like a pistol…and the deep clefts into which the corners of his mouth curved… I collected myself.

"*No one ever accused me of being a gentleman, ma'am. Watch you? When you, ah…screw, fornicate, make love, hide the sausage…?*"

"Don't be crude!"

"*No, I 'spose I'm not a gentleman…*" he said without irony. "*Besides, I've been around the world a few times. I am not easily shocked. Why, I even went to Kansas City once.*" He flicked the whip. My drapes stirred.

"*I do apologize, however. Surely, a gentle, cultured, naïve young maiden of your blushing refinement and careful, meticulous upbringing—was it in a convent, I wonder?—would naturally be offended by my ill manners and uncouth japes.*"

I rushed to smack him without thinking. The varmint held up his hands in mock terror though my hand swished right through him. I spun myself backward, nearly falling in his lap. I jumped back as if I spied that yellow-bellied racer.

Swatting at shadows. Would I have no satisfaction?

"*Ah,* paloma, *I have no voyeuristic tendencies.*" Distaste curled his voice like a dead leaf. "*Amusing at first…then, uncomfortable.*" He did not elucidate further. "*Ah, well. I see I cannot please you. Perhaps I should go.*"

I demanded. "Go? But—where *do* you go…? If you cannot leave this room, as you said?"

"*Where? Difficult to explain.*"

"Try it!"

"*I—fold myself…into myself.*"

"You don't!" I could not picture it.

"*I said I could not explain!* Bueno*! I go away. I go into myself. I gaze out the window. I recall more pleasant times—places I've been, until you're—finished, rather than watching you romping about in bed with an amazing assortment of men and having your pleasure! Frankly, I think you could do better!*"

If a phantom could "*Hummmpf,*" he did.

"And I am to care what you suppose? I am to hie myself to a nunnery, giving myself to God, or, perhaps become a spinster child-minder until I am a doddery, dried-up old hag thrown out on the midden heap?" I paced, thumping my feet on the floor. "Or…I could marry a farmer!"

I whirled, facing him. "His field hand by day and

doxy at night! Or clean up spittoons down in the saloon…or…"

Oh, I was wound up like a clock-spring. I stopped, heaving.

"*Little one.*" The voice was weary, bored. "*I meant no such thing.*"

I viewed the phantom stalking bare-chested to the window, staring balefully out.

"*You appeared* muy guapa *last night.*" He spoke facing away. "*I like your hair that way. But can you not do better than a cowhand right off the trail?*"

"Oh, back to that, are we? I suppose *you* would have been better. A greater lover? Whatever you were!" I grinned sheepish, then, at the thought of my conquest of the evening before. A slow night. I was lucky to snag Willard. Earnest, shy, freckled, and clumsy Willard, but mercifully quick.

We shared a grin before my phantom remembered himself, scowled, and resumed swatting curtains with his whip. The bullwhip disappeared into them. They stirred, however.

"Why?" I continued sharpish. "Are you a hoity-toity?"

"*Hardly. I can't brag about my pastimes, nor my illustrious ancestors. Nary a prince, city mayor, nor dogcatcher among us. Yet—no one stole from me.*"

"So, you suppose. Are you any better than Flint? Weren't you a thief too?"

The long pause meant my arrow hit its mark.

"*If you put it that way. Yet I did not vow undying love to my victims, either, madam!*"

I had no rejoinder. I wasn't even sure what he was in life.

I was readying myself for another evening and already late, courtesy of my unwanted tenant. Unconsciously, I noted I had piled my hair in the same manner he admired, yanking it loose from the combs and set about disregarding him.

And he disregarded me. When I searched my looking glass, he was nowhere in the room I could see.

Chapter Ten
Another Tarnished Star in My Crown

I tossed, dreaming darkest revenge, awakened glaring at the moon, wanting to burn the bank down. Yearning to kick the smarmy clerk in the caboose. And to kick Flint where it hurt worst, and apparently where he kept his only feelings…and most of all, despising the nosy, irritating, heartless phantom.

If I could.

A zephyr brushed my face.

I touched my cheek.

I fancied a hand on my shoulder. I stiffened, and gasped sharpish, ready to snatch the derringer from the bedside drawer. Fingers like steel gripped my shoulder till it hurt, stubbornly shaking me awake. It was him! Suddenly I felt like an untried maiden. Petrified he had invaded my bed. Terrified of what he might do.

"Please! Go away. Why are you bothering me?" My voice was a frightened mouse squeak. I had been sliding in and out of dreams like a hole in an ice-covered pond.

"This is not about you. Hush, listen!"

Strong rough fingers shook me again.

"Listen, lazy slugabed!"

Then, I heard it.

Poor little Flora, softly weeping. One could scarce hear her kitteny squeaks. Hopping out, I forgot all about what woke me and ran down the hall to tap at her door. How I could have heard her is beyond my mortal soul. But then I didn't.

Flora really *was* sick, poor little scrap.

All the fellas liked Flora, 'cause she seemed like a Frozen Charlotte doll, just made for saving—if saving meant taking her to bed—from old Gustavo, the Italian gold miner, to trappers with dirt tattooed under their skin, to leathery old range riders who hadn't been under a civilized roof in five years.

Flora always looked about twelve, though professed to twenty-six. I figured around eighteen. A toothpick. A fairy sprite, a dandelion fluff with wispy shimmies floating round her frame—so huge they accidentally showed her small bosoms like she was all unaware, enflaming the johns even more. They all wanted a taste of Flora's little green May apples.

Poor Flora didn't ken how to take care of herself, though, or how to refuse the rough ones. She seemed to actually invite punches, pinches, and harsh words with her sweetness. I meant to be nice, but somehow, she always got overlooked. Always said she ran into the dresser, or some such, so afraid Madame would kick her out in the street if she fussed. I figured the dresser ran into her. She never complained, but I suspicioned Flora would be paraded more and more past the less savory if she didn't perk up some. A few doxies can be sullen and hard on a guy, ordering him about and even taking a riding crop to him. Some fellas gobble that up, like a cat does fishcakes.

But Flora wasn't one of them. Flora wouldn't smack a fly with a feather duster. Earlier, she had a hard time keeping watered whiskey down, I noted, and when Big John—not too bad a fellow—strode up, she cast fearful eyes and made a small noise in the back of her throat.

"Here." I walked up bold, nudging Big John. "Why do you want that little old pail of skim milk when you can have cream?"

I'd used that line before, but it had never felt so appropriate. I motioned to Flora, *Get gone!* Rubbing my bubbies on his arm, I brushed his favorite bits with the back of my hand. John wasn't so bad, just clumsy as a bull in a pastor's wife's parlor or at grandma's quilting bee.

Flora nipped out, dimpling a smile. I was shameful, though. One should not be crowing over Christian duty. I grinned at Big John. He wasn't called big for nothing. He grinned back.

John left much later without a word. We kenned each other too well to chat. Besides, I was still aglow with the notion that Flora wouldn't have to do anything heavier that night than lift a spoonful of milk custard.

Yet now, Flora was hot as a poker. I rushed to the water basin and wrapped her brow with a wet cloth. They say to sweat a fever, but I did not have the heart to smother her in blankets on a close night. Opening the window, I removed sweat-soaked sheets, made her drink water, soothing her from the night-horses galloping through her head, all the while checking for dread spots that could mean scarlatina, or the pox.

I kept doing that until dawn, and her bilious fever broke, so I covered Flora with a clean sheet and tidied her hair. When I crept back, I felt a lightness in my room, as if spring entered after a hellish winter, and a breeze like velvet scented with white lilacs blew through my windows. Fingertips moved across my lips.

"*That was a right nice thing you did. Well done.*"

My eyes wetted, and face screwed up, all unbecoming.

Nobody had spoken caring words to me for so long. "What do you know about nice?" I snapped. I did not ken how to act in the face of his kindness.

"*I regret about what happened that day. I should have warned you, but you're stubborn as a pack of mules. You wouldn't have listened…*"

"I don't have any notion what you are on about."

"*Only money, dear girl. It means nothing in the end.*"

"It does now. To me! What have you to do with anything? You don't need money. I was going to be somebody!"

"*I was away…or I might have…*"

"Stopped Flint?"

"*Somewhat like that.*"

"Quit prying in my affairs! I was doing fine without you."

"*You are an unforgiving, ungrateful little hellcat, aren't you?*"

After an interminable silence, I ventured. "Are you still here?"

"*You know I am,*" floated the whisper of despair.

"I am too."

I closed my eyes and turned my face to him.

****

We collided like runaway freight trains, as two lovers after a quarrel, desperate to make amends. I gulped hard, refusing to dwell on what it meant when strapping arms crushed me. A thick-calloused hand cupped my cheek—a hand of hard use, feeling the rasp of pads of muscle, toughened, as one used to the rope, the reins, pistol grips, and a hardscrabble life, pleasurably scraping my flesh. The phantom—I would not give him a name; it would make it real—explored my body, rounding my breasts, running hands down, shaping my waist, cupping my fanny, and dipping between my thighs, as if not kenning what part to ravish first.

"*You should not be so—fetching...*" The voice groaned out. "*So touchable… I could no longer resist you than if you were sent by the devil to torment me with red hot pincers.*"

His word were harsh, bitter as the Longhorn's cheapest rye whiskey and just as potent.

The phantom lover said all this between kisses, his lips on my flesh hot as a devil's brew, cool as an angel's wings, harsh and soft, melting, and brutal, as if he, this phantom or ghost or specter wanted to regain all the earthly pleasures denied him in whatever nether world he inhabited in one twinkling. I felt myself—to my terror—respond to his ruthless, needful caresses.

I finally struggled to breathe, pushing him away, still not opening my eyes, terrified of the glittering gaze, the hard mouth with bracketing lines…

"*You are indeed a sorceress. Or I am a...*"

"A demon?"

"*I can be, if that is your desire. I can be very wicked.*"

I shivered, wondering how deep my wantonness would plunge me.

I'd gotten to ken my regulars. Too familiar sometimes. Ofttimes, near dozing off no matter how pleasurable the ride, like a cat being scratched behind the ears. This phantom's touch, was unknown, alien. However, in too short a time for my conscience, I sank into sinful surrender, no longer caring, especially when I felt a body, his body, unaccountably solid and strong, smelling of saddles, aromatic cigarillos, and rye whiskey rolling heavily, full-length, atop me, clutching me to him.

"*I vowed I would not do this again—the hell with it!*" Thrusting a rough hand between my thighs, he explored me, pushing my legs, warm to his cool touch, farther apart, and I felt him—solid and stalwart and harder than any man—find his way, gently at first, then thrust with a final end of forbearance, accompanied by a deep blissful groan, matching my own moans of ecstasy as we, this stranger and I, made slow—agonizingly slow—love, as if he wished to treasure the coupling, not the brutal desperate mating I had come to halfway expect. He lay still, as if savoring, full length into me, not stirring a muscle, though I felt his member twitch. I wanted to scream. Feeling my desire, he favored me, thrusting deep and long, varying his strokes as one well-schooled. I didn't mind how many women he had practiced on, as long as the master ended with me as the favored student.

****

It was dawning.

I felt no warmth where a body had lain, no matter how lightly.

Yet his long depression amid hopelessly tangled sheets told me I was not a love-starved, crazed female. I still felt the sweet fullness between my legs and thighs and on my tender swollen breasts and puffed lips.

"Come back," I whispered, recklessly. "I don't care!" Propped on an elbow, I narrowed my eyes, scanning the room. Not a shadow or sound. My body stiffened like a plank. Reality flooded in, dousing memories with the coldness of snow sliding off a roof down one's neck. What was I doing!

"*Don't be afraid. I watched you for so long. There are names for men like me.*" His dry humor was unmistakable.

"You are not a man," I accused, feeling terribly, sinfully, guilt-ridden.

"*Oh? I beg to differ. That was not what you attested to last night—frequently. Yet my spirit is charged by what happens here in this room as any normal male—and by my long captivity.*"

"Oh, not me, I suppose!"

"*Vain, too, I see.*"

"You would know all about that!" He ignored that comeback.

"*That—energy. It does something. Lately, I ventured as far as the hall after I watched the street outside your window. I pray it does not end there. I've never been that strong. Never able to break these invisible ropes or leave this miserable chair. Do you know how uncomfortable that blasted red chair is?*"

The comment made him oddly human.

I couldn't imagine how it felt, chained to this room for untold years, knowing only what transpired between those passing through for days or possibly decades.

"But who—who were you, really? Should I be afraid?"

"*Afraid? Why, I am the other resident. One might venture, I am the legal resident. Hell has more lawyers*" *than a dog has fleas.*" His bitterness seemed black as day-old tea, as if he too felt unease. "*Apologies. If you could see me, I am making a courtly bow.*" His sarcasm was detectable. "*I will not touch you again. You need not fear me.*" Now the voice was behind me by the windows.

I felt hurt, used. I willingly took part in an act that was, if not sinful, I was certain there was no word vile or perverted enough. Cast aside, by a demon. How dare he?

"You cannot stay, or I will go mad. I already am, to believe in you."

"*I will keep out of your way…I will not make my presence felt.*"

"But where would you go? Why mayn't I see you, now?" I asked contrarywise. "I did—a little." I waved my hands stumbling hither-thither, determined to make contact if only to strike him, in the end swatting out in frustration. A hand from nowhere caught me before I fell.

"Damn you! Show yourself!"

"*I'm tired. It tires, you see, to be startled out of— whatever I was, or wherever.*"

"But you are a dad-blasted—" I closed my eyes, barely letting a sigh escape my lips. "A *ghost*…you can do anything you wish! Fly to the moon. Float to the damned ceiling! Did last night mean nothing to you?"

"*Of course!* Por Dios*! Say it! Ghost, shade, specter, apparition, phantasm, spirit, haint! Pinned to this damned blasted room for—Hell! Far too bloody-blasted long! Now leave me be, before I forget myself!*" I witnessed a hand hover in the air as if to strike.

Backing to the bed, I shivered, wondering if his

changeable moods affected the air, for the room chilled again. "Why aren't you in Hell? What are you waiting for?"

"*I don't know,*" came the melancholy voice.

"Sorry. Did not mean to offend."

Like heck I didn't. "You won't leave, then?"

"*What? Are you deaf, as well as rude and nagging? No fear! I can't! Didn't I mention that?*"

The air stirred as if he waved an angry hand. I detected a fist punching the wall, sensing him striving for the right words.

"Please try to explain."

"*My form—is coming together. That's not it, damn it… I see my hands. My face in your dressing mirror, just for a few ticks of that silly bedside clock. Something new. I wasn't aware I could be seen.*"

I glanced at my offending gilded cherub clock, which had set me back a silver dollar and five cents.

"*This… 'forming' is fiercest in times of the passion and hot blood, especially while you—*"

"You said that!" I blushed.

"*Don't flatter yourself. When I'm riled or hankering for my former life, and regrets turn bitter—*" His voice faded, or softened. "*Not all regret. I…enjoyed that. I feel I took advantage.*"

He felt guilt. That was why his mood. I detected him by the window. Hesitantly I touched his shadowy shoulder. The form wavered as if he flinched. "We all have regrets, whoever we are—or were. I did not mean to insult."

"*My past debaucheries, the road untaken. Bah! Such weakness. I am become maudlin in my old age.*" As he spoke, I fancied brass shells fired at the world.

"*You give me strength. I do not fancy being dependent.*"

"If you cannot, how can I?" I felt snappish and weary, of a sudden. "I can hardly help it, nor do I want such ability."

"*So be it.*"

I was left abruptly alone. I wondered what hellish world he inhabited when not invading my room, my comfort, my sanity—*my body…*

****

We girls generally slept till eleven, straggling down soon after for mid-day breakfast, or for a special treat. When business was good enough for Madame, we headed to the Vincent Hotel on Wylder Street. Until then, we could sleep 'in the arms of Morpheus,' as Madame liked to say when putting on airs for special gentlemen callers—lawyers, the circuit judge, or mining owners. Anyone who looked like he owned more than two pairs of boots and read a book.

"They sleep in the arms of Morpheus, so they will be fresh as daisies for all you stalwart hot-blooded stallions," she'd trill, setting my teeth on edge. Seemed we ate cinders, our teeth grated so at times. Then she'd give a roguish wink, crinkling her cheeks like cracks in plaster, and suck on a cigarillo holder in what she supposed a sophisticated manner. I scorned the whole performance when feeling 'specially fractious.

I think he—Morpheus—was a Greek god of sleep. Makes sense, I reckon. Either way, I looked more a bedraggled, stepped-on daisy after my night playing Florence Nightingale and verbal and physical acrobatics with my demon tenant.

****

He did not manifest for days. The room, seemed

empty as a house on moving day—furniture gone, echoing spaces, dark rectangles where portraits once hung—though I ventured to draw him out. I even sat in his chair. After a sensation of entering another soul—a disturbing happenstance, I can tell you!—it was as if he traveled on to that shadowy place I could never enter. Perhaps he had gained his reward, or Hell's fire, as the pastor liked to preach.

Perhaps the room was mine again.

Chapter Eleven
Return from the Devil

He came to me in the night.

I stood by the bay windows after my evening clients left, searching the quiet streets for what I could not identify, with a yearning I dared not name. By a cool stir—a velvety smoothness to the darkness, I sensed his ghostly presence. His hunger was crackling energy, my appetite whetted by remembrance, his by what forces of denials endured—for how long, I could not fathom, yet his touch was thistledown—a hand wafted over my shoulder caused my skin to vibrate and tiny down on my arms to lift, as if a storm raged outside, in place of inside me.

Iron bars clamped my body to his, back to chest. He bent his head to my neck with no ceremony or gentleness, his want fueling his kisses, biting my ears, brushing his rasping jaws against my enflamed cheeks as he searched my mouth. *"Don't say no. Don't. I cannot…"*

He left the plea unfinished in a strangled moan as he gripped my hair, thrusting strong fingers through tangled curls and, turning me, held my face in a vise. *"I tried to stay away."*

I could no more resist than stop a gully-washer rushing down a ravine.

I felt myself lifted, floating in unyielding arms as

he wafted me to bed. The bed lurched; a weight fell alongside me. I had promised I would deny him, but I dared not breathe as calloused hands fiercely sculpted my body, then lightly trailed fingers back, silking my flesh, as if delaying the delights to come, while I trembled with need, feeling resolve weaken.

Usually, I was the tease. This was unprecedented.

I fumbled my hand down, instinctively groping the hickory hard strength of him, the hugeness. My tender bits quivered, pulled to him. An equally powerful pull yanked me back—I came to my senses, with the same shock as when I fell though ice in the bathing pond last winter.

I screamed impetuously, hagridden with confusion.

"Stop! Don't. You mustn't! I—it's not right." My body turned into a stone angel like in Wylder cemetery, rigid with cold and with fear of the unknown, the impossible, and my own unquenched, shameful craving.

His hands abruptly left off exploring.

I sensed a breeze as chill as November as he removed himself. Winter rushed into my room like a whirlwind, with icy words flung like sleet.

"*I have never taken a lady, baud, virgin, or maiden, disinclined! Then, I have had no such problem!*"

I propped on an elbow, peering, striving to see him. "Oh! They all beg, do they?"

"*I would not say precisely—beg! But I am looked upon—favorably. Before and after! And you are not exactly choosy, are you, nor inexperienced. So quit acting the flaming virgin. I am not the most peculiar lover you have ever—entertained.*"

I inventoried my parade of lovers. My face heated. "I *like* my job. I like men! Just not *you*!"

I'd never pardon him, I vowed. Yet I still shook with unrequited need. "I would never choose you—in or out of bed, alive or—or dead! Besides, this is wicked. It's wrong. This must be against natural law, or—?" I played the ace card. "Or *God's* law!"

"*I doubt God has anything to do with us. And you care so much for rectitude? Hah! You don't mind servicing married cusses.*"

"I—I don't ken *who* they are, or *if* they are. I don't pry!" I announced with all the self-righteousness I could dredge. "You are an—an *abomination*!" A word the pastor liked to shout from the pulpit. I was not certain what it meant, but it seemed appropriate.

Another gale entered, forming whirlwinds, twirling about my body, silking my breasts, swooping down my arms, invading my privates, skimming legs, tickling the arches of my feet. My skin was lightning. My toes and sex tingled with delicious shock. My breath quickened with my body.

Abruptly, the touches left off, followed by a basso chuckle.

"*No need. As avowed, I do not force unwilling females—even hellcats who are asking for it.*"

"I wouldn't ask you if you were the last man on God's green earth. The least of my clients is more skilled than you. Any farmer! Any greenhorn schoolboy from the East, any—"

Then he kissed me. I felt my body as if invaded again, swept by a tornado, crushed, toppled, every crevice sought out, his mouth hard on mine, unyielding, bruising with his clever lips, harsh with anger, his tongue battling mine.

He drew back. "*Of all the women who could have tarried in this room, why did it have to be you? A bloody head-hunting Salome. A backwoods Delilah wanting me weak and unmanned. Won't happen, sweetheart. Take to your unloved, overused bed, and stay there!*"

And he was gone.

I was used to sensing his absence by a hollowness in the atmosphere.

The whirlwind passed, leaving only devastation.

****

Waiting for what? For some phantom lover to grace you with a visit, causing trouble? Wouldn't the girls and Madame have a right hootenanny over that? I quizzed myself crossly, glaring in the looking-glass whilst getting ready, all the while hoping I'd catch a glimpse of the striking highwayman's face, at least how I imagined a highwayman *might* look. A preacher's son wanting to impress me recited a poem once, called "The Highway Man." I always meant to read it, but Wylder wasn't big on books yet, outside of church or the schoolmarm's McGuffey's Readers.

Were my lustful thoughts only the body's tyranny? Like saying the sun was a lucifer match, warring between burning the Longhorn down and sending him to Hell on a red-hot poker, or accepting him in a surely diabolic arrangement. Besides, either *I* left, or *he* did. It appeared he had little say on the matter, and so I half-waited, half-feared, atop my counterpane, hands folded across a virginal nighty like that poor mad Ophelia I heard tell of from a down-and-out actor passing through Wylder last winter. All I needed were white flowers on my too-white breast, with the lowering moon bathing my body with purity, I avowed chastely.

Would I pay with damnation? Would it show on my face, in my manner? Surely my meetings with the specter were sheer debauchery, if not full depravity. Shamelessness, if not immorality. Wicked—against all nature.

"Maudlin as a ten-penny novel!" I snapped and leapt from bed.

I discovered I did not care a whit. A wild part of me, the part that jumped on that freight car back in Indiana with nothing but a bandanna holding my belongings, was too eager to explore the passionate limits of this nether world.

Chapter Twelve
All's Fair…

A month went by, as fall turned to winter, before I beheld him again. My heart thumped a beat. I detected a shadow, a shift of light, a momentary blotting of the moon, and he was here. As earthly sweethearts, we quarreled, kissed, drawn to each other like a magnet to a gun barrel, gazing longingly at the other across space and time and unkenned worlds.

He strode to me, his boots making no sound. *"The devil's mistress tempting me to the fiery pits of Hell could be no more perilous, you damnable tormentor."*

My own tormentor, my dusky mercurial phantom, was garbed once again in skin-tight black leather that seemed painted on, with silver medallions down the side, his broad chest shirtless, the long dark mane wafting lazily in an unseen wind. His figure had color once more, no longer a faded watercolor, his skin a warm coppery satin…

I hurled myself into his arms, which fortunately held me fast and close, not letting me fling weightless through the air. We clung as drowning sailors cling to a rock in the midst of a typhoon. Perhaps Hell itself was opening its fiery jaws, as I opened myself to him.

"It is poisonous to see you with another. I must accept it, but I will always be there. Do you think it easy, observing you? I want to pick every bastard up by

the scruff and toss him headfirst out the window or kick him down the stairs. And then you!"

Giving life to threats, he picked me up and tossed me over his shoulder and literally chucked me on my bed.

Supporting his weight, he rammed both fists deep in feathers beside my head, glaring down with charged green-glass eyes. "*Is this what you want?*"

He threw the question as a gauntlet, daring me to pick it up. I nodded numbly.

"*Then you will have it, until you beg me to stop!*"

He crammed his mouth on mine, kissing me thoroughly with long-held fury, invading me with his tongue, then worked his way down as I sank limp, the last reservation melting with his fevered mouth, with stops along the way to my belly.

Oh, yes, his mouth was warm, by turns hard, intrusive, soft, rasping, hungry, greedy, lingering over my tender parts until I wanted to scream as if at any second the gods governing such phenomena would tear us apart.

I touched him, rock solid and growing until I could not grasp him fully.

Disturbingly, he held back, even jerking away.

He reached down, harshly gripping my hand, making me gasp, staying it in place, locking me from exploring him further. Yet he held on to me. His compelling rein-calloused hands carved my back, pressing the groove of my spine with strokes firm as if peeling paint over my fanny; one hand held one cheek, exploring with his fingers, as I wriggled and groaned for mercy, for release. "What's taking you so long?" I growled.

In the end, it was not fate that separated us…but the phantom demon.

The cajoler.

The taunter-in-chief.

The avenger.

Breathing hard, or what was for him, with true madness in his gaze—I had once encountered a wolf in the woods with the same hungry gleam and feral glitter with no pity behind it—only the desire to rip into me…

With inhuman effort, it seemed, he got himself under control, like pulling reins hard on runaway horses.

I raised on my elbows, staring uncomprehendingly. He had waited so long. I could tell. I kenned men! His naked form wavered above me in and out of space even as I viewed him.

"Why!" My anguished cry reproached me. Anger, mortification replacing ardor, boiled up inside.

He swooped from midair as if he meant to crash into the floor, stopping just short, raising himself upright. "*Now you see…*" he said with a twist to his mouth like the flick of a cat's tail. "*Now you know.*"

"Damn you to hell! It hurts you worse than me."

I pointed to his upright soldier. He only smiled colder, swiping the offending part of him with one hand as if reprimanding a horse.

"What can I do?" I snarled back. We were two beasts fighting in a dark woods. "I am trapped. I cannot leave this room any more than you! Do you not *care*? I do all that, with all those men, for you!"

Well, a small bit for myself too.

"*Hah!*" He eyed me scathingly. But his gaze dropped, conflicted. The phantom shook his long, tangled mane. He seemed even more visible, it dawned on me. He was naked, I realized with an admiring jolt. Lost in his rough-hewn male beauty, I drank him in while I could. Why did he need to be so perfect? Rangy bones, lean hips neatly balancing his broad amber scarred chest without an ounce of softness, only tensile packs of muscle set to spring, to react, to defend. An astonishing male member, even in repose.

I covered my mouth as my eyes finally took in the blemishes, raking ridges of proud flesh of old knife slashes, bullet rips, ugly purple gouges, one beneath his shoulder, another pocking his side—I had seen such before, but never such a collection proclaiming hard living on the edge.

Abruptly I recalled the one glimpse of a scuffed black leather vest blackened further as if drenched with blood, and with angry singed holes…pondering what tale that told.

"Ohhhh," I breathed.

"*Pretty, isn't it?*"

With that he was no more.

I gazed unseeing, striving to piece together a crazy quilt of dark, mismatched sensations. I despised him. I wanted him, as I needed to breathe. I feared his coming. I waited for it with each breath, with the slightest noise where none should be, with the shifting of a light. A chill swept the room, ruffling my bedcovers, rippling drapes, rattling the heavy frames on the wall.

Chapter Thirteen
Change of Seasons: The Ill Wind of Autumn

The air was boiling and humid—oddly hot for October, cooling the ardor of any customer. The time women eschewed stays and sat, legs spread, with hiked skirts, fanning themselves on rude front porches. Madame Solange gave us all leave. I was gratified when the girls knocked on my door brandishing hard cider and bacon-fat cookies, or burnt popcorn from the Longhorn pantry, and we drooped dustily to the watering hole, soupy warm, but the air cooled us some, in our all-togethers. A respite too, to get away from the turmoil wrecking my peace of mind.

"Miz Solange's right." Big Bertha grunted, swigging from the clay cider jug. "All the pleasures without the weddin'." Bertha's favorite grumble.

Flora piped up in her kittenish little squeak. "But ain't that what they pay us for? The favor of *not* marryin' when the itch is on?"

Little Mae sighed. "Seems not much different than what women do anyhoo. We pay the price, weddin' ring or no."

"Didn't you see that little white line on his finger? His *weddin'* finger?" That was also Big Betha's most cherished line whenever Flora got too sweet on a fella. Most fellas, at least hereabouts, won't truck with a wedding ring anyway. Mining, roping cattle, breaking mustangs can rip a finger right off if it's got a ring on it, even slaving in a blacksmith shop. My thoughts reluctantly returned to my missing cowboy and the missing sums, wondering if he had a white band about his finger. Thank the Lord, the bank was not prone to bandy about information, no matter how juicy...I hoped.

We sat about glum but getting happier, thanks to mule-kick cider. Talk lagged. With the pond shimmering in my eyes in the heat of day, and the effect of the cider, my apparition now seemed unlikely, as if I had been under a spell. Besides, I had aspirations, I drunkenly recalled. I couldn't be derailed like a runaway train, mooning over fantasies conjured by too much drink, fickle cowboys, or tall dark strangers found only in novels.

That all changed in a manner I would never have expected.

****

Fresh news blew in with an untimely prairie blizzard soon after, rippling through the saloon and finding Madame Solange's ears faster than the telegraph wire. A special contingent of mining and machinery officials from New York, Chicago, and Indianapolis were on an inspection tour and some business, according to the scuttlebutt, about railroads. Investors, too! Real high-steppers.

We were in undeclared but ferocious competition with the Wylder County Social Club to get at least a small portion of this rarified custom, and because of the unseasonal storm and proximity to the train station, they might tarry in the bar, ready for strong whiskey and willing companions as they scurried in brushing snow, whooshing great plumes of frost, glad to be inside the warmth and anticipating relative festivities, if one counted ByJingo's, Rattlesnake Jake's, and Mr. Gruenvald's scrimpy good will, made up by Madame's keenness and our ever-willing natures and soft warm beds.

We girls did have the advantage, 'cause we were right across from the rail lines, but unfortunately, the Social Club owned the reputation.

Indian summer had turned into winter with the return of an arctic blast surging down from Canada like a stampede of ghostly cattle, even though it was more than a month before Christmastime—the last of October, in fact. It was indeed fortunate their arrival coincided with the annual Harvest Festival.

Madame decided to put on the dog and bring on seasonal celebrations early in a messy merge of fall and Christmas decor. Levi put out small cedar trees in whiskey barrels fronting the swing doors, warned there'd be no tobacco-spitting on the boardwalks, shooed disreputable duffers gumming out thrice-told tales of mining disasters or Indian perils that befell them, shined the spittoons, polished the Longhorn's murky bar mirror, and begged a few bottles of good hootch from the Five Star Tavern.

We girls helped spruce too, nestling concoctions of pumpkins, winter gourds, and prickly holly anywhere we fancied, nailing wreaths and fir branches above the bar, wound the railings leading up to Paradise, and freshened up the place with vases of spicy pine and cedar in place of the tobacco juice and beer fug.

In a flurry we mended petticoats, purchased new laces, ribbons, tacky jewelry, and sundries up at the

Wylder Mercantile. I curled my hair in bouncy gold ringlets atop my head, letting a few spiral all careless-like down my neck, with one dangling over my forehead, and tying a velvet choker 'bout my neck.

I fumbled with the bow at back.

Breathing hard, though I would not show eagerness, I felt hands at my nape plucking the ribbons from my fingers, deftly tying them—or attempting that task. I gulped. It had been a while, to say the least. I had almost forgotten him.

It's true.

Honestly.

I hardly ever gave him a thought.

He had been good to his word.

I wasn't sure how I felt about that.

Pressing my lips, nipping in a comment, I remained mute. I would not spoil this, like a nagging wife, asking where he had been. In my looking glass, I silently appraised the fierce bronzed face concentrating mightily on tying my choker. The contrast of his rough, scarred visage, wicked brows meeting in the middle as he bent to the humble task, nearly undid me, however.

"I thought you gone forever," I finally managed, cool as a root cellar in December.

He flashed me a ferocious look and returned to fumbling with the tiny bow in his big hands. At last, the job was done. Fingers grazed my flushed cheek. I shivered, wishing Madame would summon me.

I looked up, catching both of us in the mirror, gazing inscrutably at each other—as if this was all that Heaven or Hell allowed, I thought grimly. As he assessed me, one brow raised over a blue-green splinter of eye, he nodded approval and backed slightly into the mist. "*You are most beautiful, tonight…*" His voice was uncommonly husky.

"You have a mustache now," was my only comment. A fierce black glossy mustache, slightly curled downward at the tips, added to his pirate image and made him even more appealing, damn him.

He eyed me sternly for a gibe. "*Yes. I come back different at times—as you realize. It has nothing to do with me,*" he answered with the stiffness of a starched shirtfront.

"It—it suits you." I replied just as dry, shameless strumpet that I was, already anticipating how delicious his rough whiskers would feel brushing my delicate skin.

He strode back, if that is the term used for boots striding across my carpet without sound.

"*This…*" he mused, gently tugging my choker, "*is specially effective to parade around in when you shuck off your clothes.*" His form grew clearer. He was trying to make amends, I realized, in a clumsy man-like manner.

"*Makes you seem more buck-necked. Men like it. I like it,*" he said with a ferocious scowl, meaning that all other men who might view me thus were useless varmints.

I spun finally, laughing; however, he wasn't even a wisp of candle smut.

"I *despise* it when you do that. I mean just *disappear*! Vanish!"

"*I don't always have choice…little one. I mentioned I would be discreet. It is better this way. You do look—most beautiful tonight. I wish it were for…*" And the voice seemed in another room, or world, fading, as I listened.

"*Pluto*," for all I kenned.

Grimly, still cursing a blue streak, I carefully robed in my most expensive green velvet, the shade of river moss, that set off my eyes and showed my ankles (up to my knees in front), the neckline of which plunged almost to my waist, guaranteed to stun any dignitaries like felled oxen—or so I trusted.

Madame Solange hung a too-obvious mass of pre-Christmas mistletoe over the top steps to rachet up the mood, and also at the bottom step leading up to our so-called Paradise, to take advantage of our illustrious guests.

It turned out to be anything but 'Paradise' for me, however…

Chapter Fourteen
A Man Hath No Fury Like a Ghost Angered

"Paradise on earth! This way, gentlemen," Madame cooed as she ushered the eminent guests in and played surrogate host, whilst Levi hung back polishing the bar and hauling up the best liquor, with Jake wearing his usual sullen expression and ByJingo pounding away with gusto at the rinky-tink piano. He kenned "Rosie You Are My Posy," "Beautiful Dreamer," and "Camptown Race Tracks" like nobody's business. His ragtime was even commented on favorably by one prominent visitor as a novelty he'd heard only in Chicago.

"Of course!" Madame trilled. "We aren't the backwaters here. Only a few steps away…come and meet my very, very naughty angels!"

I was entertained, okay—flummoxed—by Big Bertha's and Little Mae's appearances. Bertha, downright scrumptious as a slice of hot cherry pie, decked out in red damask, launching her generous bosom to perfection, and emphasized by a cinched corselet affording her a stunning hourglass, her glossy chestnut hair in bouncy ringlets secured all over with tiny scarlet bows. From her ears hung chandeliers of paste ruby earbobs. She looked elegant.

And Mae! Her little tailor had done her up proud, resplendent, and glowing in yellow satin, around which she threw a lovely paisley shawl in gold and green matching her eyes. Finishing it off, a rich gold-and-jade pendant hung between her mounded bosoms.

Their display had not caused my delighted grin, however…

I saw *him* immediately.

The girls, even little Flora, with an interesting waif-like pallor and gowned in diaphanous virginal white suspiciously like a nightdress, snapped 'round. Little Mae and Bertha sucked in bellies. Flora didn't own one to suck in; nevertheless I watched her tug at her neckline. The rest, including me, flung out our chests to beat Lillian Russell, eyeing true, big-city, back-East gentlemen of class as they strode like kings into the Longhorn.

The first dandy, ruddy from cold, burly, silver-tongued, and established, laughing as if the snow he brushed off was icing sugar, entered like a visiting prince in a rust-colored three-piece suit, sporting an emerald velvet waistcoat and lapels that played well with his fox-colored hair.

To my detriment, I didn't note his face, half hidden behind a mustache, also fox-colored, or his glasses as I perused the other business men of industry.

We girls' speculation flew to glittering stick pins, watch fobs, and hefty rings. This particular gentleman braced an elbow on the bar with one gleaming patent leather shoe, unsuitable for Wyoming in the winter, perched on the brass rail as he raked the room, hidden behind spectacles pinched on the nose, without ever moving his head—like a hunting wolf studying which fat deer to take down, I thought later when it was far too late.

I kind of shivered at that, but faint heart never won feral gent, as they say.

Still, I felt shy, uneasy of a sudden about installing him in my room, resisting an intense urge to flee. However, it wasn't *that* long after my cowboy vanished with all my savings. I was ferocious about building my funds back up. *This* big spender might slip extra greenbacks in my garter. Plus, I sorely needed to add glitter to my tarnished reputation.

I held myself back like a lady, though, tilted nose in air—I have a pert profile—not casting a flutter of an eyelash his way, nevertheless taking it all in. Silver stick pin shaped like a horse, with emeralds for eyes, adorned the green silk cravat. Pocket watch big as a gold turnip. The ring resembled a cluster of gold nuggets winking with diamonds. Shiny patent leather shoes, so unlike muddy clodhoppers most men wear, and sporting those little cloth covers called spats.

I'm tall and stick up like a sunflower above prairie roses and some of the revelers. So it made me prideful but unsurprised when he held my eye, this city-born man in store-bought tweed with velvet collars and gold-headed ebony walking stick. Boldly I held his gaze before turning and smiling at a man I didn't even see.

He gave a princely nod when I glanced back as if casually. Twisting his rusty mustache and pursing his lips, he beckoned. I preened as I led him, arm in arm, up to Paradise, tinkling away like a chandelier in a high wind over the salesman's slightest pleasantries, whilst he whispered in my ear. Glancing up at the mistletoe, he gave me a hard lingering kiss to the *hooraw* of Longhorn's celebrants.

My better angel hid her head in shame at my

fanfaronading air, nose so high I nearly tripped, but I clung to his arm like a shipwrecked sailor clings to a rock.

I should have had my first warning when he nipped my lower lip with surprisingly sharp teeth.

Despite my giddiest intentions to get back under Madame's benevolent eye, there was a darkness when I sashayed into my room that had nothing to do with light, urging me to come down with a sudden ailment and shoo him off.

Instead, whirling like a debutante at a Boston ball, light, gay, very arch and determinedly flirting, I ignored the forbidding sensation. Yet. *Yet,* my heart fluttered broken beats. I could not put my finger on what was wrong, to save my soul; however the threat of menace filled the room like a sour fog the instant he stepped over the threshold.

"Just let me turn my lamp a little higher, sir." I hoped he supposed the quaver in my voice was passion, fake or not.

"Turn it down," he barked. Which startled me, as most gentleman callers want to get their money's worth. My long legs and short, tiny-waisted torso and upright bubbies delight most men, 'specially in full light of day in front of God and everybody, but kerosene lamps do nicely too.

He kicked the door shut in answer.

I turned down the wick right quick. Then he plucked me off that rock of safety, pushing me to the bed, hard, till my head thunked the seven-foot-tall headboard and my ears rang.

I put my knees up to ward him off. "Well, hey, sugar! My, aren't you the—" I tried to make light before he cut me off with a sharp barb that hooked me in my pride like a gaffed fish.

"You really think you're somethin', don't you," he snarled, removing that fine coat, slinging it on the red chair, and loosening his cravat. I scrutinized the red chair. Nothing. Not sure if I was relieved or not.

"I guess I am, handsome." I tried a roguish smile. "Why not find out for certain-sure?" Pride said that, as smooth as if practiced in a mirror. However, I was uneasy as a mouse at a bobcat's barbeque.

Reaching a meaty hand out, a steel-like grip pinched my upper arm. He dragged me to him. Not in desire. With a glint of rage. I saw now how muscles strammed the fine shirt linen, now he'd shucked his gentleman's vest, and his chest above the pudgy belly was brawny as a bareknuckle fighter.

His kisses felt like barbed roses, red and sharp, as he dropped his head like a bird of prey jabbing at my neck and mouth. His whiskers ground my chin. I touched my lips to see if they bled.

They did not, but not for lack of trying, with his sharp teeth and tongue, and how he spat a string of savage words like darts. "Harlet and filthy little slut," were the least of it.

His voice rang a dull bell in my head.

It seemed oddly, horribly familiar.

Sticks and stones, I told myself.

Get this over with.

Smile.

Pretend not to hear.

Edge to the door if it gets too rough.

I thought of Madame, then. Live coals would rain on my head if I offended this wealthy client.

My dumbness seemed to swell him like a boiler ready to blow. His face reddened, eyes flickered. His panting mouth, akin to that of a rabid dog, hung loose and wet. "Ya like that? I have more, or are you used to being called a filthy trollop?" His excitement increased.

"Please, sir, no call for that." I spoke like a wind-up automaton, determined this troublesome client would not out-master me. I *would* see it through. I'd show Madame Solange I was up to anything, temporizing soon he'd be gone, even when he painfully pinched my bottom and hissed in my ear, "You vowed, comin' up here, you were gonna show me a *good* time!"

That word *good* took on a sickly new meaning.

He dared not strike me, though. I'd call Big Bertha. Hoping she was not engaged. Or downstairs drumming up business. Or refused to come.

Big Bertha, at six feet some and needing to weigh down at the feed-and-grain scale when so inclined, was our—as Madame Solange liked to say—lady sheriff, along with other specialties, that I made certain I never inquired about, however her clients appeared pole-axed when they left, but well-satisfied. Still, if he got rough, would she fancy mussing up her fancy getup to rescue me? I sighed. About as likely as flying pigs. I refocused on his mad gaze through his thick glasses. There was something about his eyes. A curious brown, almost pale yellow.

"Looks to me like moonin' about's your specialty. What'sa matter?" He sneered, showing small sharp teeth in a snarl as he flung his suspenders down. "Ain't I every young girl's dream?"

Fair enough. Half my mind *was* on Big Bertha.

"You would be, if you'd quit calling me names."

"I paid top dollar to that old armored gunboat and intend to get my dollar's worth! I sprung for all night," he promised cruelly with a lopsided grin, "and that don't include a smart mouth."

I shut my eyes as the salesman flung himself on top without removing his clothes, only unbuttoning, grabbing at my skirt hem, and began his ravishing in earnest. I heard my precious velvet rip.

"Wait!" I wailed despite my intentions. "Don't you want me to undress? I can do you a—"

"Oh, I'll undress you all right." He grabbed at my neckline, yanking at it. I heard more stitches pop. "Wait a cotton-pickin' minute!" I roared and dropped my ladylike air. To Hades, if he thought I'd let him destroy my best dress for sport!

He glared as I grabbed both his fists with the hefty rings cutting my palms and glared back. "It's hard with you pressin' down on me like a wagonload of bricks, to show you *anything* but how to play *dead*!"

"You don't listen! I said no sassy tongue. Now I have to punish you!" He flipped me on my stomach before I could react, never taking cold wolf eyes off me; pressed me down with one hand. With his other, he stripped off his suspenders. Leather, I understood with sickening intuition. Now I knew why he didn't venture to the Wylder County Social Club. They had true enforcers on the lookout for his kind. Moreover, they had a way of dealing with them.

Gripping the suspenders, wide-eyed in anticipation with his yellow, red-lashed eyes—unfeeling animal eyes, except for anticipating the pleasure to come—he flipped me back over, so I could better see what he intended. I put my knees up again.

I could not keep terror from my own face, hating that fear gave him further pleasure, watching his gaze glitter and teeth grit in a mean parody of a smile. The pale-yellow eyes gleamed rat-like as he bared discolored teeth, hissing, "Salesmen are unrelenting, my dear, merciless, shrewd bargainers, as you will soon discover to your torment." He had turned from a gent to a beast, in the time a knife flicks a small target.

Me.

The word "salesman" rang another dull bell as I gave him a mighty kick from my drawn knees, not caring where it landed. He jumped back in time not to take the full brunt in his stomach, or his jewels. Still, it halted him some. He liked it, though, I realized to my dismay.

"Aha! Wanna play it that way, do ya? Take off those rags, if you don't fancy my rough hands on your fair white body." He sneered as if he hadn't already ripped my neckline and torn at my best petticoat.

I leapt from the bed and held my hands up as if in combat. A street boxer would not be impressed, but I envisioned a flicker of anticipation. The yellow eyes tracked behind the glasses. I held up my palm, commanding *Stay*. "Yes, sir! Allow *me*."

Plastering a grim smile, I performed an awkward striptease while he crouched on the bed as if he had springs in his legs. Some girls have a knack for drawing things out. Me, I prefer stripping more natural-like, as if redding for bed, pretending I'm alone. Now, I was clunky, ugly, and awkward in my reluctance, mixed with haste to get it over.

Me as a ten-year-old drawing on my nighty, gazing

out my farmhouse window at apple orchards glowing amber in waning days of summer, hovered like a sepia tintype before my face. I gulped. Tears unbidden runneled face powder onto my pasted-on fake smile. I shivered, shame clothing me in cold sweat. Tasting salt on cracked lips, I continued gyrating.

"Hah!" He licked his own lips already wet. "Time enough for crying—later. Don't much care for your mawkish attempt at burlesque. Disgusting! I have more refined pleasures in mind." Giving action to the promise, he leapt up in one powerful motion, again like a beast, and indeed, began clawing at my choker. "What can ya expect in a cheap whorehouse?"

I laughed bitterly. The choker was meant to enflame, I recalled queasily. The simple innocent ribbon had done its work too accurately.

"I said all!" He grunted in my ear as his fingers dug into my neck. "And when I say all…" Drool dripped on my bosom. I grimaced, choking from his tugging, battling his hands despite my resolve. I jerked away, near strangling myself. He tracked me, *thwapping* the suspenders in the palm of his hand.

"I threw extra silver into the old bat's claws. As I said, *he-heh*—we have all night for amusements."

I crossed my arms over my bosom. I'd never felt so unclothed. Me, disrobing, performing my "dance of the seven veils" aplenty before gents, high and low. This time, I wallowed with animals down at the stockyards.

I kept backing—circling. He thought it great sport. His eyes flicked my body, penetrating my flesh like hot bullets as he *thwapped* the suspenders. Where should he strike? The tender bottom? Creamy thighs? The thin back? The delicate-skinned breasts?

His glasses hung askew. He flung them off.

Of a sudden, it flashed across my brain, as illuminating as a lightning strike, stark, sick, and yellow.

Yellow as his eyes.

I recalled him.

My Sweet Lord, it was him! I even recalled his name.

Petersen!

My tummy seared with acid. Bile scorched my throat. I choked on it.

It was the mustache, the glasses. His gingery hair covered in the past by a derby had been more orange than rusty gray. Older now, too, with lines drawn in place of the shiny red face of long ago, when he tore my petticoat off in the hayloft, and I not yet thirteen. What bad providences crossed our paths so far apart in years? But then, he was a salesman blown across country like a bad wind or sick tumbleweed.

He did not remember me.

Of course. I was a faceless female, then and now.

The man he was, the bad seed, blossomed like a deadly weed into what was foretold, with treacherous new cravings. I was a child then. My childish body was full blown now, too. Most likely he had never looked at my face, even then.

I recoiled, wincing, recalling the filthy muck-coated hayfork sinking into his bare flesh.

The *pop* of skin and the slick slide of tines entering soft fatty tissue like chicken fat, yellow and lumpy. The holding back a trifle, at the last second, that gave him his life.

He lied to the world when he vanished.

He lied to his wife.

If—*when* he disrobed… I flinched, kenning well I would see a row of red circles from the mucky tines, or purple raised scars of infection tattooed on his paunch. I curled my lip, little caring, not wishing to see his white abdomen.

"A tweed coat with velvet collars and stick pins in fancy cravats doesn't make a gentleman," I hissed. I felt like emptying my chamber pot on his head. I was far from my bedside table or dresser. *Where had I placed that danged derringer last?*

I backed into a bay window, briefly considered leaping out on the roof in the cold, naked as a jaybird, but kenning I would never make it, veered to the bed, grabbing a sheet to my chin instead, arousing him even more. He paced crouched—a stalking wolf—ripped the sheet away with his teeth, shaking it, letting it drop. "And a trollop don't make a lady," he sneered. "You're skinny as the rails I rode in on. Slender and willowy you may now be…"

And he said the worst. What I secretly dreaded, but would not be dragged out of me with a winch and a pulley: "In a few years you'll be scrawny as a plucked broody hen, and this yeller hair?" He yanked one of my curls. "Dry and dusty as that godforsaken prairie we rode over. So don't go all muckety-muck. Your future's writ. In fact, you and all your pox-ridden whorish friends should just end it one night with a rusty razor."

He hated women.

A few men were like that.

They needed you but despised the yearning.

They had the sick lust, so they brought you low to their level.

The salesman did a strange thing then.

He snapped his head and scanned the room, suspicious-like, with narrowed eyes.

I felt it even more intensely than he. Of course, I kenned what he only felt.

My heart beat a little tom-tom of hope and fear that made me dread I was headed to that Cheyenne asylum. Thick, turbulent close air invaded the room, congested as an approaching cloudburst, tasting bitter, like swallowing cigarillo smoke. Sulphur. Blood. Iron. Copper. I detected a crackle, as when lightning lifts your hair and sizzles your eardrums. Like that.

The salesman from Hell sensed it too—this odd *buzz*.

He shook his head, not unlike avoiding a pesky fly, raising his whip hand as if to swat.

His suspenders were unique, I realized too late, evolving into seven or eight twisted leather strands with cruel knots on the ends big as blackberries. Forgetting the odd buzzing insect disturbance, he lunged, clamping one hand over my mouth, whisking me round, and bent me over the bed. As he pinned me with the flat of one skillet-sized palm, his whip hand swung high; the leather cut the air.

I twisted round to cry out for Bertha. He plunged my face into the bed. I breathed in feather chaff. Coughing, choking, bearing the first light sting of the whip's hard knots as if he were testing or teasing, I struggled, pushing against the suffocating down.

Clawing back blind, snatching a tuft of his ginger hair, I arched my back like a cat, kicking my legs to toss him off.

Suddenly the weight lifted. I looked over my

shoulder, my hair hanging all loose and tangled.

The salesman seemed gut-shot. Jerking. Clutching his stomach with a stew of astonishment on his twisted face.

His head swung sharply, whipped back and forth as if struck from side to side—how a neck could bend that far—followed by a meaty *smack*, like a hammer pounding a side of beef.

A red mark blossomed on the salesman's jaw, like magic. A goose egg formed on his cheekbone. My attacker looked pole-axed, shook his head like a bull stunned in the stockyards, and blindly raised the whip, not certain where to strike. The whip suddenly hurled itself across the room, then swung back on its own, striking him a stinging lash across his shoulders. He cried out, shock, rage, and bafflement warring across his battered face.

A smile spread across mine like the sun rising across the plain.

I kenned what the salesman could not possibly. Let him wonder, I savaged, how his whip could have a will of its own and strike him senseless.

This time Petersen seemed to plunge, tripping, rucking the carpet as the toes of his patent shoes scudded across the floor, while the seat of his pants and jacket shoulders lifted in peaks. I watched him sail airborne across the room, landing with his chin on the edge of the washstand, wincing at the bone-cracking sound. Petersen swayed on hands and knees, watching me, befuddled and insane with rage.

I was uneasy, no matter how much he'd earned his drubbing. I strained to see my phantom—who appeared as a swirl of slashing color at the same time I detected the unmistakable *snap* of a whip, followed by an aggrieved outcry as a welt appeared across the salesman's back through a slice in his fine linen shirt.

I scrabbled near the rickety headboard, in a dither on whether to leap for the door or try to stop the mayhem. The salesman seemed in a bad way. "Stop now!" I yelled.

The man on his hands and knees snorted blood. Rubbing his chin, noting gore on his fist, he swayed to his feet like a lurching bare-knuckle fighter or an ape I remembered once from a picture book, arms curled wide, fingers in claws, small teeth in a toothy snarl, all self-possession lost, leaving in place the feral animal he was.

"Trip wires," he growled through a ruined mouth, furiously scanning the floor. "How would a whore like you…?"

"Hold your filthy tongue, you unnatural bastard!"

The phantom's voice hissed with the chilling menace of a striking snake, followed by another meaty *smack*. The salesman's head jerked violently back as a hazy fist landed on his jaw. Blood spurted from his nose, making a red bib of his fine linen shirt.

"Enough!" I cried. I had to get him gone before he killed him!

The salesman made an *awk*ing sound. His mouth slanched sideways, uncovering teeth and gums. Another tooth flew across the room, pattering against my rose wallpaper.

I got to my knees. "Stop! You'll kill him!"

"Don't insult the lady, then, and get the hell out, and I won't!"

Rubbing his face, the salesman shook his head

drunkenly, as if from a three-day binge, glaring murderous rage. To my astonishment, he howled, exultant. With real blood in his eye, he hitched down his pants, scrabbling frantically through the slit in his long johns.

With sick awareness, I realized that his mysterious injuries fired him up. His nose stopped bleeding, but there was enough in his eye. I had known men like that. The ones akin to those who enjoyed jumping out and frightening you. I always gave them what-for and made sure they kenned I was not a shrinking violet.

But not this one. For the first time, I could not have handled him with cunning words, coaxing ways, or even my sweet little pistol. Nevertheless, I pleaded, "No more!" Sooner than later Petersen would either be killed or leave in this sorry state. I *had* to end it. One blessing—the girls were still downstairs in the Longhorn. I hadn't heard them twittering down the hall, clients in tow, or their doors slam—yet. With no time to reach the derringer, I clawed for the clock instead, the heaviest weapon in reach. I would finish this myself. I wasn't even thinking of aftermaths, in my fury.

"Stay back!" I warned. Not Petersen; *him.*

"I'm going to get my pound of flesh," Petersen growled. "I'll get it with *your* pound of flesh, you bloody bitch!" He snorted when he caught the weapon in my hand, sneering, "Think we have *time* for it?"

I laughed bitterly. I would not come out a winner, but I could give him a pound of hurt. I hurled the clock. It bounced off his forehead. He jerked aside but kept coming, bloody teeth bared in a strange rictus of a smile. I scrabbled for the derringer. *It wasn't in the bed table.* I dove across the carpet, wrestled with the dresser drawer, snatching it up, gripping the lady pistol with both hands in front, tightening my shaking finger on the tiny trigger as—

I felt a hand on mine, forcing the gun lower.

"None of that, darling girl. He is not worth your sweet bottom languishing in jail. Or your neck suffering noose burns. 'Sides, they will all come running."

"I don't care!" I had blood in my own eye now. His words sank in. I ground my teeth and howled, letting the gun droop. "Okay…then help me."

"That's what I was attempting, you insufferable little wildcat."

The beastly salesman, listening to this exchange, looked momentarily confused before animal madness descended once more, changing into a smirking, entertained bully. "Help you!" The salesman guffawed. Bloody spittle flew between broken teeth. Yet he looked uncertain for the first time, checking to see who, if anyone, crept up on him. Seeing nothing, he approached, crouched and ready.

I sidled for the door. My knee struck the end of the bed. I staggered off balance. Snarling, gleeful, he moved to block me. "Trapped now, girlie! You'll pay dear! Wish ya never denied me?" His puffy lips slurred, "You won't be so pretty when I get through with you. No one fights Petersen and wins!"

The chest of Petersen's shirt lifted, pinched as if cruelly twisted in two great hands. He looked startled down at his offending shirt before his body hurled backward to where he landed on his tailbone on my patterned carpet. The resultant *thud* made me wince. Surely, that alerted at least Jake! My room was closest above the bar. Vain chance, though, that Rattlesnake

Jake would react to the occasional thud and cry.

I watched with detachment as Petersen's head lifted and smashed back on the floor. . A new bruise, stained his jaw. However, in his zeal to get to me, he shook his fading ginger hair from his eyes, ignored the odd circumstances, and scrambled to his knees, insane with fury.

"*Stay down, jackass! The lady said I shouldn't hurt you,*" brayed the deep rumbling voice behind him.

I clambered back up on the bed. An island of safety.

"*Like Hell, I won't!*"

Petersen lifted.

I looked…UP….UP… I laughed in wonder. The salesman's shoulders peaked as if pinned to an invisible clothesline, only the clothesline was seven feet in the air.

I cricked my neck and gaped—as Petersen appeared to be lifted in invisible arms even higher.

Flinging out his arms, kicking his legs, Petersen scowled down at my crazy plastered grin, when he wasn't shooting panicked looks in disbelief at the ceiling and then the floor. "Ge' me *down*," he howled, dangling, swatting wildly, reaching vainly behind him, above him—anywhere to gain purchase in what must seem a perilous, unimaginable situation. I covered my mouth, laughing, crying, or someplace in between.

He did not come down.

"Help!" he bawled. I threw frightened looks at the door, running to make certain it was locked. The salesman's limbs flopped like a Raggedy Andy. He spun. Then, my phantom hurled Petersen across the room. He struck hard onto Little Mae's wall, knocking a picture frame loose before crumpling to the floor in a stunned sprawl.

My mouth was so far open a bee could have sailed right in without my knowing. I prayed Little Mae wasn't home.

Petersen shook his head, wriggled his jaw, and plucked out another tooth, stupidly staring at it pinched between thumb and forefinger.

"Wha' the Hades's *tha'*?" the disheveled salesman finally slurred, bleary-eyed, through numbed lips. "Wha' the Hades ya do ta me…?" He looked at me in wonder.

A small part of me—okay, a sizable part—rejoiced, until I watched him crawl to the bed like a broken spider, drooling pink through a grimace of teeth. I kicked the whip far from his groping hands.

"How could this happen?" I asked the air, more to cover myself. I had to get rid of him before the phantom slaughtered him or at least did him serious damage that I could never explain.

"Where are you?" I hissed, gratified when a shadowy form hovered over the salesman.

"*Here, hunting down rabid dogs.*"

I gasped, rushing over as I perceived my defender held my dressing table chair over his head. I held my hands up to ward off the blow.

"You can't do that! Don't!"

Petersen, stumbling in stages to a standing position, darted stunned looks from his one open eye, behind him and over my shoulder, then fixated on me.

I saw death there. Mine.

"Oh, *can't* I?" he slurred. "Who gonna shtop me, li'l bish! You?" His hair was a briar patch. His fine shirt ripped, face blossoming purple lumps and bruises. Still, he kept coming. He lurched, favoring one leg, tripping sideways over his own feet, landing heavily.

"*Getting tired of you, hombre! Let's end this.*" I heard a low growl. It did not come from the salesman.

If only I could make it to the gallery, I could draw Petersen, toss out his clothes, pretend I never laid eyes on him. Maybe. If no one had watched us ascend to a paradise that turned into hell.

While I was furiously thinking, the salesman rose up in parts, relentlessly stumping toward me. "Please, mister, for the love of Heaven, stop!" I fumbled the brown china knob. He vaulted, hands out, suddenly upon me, clamping a vise of fingers around my neck as he landed atop me in the hall. The clamor from below blasted full-force—merry drunk voices, the *clink* of glasses, ByJingo's piano plinking away a noisy jolly ragtime, while a madman's eyes burned hatred into mine.

Bloody spittle flecked my face. The dim hall spun, stilled, darkened. Bony thumbs slick with blood pressed my windpipe. I clawed—gasped, kicked. He thrust me back over the gallery railing. As if from far away now, the gay *tinkle* of ByJingo's merrymaking, the carousing and laughter faded as if muffled in cotton.

Back bent, my head upside down, I desperately viewed the bar littered with bottles and glasses. I caught the eye of Rattlesnake Jake, who'd seen it all, gazing unflappably up, and he bent back to polishing glasses with a dirty cloth, as if a doxy being murdered before his eyes was stale news. I kenned it was hopeless. My phantom could not leave the room.

Thumbs pressed deep into the hollow of my neck.

Petersen's hideous face grew shadowy. My back strained to straighten before my spine cracked. I clawed blindly.

"*Let go. The lady seems to want me to let you live. Might consider it if you release her—or not.*" The mildness in the voice chilled the air with menace.

"Hurry!" I wanted to scream. With my last thought, I realized my defender was in the hallway! The salesman's peevish face swiveled. Squeezing my throat tighter, he angrily sought out the interloper. My feet skittered for traction…my back was breaking…the hallway…his ballooning face blotted out. All was over. My dream. My life. His were the injuries. He would say I attacked him. My sight narrowed to a small crimson dot.

I was dying.

Petersen pressed harder, as if he had to hurry now. His hands eased a mite. His thumbs sprang loose. He threw me an almost comical look as I struggled to straighten, hawking and heaving. A whip snaked out of nowhere, wrapping Petersen's neck with the *crack* and *snap* of sawed air. He clawed at his throat.

I arched from the railing as if shot, sucking in like I'd swallowed barbed wire. Enough! Hands in fists, I staggered to Petersen. He looked bemused, sneering at my balled hands even though the whip tightened about his neck. I socked his jaw. The noose loosened. I heard a deep rumbling laugh like a freight train running across rusty rails.

Squinting narrowly, with a sly grin, Petersen barely reacted as I propelled him into my room, kicking the door closed. Behind Petersen came another low, ominous chuckle.

Petersen's ravaged, bloodstained face assumed a clever look. He wagged his finger at me. "Are—are you a man? You one of them vaudeville acts? Like in Chicago? Don't mind a little fun and games!" With an uneasy grin, he scanned the room for further trickery. "Didn't think to find it in this tinhorn backwater. You're a cheap ventriloquist! And you got a sidekick here, somewheres, hidden. Whad'ya do? Knock 'em out, take all their valuables? Kick 'em in the alley? Whad'ya think I am, some greenhorn? This ain't my first roundup."

"Look, mister. End it," I pleaded. "No good can come of this." I was hurting all over. Why was not he? He was a mess of bruises, cuts, and missing teeth.

"Oh! And what's a little piece of trash like you gonna do about it? It ends when I say it ends, girlie-girl. Just gettin' my second wind."

I began laughing. My laughter took on a new turn, jetting tears even after I felt a breeze swish past so fast it left a watercolor blur.

He blinked. "You like games…do ya?" he slurred, clutching his jaw. "Well, ya conniving little slag, I gotta lollapalooza for you." Petersen jangled hefty, winking manacles in one hand and a straight-edge razor dug from his pocket in the other.

The manacles clattered to the floor.

The salesman resembled a flying carpet, dropping with a spread-eagled, floor-shuddering *thud.* Stunned, groaning, Petersen rose like a ninety-year-old with the rhumatiz, nailing me with not quite stable eyes.

"Please end it!" I begged. "Something really bad will happen."

Like the monster, the one Mary Shelley wrote

about that wouldn't die, Petersen stubbornly got to his feet, shakier now but still waving the razor, the wicked sharp blade flashing orange from the kerosene flame.

"*You don't learn,* gallito*! I said, Don't hurt the lady!*"

Petersen bent double, letting out a weighty— "*Oooooff!*" Clutching his midriff, he curled on the carpet like a stinkbug finally done in, moaning, "think…ribs…broken."

Oh, lordy! Any second, Madame would come poking around. But what if what he said was true and he paid for the night? The ungodly rumpus couldn't go unnoticed this long. My mind was a fox in a spring trap. Petersen lay still. I skirted past to fetch some water.

The salesman snatched my ankle. I fell on my elbows, yanking my foot, kicking with the other. My pretty oil lamp keeled off the dresser, smashing on the floor, leaking a pool of stinking kerosene and thick fumes.

Fire traveled from the wick, making a small crimson-rimmed lake, greedily licking the carpet and, to my horror, spreading beyond the lit pool toward me and Petersen. I slapped flames with my hand without thinking. I saw a footprint in the oil, impressing the oval of licking fire traveling toward the bedskirts. A sooty smudge floated in the air. I checked my hand. Hurtful—not unbearable. The greedy flames were stamped out.

"Thank you," I gasped.

"*Time to end this,* cabrón*!*" My phantom's voice rent the air with violence.

A thick brown glass whiskey bottle Petersen had brought with him swished through the air, smashing against his cranium, making a *bonk*ing sound. Petersen slumped, eyes rolling to their white underbelly with the bottle still rolling across the rug and coming to rest against the fallen picture frame.

Two casualties of a private war.

"Is he…? Is he—dead?"

I realized I shakily held my derringer. *I will hang when the next circuit judge comes.* I must have snatched it up, though I had no remembrance.

"They will say I did this," I said, feeling as dull as my voice sounded.

"Of course not, little one. The hombre had it coming."

"You don't ken that. It won't matter to you."

I was unfair but nervy. Perhaps Petersen was alive. I was feverishly hoping, though I cared as little, as far as one could spit, if he still inhabited even a pigsty, let alone life…though that turned out prophetic.

However, the character of the air ceased to be a whirlwind, cleansed with the sharpness of new snow, save for a lingering burnt wool smell from the carpet. It was over.

"He didn't see you," I whispered. I wasn't certain if that was a good thing or ill.

"*He will have a hard time explaining, little one. Hah. How can he? A woman doing all this? I haven't had this much fun since…*" He left the sentence unfinished.

The deep rumbling chuckle irritated my soul. I began to make a sharpish reply, when in the corner of my eye I saw Petersen's inert body sprawled broken on the carpet. I agonized all over. However would I explain this? Events went far beyond rational, if

Petersen took complaints to Madame, Levi, or even the sheriff. "*If he is alive,*" my devil whispered. Moreover, I still held the gun, till my fingers shone white around the pistol grip. I looked in horror at it. For a ghastly instant, I recalled wanting to put a bullet in him. I noted a faint rise to Petersen's chest. I wept great ugly, heaving sobs, drenching my bosom, like the fainting violets I so despised.

Out of nowhere, Big Bertha materialized in the doorway before I had a chance to wipe my telltale swollen eyes, or straighten the shambles of my pretty room. I whipped the derringer between the froth of torn petticoats.

I did not look in my ghost's direction to see if he folded into mist or sprouted wings. I examined Big Bertha closely—no reaction other than her squinty eyes narrowed, taking it all in—dead-to-the-world salesman. Battered face. Crumpled limbs. Disarranged clothes. Whip, manacle, and deadly razor. Me trembling, disheveled—

Okay, I was being dramatic, but inside I was shaking like an aspen.

"*You* did this?"

I nodded, mute. "He—he tripped on…" I looked desperately about. "On that!" I pointed to his whip—I remembered now, the real one was called a cat-o'-nine-tails—tangled on the floor with one of the whip-strands around his ankle.

She grunted, studying the cruel knots ending each twisted strand. "Looks more like he tangled with a sack of bobcats, but I see." Nodding, with a smirk of understanding, her small eyes still raked the room, not missing the overturned chair, broken oil lamp, singed carpet, or bed that looked like a giant eggbeater had been after it.

But you don't! I wanted to wail.

She eyed me, cocking her head.

I tried on my most pitiful, scared, helpless look—not far from the truth.

Toeing the bottle, she finally snorted, "Drunk as a hooty owl, too." Her voice, always like saws scraping sandpaper, held distress that she'd lost an opportunity to show a man—any man, the ways of her world.

Narrowing shoe-button eyes, she eyed my reddened neck. "Hurt ya much?"

I shook my head "no" even though it felt like I'd swallowed broken glass, aided by lingering kerosene fumes.

She growled admiringly, "Ms. Tits don't need to know," and grinned, showing picket-fence teeth. "Might wanta cover that." She pointed at the dinner-plate-sized scorch pattern in the carpet. I nodded, mute, as she hipped her fists, sneering at the sodden heap of Mr. Petersen. "Now, what do I do with inebriated skunks?"

My mind waded through cold molasses. My only desire was that Madame's gimlet eyes had not taken in exactly whom, or *which* dandified gent I whisked off so hopefully. I glanced at my cherub clock.

Could it only be a bare hour ago? In the swarm of the well-heeled hatch of clients, I might be lucky.

"You don't wanna know that, neither." Bertha winked ominously, hefted Petersen over one meaty shoulder, and with no further effort, favored me another wink and clomped out. I watched her proceed mountainously down the upper gallery, to the door by the one leading to the attic, and from there down to the gap between the Longhorn and the barbershop. I shut myself in, to set to rights not only myself but the torn-up room.

I'm one of Bertha's favorites, though Lord alone appreciates why. Maybe 'cause I take time to talk to her out back when evenings cool some in the summer, and share a nightly tipple and cigarillos laced with a pinch of peyote.

Nobody apparently missed the salesman.

No one asked after him, and with all the Harvest Festival rumpus going on at the Longhorn, the ruckus upstairs blended right in. I queried Big Bertha, and let's just say she tapped her nose.

"Pigs get along right well with him."

I sucked in and asked no further word.

I did not realize this was only the beginning. How could I?

Chapter Fifteen
No Good Deed Goes Unpunished

After Bertha left, I stood in my once-pretty room, revolving like a lighthouse beacon, hands over heart, not in gratitude but to keep the thumping down. "Guess I oughta thank you." My grudging tone was strident as a fire bell.

I was riled, distressed, hurt—chagrined, my careful world crumbling under my feet. An unwanted tenant I scarce dared believe driving me mad nine ways from Sunday, robbed blind by the man I had adored and Lord help me, still did, and then my lack of control of this damning situation.

I heard a snort of derision. "You can show yourself now, as if I had choice!" I snapped.

Part of me was shamed, furious that I needed interference, still writhing with annoyance I hadn't read the signs and the wretch's unwarranted comment about my being "a mere woman." I was a professional! It made my plight seem tawdry and me seem weak. Nevertheless, I supposed it common courtesy to show *some* appreciation. I plunked down at my dresser, making a face at my disheveled self, eyes red, mouth swollen and cracked, but still, I was relieved it had not been fragile Flora that the bastard chose.

As said, my gratitude didn't last long.

"I could have taken care of it myself!" I blasted,

more to goad. Wincing I recalled the last time I had "taken care of myself." Was he still here? Or had my phantom returned to Lord only kenned where? I crossly realized I had no way of kenning, and my ire was for nothing, perhaps.

But then his rum-smooth voice floated from the bay windows. "*So, you would have me dismount from my white horse? Although I've no doubt your, ah, friend looks as if she could stop a herd of stampeding buffalos with her little finger.*"

"I had this! I'm not afraid to use it." I scrabbled for the dropped derringer, uncertain in which direction to wave it.

"*Hah! In your dresser among that litter of pomades, powders, cologne water, gewgaws, and maquillage. A wonder you did not brandish your hairbrush or curling tongs.*"

I frowned. "Maquill-age?"

Abruptly, my lip rouge and pomade containers danced cheekily before my nose.

"*This. Your cosmetics, one who kens everything. Not that you need any. Pretty enough without all that artifice.*"

I snatched the tins from midair, snapping them back onto the dresser. "Do stop playing the fool. I have to go back down." I was near weeping. My face was a mess of tears and smudged cork.

Angrily, I watched my derringer lift from the dresser and bounce in the air. What next? My phantom pest tossed it hand to hand. I tried to recall if it was loaded.

"*Good place for it.*" The words scathed. "*Should be on your body.*"

He failed to say that most times my body wouldn't hide a hairnet.

"Oh! Go away!" I demanded grumpily. "I'm in your debt, but I need to get back."

To what I knew.

Familiar routine.

To show Madame nothing was amiss.

"Why, no. I have no notion where Mr. Petersen got to. And who might he be?" I'd say.

I cooled. My bones slowly filled with aches.

Reluctantly rising, I smiled grimly—*I really must get back.* If Petersen were missed? If any noted Big Bertha with a large fox-haired man slung over her shoulder? I had to find out. I glanced at my cherub clock. Not yet midnight. Madame usually refused visitors after midnight. I suspect Levi had something to do with that edict, yet this night was different, with such an important influx. I dared not avoid the Longhorn, for fear a client from among the profusion arriving with Petersen might refuse other girls, or if they were all occupied.

Clumsily dusting on great gouts of pearl powder, making my eyelashes resemble spiky icicles, I shakily applied pomade to cover cracked pale lips. Like a wind-up doll, I repaired the damages—sorely aware my evening mightn't be over, and I must return to the "mad social whirl" before Madame came rounding up the cattle... Truth, I was not thinking sensibly.

"*You can't.*"

Muscular fingers, encircling my wrist, slipped to my hand, turning it over, my palm lost in a bearlike paw. He could have crushed every bone, but he held my trembling fingers as gently as a newborn chick. A kiss brushed my palm. I bit my lip, near crumpling from rattled nerves.

Addressing the looking glass, I refused to meet his disturbing eyes blazing blue-green in the remaining lamplight. Shaking him off, grimly burning cork, I re-smudged my eyes and smeared rouge, all the while accompanied by visions of Petersen tossed to the mercy of pigs, pinching my eyes tight to shut out the picture, which meant that I now resembled a raccoon, and yet another application of burnt cork.

"*Don't, love.*" It was an angry command.

I halted mid-smudge. My cheeks were dotted with drifted cork.

Love. Not "*querida*," but "*love*."

The fearsome wretch wrapped his arms about my waist and neatly plucked my bottom from the seat. I stubbornly fought to get back to my dressing table.

"I need to at least pretend, or mama bear will be after me." I attempted a shaky laugh, indicating my ravaged state with a rueful smile.

"*Not tonight!*" The deep bark set ceiling lights atremble.

"But I need to!" *If I were banished, would he care?*

"*I never know how long I can stay,*" he answered with the harshness of despair. Time was no friend to either of us.

I squinted, viewing his form dimly through the room's gloominess. To my surprise, though I should not have been, he was nude as a statue, bronzed body gleaming in the new moon streaming through windows, throwing us in sharp relief like cut out silhouettes.

His body had been—*was* beautiful, more so by the contrast of scars and bullet wounds marring muscle and flesh, and the cut in his brow saved his face from magnificence to near brutalness.

Perhaps Petersen *had* told the truth and paid for the night, as others of their illustrious company, I warred. No one expected me. All still below. Only a solitary tune lightly played by Mr. ByJingo as was his pleasure after all left the premises.

The rooms beside me seemed settled, though I heard a man's rumbling howl down the hall. Probably Big Bertha's client.

I was safe for now, I thought too soon.

He bent and bruised my already bruised mouth with a lingering hungry kiss. Moreover, I could tell the bruhaha had lit an inferno of lust over and above our previous passion, one that could not be quenched with a mere dousing of rain water. It would take a waterfall and matched my own hunger as I stripped what remained of my clothing. I needed him. I hated him. I craved reassurance.

My eyes flashed to the bed. My heart pounded to his heartbeat.

We did not make it.

In the shortest time possible, we found ourselves on my flowered carpet, clutching, groaning, feasting on each other, whispering words I dare not repeat—silly, flaming, irreverent, loving words. We repeated vows on the bed after he dragged me up to it, ramming me deep in my feather mattress, insatiable, as if for the first time, while I gasped and laughed at his ardor, matching my own with each fevered stroke. I was astonished as always over how solid and hard he felt, how deep and more satisfying each pounding thrust, more than any mortal client. He kenned instinctively this would erase self-doubts, erase the past with passion that was pure and honest and lusty.

Later, in catlike contentment, spitting a few feathers, and scented with the perfume of musk, I languorously unfolded, stretching arms overhead, bringing them around his neck, sleepily nuzzling.

It was near dawning.

Light the shade and sheen of oyster shells filtered through my curtains. It was the moon, I realized, of a long winter night. Abruptly, I recalled Petersen and the mayhem last evening. Nothing had disturbed our peace. A miracle. Did I dare believe there would be no repercussions? I swiftly turned my head to finally gaze upon my phantom in the wan light, yet the room was hazy. I made out an indistinct shape and illusions of a tousled head. His long black mane lay across the pillow like a pirate's flag. Stealthily, I studied him—Lord forbid he should catch me. The broken-nosed face, brutal even in repose, thick brows with wicked peaks, scars, the sweep of black lashes fanning bronzed cheekbones, the mouth, stern even in slumber—or what passed for sleep.

Closing my eyes with the lingering sensation of ardent kisses, and a body well-used, I drowsed, delaying the moment I had to rise and recall the night…

My bruises, fusing with the burns from the carpet, had melted away. The welts on my throat healed under harsh kisses of his ferocious passion, yet a curing bliss too, as he had savaged my body with pent-up lust, kindled by the brutal encounter with the salesman, and mine by vindication—erasing the past, we had battered each other, pummeling, ripping, clawing in an insane fever. Me on top, tumbled-down hair dripping on his shoulders, with him rolling me under finally, capturing me, crushing my body spread-eagled beneath him, with his hands capturing my wrists on the blue-bonnet carpet—each fighting for ascendancy. I could still feel the plush wool abrading my fanny.

Was it any different than with Petersen?

Yet I was a willing captive this time, as I realized he was studying me, as if drinking me in with an unfathomable expression—sadness, desire, regret, fear I would leave as unannounced as he? He raised himself up, reaching for me as I for him, feeling an iron bar encased in velvet as he thrust forward, entering—"*Is it well with you?*"—he asked with barely controlled hunger, his face bearing down on mine, and even though I kenned he might not be *real* flesh and bone, the sensation of the warm throbbing part of him sinking deep and blissfully large, was well with me. I was shocked for a familiar instant at his initial invasion, yet feeling the sensation of a man's member, a bit cooler than normal, but otherwise amazingly different and exciting, force his way between my soft invitation, into my surprisingly narrow walls.

In my delirium, I did not care if it were the Devil himself. I returned a sensual smile as my answer and dug into him, clenching my legs about his form, like urging a horse on. We both moved to the same tempestuous rhythm as I stifled screams, biting his broad, muscled phantom shoulder.

After what seemed hours, he eased, gentling, and started the ride again where we both rippled and spasmed deep in our souls and throughout our heated bodies. At least mine did. He seemed to wish to continue, as if he never kenned when this amatory interlude might be allowed again. Marveling from whence his inexhaustible energy came, we lay side by side after I demurred, laughing, and by that laughter, erased the hideous encounter with the Hell-bound salesman.

I smiled. The downy mattress altered slightly. I rolled into the hollow left behind, as if he never was.

I searched the room lit only by a waning moon, to find my maddening tenant fully clothed in worn Levi's, with a leather band tied about his glossy black mane flooding his shoulders covered with what seemed an Indian-patterned serape.

To my confusion, he wrapped me in a quilt, scooped me up, and carried me to the bay windows and tried to melt through, but with me in his arms, he had to suffer the indignities of actually opening the latch and crossing the sill, me clinging to his neck as he stood there, as if on board ship on moonlit seas, overlooking the muddy wake of Wylder, Wyoming.

Setting me down, he squatted beside me, still gazing out at the chopped-mud streets with wonder.

"*I ken how cards are dealt and how the game is played, little one. Sometimes three aces up the sleeve, ofttimes a run of bad cards, a sharpshooter opposite you—a ringer—or marked cards. Do what you can to survive. Win big, or top the ante if you have a bad run. I do not think less of you. But more. You did not scream. You did not panic. You fought. In the end, your opponent was too evil. Do not feel shame.*"

"You mean…you care, truly?" I breathed. "Not just—?" I gestured inside to my bed.

"*Ah, my curse and chains.*" He grinned his wolfish smile, all white teeth and dangerous humor. "*Also, a blessing for this poor sinner."*

I looked down, summoning a blush.

Okay, I preened.

"Little dove?" He sighed. *"Do you think it is easy to watch you in the arms of another, giving and receiving such pleasure, when it is I who long to be in his place, touching you, holding you as if you were life itself, or to watch idly as one of them threatens you?"*

He lowered his voice. *"Yet there is nothing I can give you."*

I shook my head. *Oh, but you do*, I wanted to say. I shivered in his arms.

"Cold? I forget."

I nodded no, like a recalcitrant child with chattering teeth. It must be four of a winter morn. "What are we doing out here? I thought you couldn't… And the hall?"

White teeth flashed in his dark face silhouetted by the moon.

"My new skill."

The words were prideful as a boy showing off climbing the tallest tree.

I huddled between his legs, leaning back against his chest.

"When I attacked Petersen in the hall? I was there. I looked down at the gamblers, spotting the hustlers, the men at the bar—all that going on…"

"I'm happy for you. It must be joyous." My dryness must have seemed rebuke. "But don't you see, it is dangerous to defend me. Or teasing them. It is hard to explain away. Hard? Impossible! How often do you think I could fool Big Bertha?"

His laugh held no mirth. *"I must have some*

distractions, if you will, to make it durable—besides, that was my nature on earth. And he needed a good drubbing! I regret my actions cause you worry. I cannot be who I am not, even to match your tender sensibilities." His gaze fixed on the dimming necklace of the Milky Way. "*You were a distraction at first, but I was drawn to you like a lodestone. I wanted to remain bitter. The existence afforded me before was deadly, what with traveling drummers...*" He barked a laugh. "*Ah, what dull lives they lead! Or widows searching runaway husbands with a miserable passel of battling brats in tow—the drunken miners! I got no sleep. No rest.*"

I raised my brow at that.

He raked the motley town hungrily, as if it encompassed the gay lights of Paris.

"What new skills?" I sulked, shamefully jealous and fearful of his new freedoms. "Sitting on a porch roof in the dead of winter?"

I shivered, as frozen diamonds winked out across the sky, vainly striving to see what he envisioned.

He chortled. "*I see no ravening wolves to carry you off. Only me.*"

Peevishly, I muttered, "Now you can wander all over the place, snooping, eavesdropping, maybe pawing through my things."

"*Hah! Secrets? That happened long ago. You have no secrets, little one. I do wonder about the small tintype of that pimply-faced youth tucked under your lavender-scented lacy underdrawers, however.*"

"He wasn't!" I began. Then my blood chilled that had nothing to do with the air.

Did he ferret out all my secrets?

Had he found my damning evidence?

I had hidden them so cleverly…

Even he could not ken my past…*could he?*

He felt me pull away.

What was itching me to make me scratch at him so? Was it only that he could ferret out my unfavorable past, or was it more? I must rid myself of them, though. Silly to hang on to them. Almost a conceit in reverse.

He broke into my random thoughts. "*Let's enjoy the dawning. An event momentous to me as connecting two rail lines, or making Wyoming a state.*"

"Isn't it time you told me who you are?" I inspected him sideways. His eyes held such longing, gazing out at this small world, that I looked away, my thoughts darkening to India ink.

"If we are to have…a liaison," I ventured when quiet knitted long gray strings between us, "I should at least ken your *name*. Know *something* about you."

I kenned I was pressing him. Yet it seemed peculiar that I knew next to nothing of his past, though our bodies kenned each other exceedingly, embarrassingly well. I squirmed a bit, recalling his tongue in places it should not have been. When at last he spoke, it was of something else.

"*Tomorrow, little one. I feel myself fading,*" he murmured with regret dulling his voice. "*And you are cold.*"

Chapter Sixteen
Revelations

"My mother. She was called Kimani."

"Ki-man-i?"

"It means butterfly."

Love smoothed my phantom's gruff voice, ironing it with tenderness.

"She died young...in a raid." His bitterness made me flinch.

"A raid? You mean...attacked by Apaches or...? Your ma was...a native?" I wasn't certain what I thought of it, other than that they were just like us, only dressed and lived different.

Contempt flavored his laugh.

"Oh! I didn't mean it that way. You mean, like General Custer, then."

"You might say the army did not look kindly on her tribe. Ma was visiting relatives. They shot her in the back." He remained quiet so long I thought he'd ended it.

"They did their fair share of slaughter, too." Bitterness tempered his words like separate bullets fired at a target—me—sighing. *"She was Shoshoni, of the Kuchun-deka of the Wind River Tribes."*

Irritation suddenly colored his voice. *"Why do you want to learn all this?"*

"I want to be familiar with everything about you."

Mercy Maud. I sounded so needful.

"*If you must dig into all my dark history…*"

Did I detect a pleased tone in his grumbling? I relaxed, clutching the quilt tighter.

"*During the Civil War, the Shoshoni raided Pony Express routes, robbed stagecoaches, wagon trains, cut telegraph lines…along with the deaths that come with such exploits.*" He went on with not-so-hidden pride. "*They were notorious.*"

He raked the empty streets of Wylder with a face like a thundercloud.

"*The Shoshoni were defeated in 1863 in a bloody one-sided battle on Bear River. Two hundred and twenty-four souls massacred. My mother was one of them. Women, children, old folks. After that, the Snake Wars. They lasted four more years. The mighty Shoshoni were bloodily beaten. Resistance to the white invader faded like morning fog, as if they never were.*"

"Oh…I am sorry." How scant my sympathy must seem. He remained stiller than death, if that was appropriate.

"*Enough sorry to go around,*" he finally uttered. "*Pa's Irish-Spanish/Mex. No better than he should be. Took to drink—the so-called Irish curse—after Ma, that is. Still around, the old cuss. Somewhere. Wish I could see him. Maybe he is dead, but I don't feel it.*" He paused. "*Ma was pure Shoshoni. I have an Indian moniker too, but I don't think I'll share it.*"

I punched his ribs. He muttered something in a language I could not comprehend, then in English— "*This sharing a room is going to be a pesky problem, I can see. You are far too meddlesome and contrary.*" His black brows fought to be ferocious, and lost.

"But what *are* you called?"

"*Zachariah Tonaioza Cortez Quinn. Tonaioza was a great Shoshoni chief. Now you know. Spanish, Shoshoni, and county Irish.*"

I peered at him, armed with new kennage, taking inventory. He appeared more solid than in the past, as if the revelation gave him strength. Zachariah. The moniker suited him.

Burnished skin, smooth as a well-polished gunstock, stretched over high bony cheekbones, crossed with that single scar that divided his brow. A long Indian nose. Yes, a noble nose, high, with a slight curve like an eagle's beak. Clear Irish eyes, green as shamrocks, blazed out at me, at times rimmed in black like the pits of Hell—if Hell was icy cold. A shock of hair like glistening tar, long and straight.

One plait twined with leather and beads.

Long, stalwart legs, stretched out across the roof.

Through his open shirt, his chest muscles, then six tight polished squares narrowed to a lean waist. Broad shoulders. Not beefy like a buffalo's but solid, straining the open-necked shirt of fine chamois, tediously stitched with tiny intricate beadwork around the collar.

I frowned. Only loving stitches made that fine work.

I thought of his mother. Perhaps a sweetheart, the woman who took him in—or even a wife? Yet what claim had I on his former life, I thought miserably. Or he on mine? I recalled the dusky males blinkered from underground mining, burly trappers in from the cold, to dusty-haired, ruddy ranchers and range riders sprinkled with town swells and men of business traveling through Wylder, that I'd had biblical knowledge of, all spread before me like a checkered deck of cards.

"The blend suits you. All should be so lucky," I commented with the dryness of day-old zwieback.

"*Lucky? I'm dead!*" I sensed his ghostly head turn. "*I cannot smell whiskey as I once did, or enjoy a cheroot! Or campfire coffee.*"

I was silent, still drunk on his ruggedly ferocious face, that perfect blend—the glinting, changeable turquoise-green eyes, courtesy of his Irish blood, and the warm caramel skin of his Shoshoni mother, his straight, shining, jet hair courtesy of all three. But most of all here.

"*Not quite true, that. Lately—*" He cocked his head, scrutinizing me with bemusement. "*I have felt the return benefit of some of those earthly pleasures. And also...*" His burnished face turned the shade of oak leaves turning red yet he remained stony-faced.

For my sins, I was not mollified. "Never mind," I snapped, churlish, still dwelling on those loving stitches.

The changeable eyes searched the distance.

I stared at the quiet streets too, as wind whipped around us. Only the desultory tinkle of a weary ByJingo up early, playing for himself in the Longhorn, disturbed the peace. I witnessed no bustle beyond a wandering cat, and a young woman hurrying to her work at the dressmaker's in the pre-dawn cold.

She looked back and up, staring straight at me for a second, before scurrying on.

I ducked, but I think she saw me. Ah, well.

A miscalculation I would live to regret.

When I turned, my tenant wasn't even a wisp of smoke. I was alone, sitting legs sprawled on the porch roof like an addle-brain. I wished I could swallow my sour green-apple jealous words. I might have been dead or sorely injured if not for his absurd conjuring tricks.

"And I could have managed it!" I yelled like a shrew, scrambling over the sill, still shaken by pigs and salesmen, and by my own mean-spirited ungrateful thoughts. I was nervy. I kenned it. The fact he did not deserve my shrewishness did not help.

****

That night, I drifted to sleep gently rubbing odd bruises on my arms and where my head had banged the headboard…

…when a hand covered mine.

"I didn't mean to be ungrateful," I whispered. "I had wondered if you would…"

"*Grace your vinegary presence once more?*"

I felt him running ghostly lips down my neck, my shoulders, my breasts, in a soothing slide. Pain melted with the touch. "*Little one…I live for your scorching temper, your tongue dipped in acid. Now sleep. Maybe tomorrow I will tell you more if you promise not to change.*"

****

I had had no repercussions from the Petersen affair, though Big Bertha winked and nudged me, near knocking me off my chair at our late breakfast, until Madame barked at her to "act a lady"—Madame, still on a cloud from her success over our recent guests, two of whom, she crowed, indeed had paid for the whole night, including Petersen.

She beamed at Flora and me. I hid my face in my coffee mug. And Bertha managed—how, I could not but wonder—or tackled, and I use the word correctly, *three* of those dandies in one evening.

"I imagine we showed that so-called Social Club!" Madame swanked. "Plucked those high-steppers right off the train 'fore they even got a whiff of those poxy gals!"

She maligned them. They were nice girls, from what I heard.

I was trying my utmost to toss the memory of Mr. Petersen into the midden heap, but that image was too close to the pig sty with its enormous boar. Moreover, Big Bertha, her face hidden behind a biscuit mounded with ham, revealed nothing either. I tried to focus on the other girls' twittering over the coming Harvest Festival and their "dates" with the wealthy newcomers of the previous disastrous evening.

"Quite spoilt us," simpered Little Mae.

Not in my case, I wanted to growl.

Flora shyly showed a gold stickpin with a turquoise head surrounded by tiny diamonds. No one had the heart to query if her gentleman had surrendered it voluntarily.

I brooded over cornmeal mush with blackstrap when Little Mae's claims entered my consciousness… "You look like somethin' a sick cat wouldn't drag in. Not the first time, neither." She watched me like a sly puss for reaction.

Madame raised her head sharpish.

I had not a drop of laudanum, or I'd gulp it like morning coffee so as to face the day. A day of wonder, loss, acting the same when nothing was. How could it? I was half mad, pleasured by a ghost that had not had carnal knowledge since God alone kenned, and I was near murdered on top of that. Plus, my phantom's enthusiastic ravaging was taking a pleasurable toll.

I did resemble a sick cat, I had already decided when brave enough to drag myself to the dressing table, for I had had little sleep the past several nights, what with Flora, too.

"And here I supposed I looked like your Lillian Russell tintype or an oil painting of Evangeline," I soured, dipping my nose back in my coffee mug.

"Enough sass!" Madame smacked the table.

"What are you so full of yourself for anyways?" Little Mae hissed through cornbread dipped in bacon fat with cracklings. "Did Madame send my big spender up to *you*? I heered *some*body in your room, after everybody else was gone!" Little Mae had a favorite she tried to keep secret, suspicious we were all hell-bent on poaching. Anyone who had eyes were aware the little tailor, no bigger than a matchstick, favored her with tent-like gowns, mostly of yards of purple or yellow satin sent all the way from Chicago on the Wells Fargo stage.

I don't even like purple.

I smiled mysteriously, crossing my eyes from sheer waywardness.

Madame threw me the squint eye.

"Have you been imbibing *this* early?" At my puzzled look, she added, "Drinking, Miss Cherry! Don't let us be coy. I have my eye on you!" Her ominous tones could curdle milk. She still had it in for me for favoring Flint, and for other small liberties—and perhaps suspicions of last night plus Mae's comments stirring the pot.

I couldn't disagree regarding my shambling appearance or get Flora in trouble by saying I peeked in on her again, feeling her brow and checking her hankies for telltale blood as a lunger and had found none.

It seemed a day for more lies. I had best get used to it.

"I—I been in my spells. Auntie Scarlett came visitin' me early-like."

"Hunh! Auntie Scarlett seems to me visited just two weeks ago."

"Humm," I said. "I'll be better soon."

"Hunh! Guess it's better than two weeks late." She gave us a warning glare promising hellfire and brimstone if that should happen. We already had two rosy-cheeked, grubby-faced squallers running about, farmed out to a childless couple and a widow woman.

I used the silk thread tied to a sponge soaked in vinegar, myself—least until I was ready for kiddies right and proper. I thought fleetingly of Flint.

Mae with her earnest look. "Miss Solange?"

"Madame!"

"Yes'm. Madame Solange." Mae halted eating long enough to put the pancake as big as a wagon wheel back in the lake of sorghum from its travel to her mouth. "She's still entertainin' cowpokes in her room after hours!"

Big Bertha joined in—the traitor.

"A real hoedown's agoin' on in there when we all know this place is closed up tighter'n a pig's ar—"

I shrunk. *Oh, no, Big Bertha!* I threw a look. She heaved mighty shoulders in a gesture that said, *I wasn't going to tell.*

"Please!" Madame held up her hand. "No vulgarities!"

Undiscouraged, Mae plowed on. "An iffen she can,

why not…?"

Madame swiveled bullet eyes on me. "Is that true?"

I calmly buttered my over-buttered biscuit while hurling sideways bullets at Mae and Bertha. No doubt Little Mae entertained notions of amusing her skinny tailor in *my* room. And Bertha? Who kenned what deep desires *she* owned? Beyond making some spare coin.

"Whatever do you mean, ma'am?" I looked innocent as Virgin Mary.

"I am *very* exacting in my instructions—my *only* requirement as I make the *delicate* arrangements, I might add, for your welfare." Her gaze raked us. "If you had any notion the lengths I must go to please His Highness…"

I had some idea that included lifting her skirts behind the log pile or late-night tipples in Levi's private quarters, but I battened down as the gale swept over us.

"For *any* of you to be part of this fine, growing establishment, I will *not* have you *wallow* with every tinhorn hustler or drunken sot you take a fancy to like common sluts. Sneaking them to your rooms the back way without a by-your-leave! *Particularly* ones whom I have not been *introduced* to." Or from whom had coins cross her palm.

We girls exchanged glances. She made it sound like our enterprise was an Eastern cotillion with beaux lining up.

"But Madame, we ain't…" Big Bertha growled. Flora began snuffling like a tiny kitten. Mae just looked sulky.

"Stuff your pie hole!" With that, Madame's past was regurgitated, her speech cruder, more lowlife.

Flora whimpered and dropped her tiny spoonful of

egg, gawping.

"It isn't as if every Wells Fargo coach delivers fresh doxies every Saturday, a trippin' off the coach, just dreamin' of being a whore for you," I muttered.

Madame clicked her cup down. "You are courtesans. Or paramours. Even perhaps"—she looked in the distance—"ladies of the night, gentlemen's escorts"—looking full bore at me—"but *never whores or doxies*. Don't let me hear such tasteless terms!" Though I'd had benefit of all, and from her mouth.

She wasn't finished, as others grabbed cornbread and sidled off. "Stay. This is for all of you."

"If you want an affair…" She sneered as if that were the vilest position on earth. "Though I would scarce name such nefarious meetings—*if* they are not steady customers, and *off* the premises *on* your own time." Not that we had much of that. Time that is, or a chance at a fella that had not graced the Longhorn, and if they hadn't, it was 'cause their ma wouldn't let them.

"I would suggest you think carefully of our future relationship. I *will* toss you out without a backward look, to ply your trade like a slattern in the alleys behind the pig lots, and don't think I won't spread your reputation, like your legs"—I winced at her crudity—"all over Wylder, especially the tender ears of the so-called Wylder Social Club, if that's what you suppose. They won't abide cheats, either, I fancy."

My biscuit crumbled to dust at the mention of the pig lots. The Longhorn's old hound dog lapped up my dropped treat.

"We strive to gain prominence over, nay *surpass* the Wylder Social Club. Social indeed! I was thinking of having an establishment known as 'The Gentleman's

Pleasure.' Chandeliers. Plum velvet wallpaper, the best liqueur from Chicago. We cannot attain that if you diddle every horny prick for nothing."

The girls and I shared glances over the glimpse of her grandiose dreams and crude words.

She narrowed eyes into slits from which flames shot. "Or perhaps, you aren't giving your favors away."

"Madame!" Flora's lip trembled. A tear rolled down her soft babyish cheek.

"Mayhap you were doing a little under-the-cover fucking! On the cheap. How long has *that* been going on under my very trusting nose?" Usually, Madame used allusions. Mr. Gruenvald peered around the door, throwing sour looks, like he'd eaten a pickle, and ducked back. There went another hole in Madame Solange's chances to be mistress of the Longhorn, I reckoned, hoping she'd wind down.

Little Mae giggled, nervous. I eyed her, wondering about the little tailor and how often he visited undercover, so to speak.

I kenned something else was eating at Madame, no doubt prickling over Mr. Gruenvald's lukewarm attentions, not just us. Collapsing in a chair, she dabbed her eyes. We stayed glued, with sawdust in our throat. Bertha and Mae shot me resentful, sullen looks. How long could I rely on them? I rocked their boat in the seas of tranquility.

Even sweet Flora. I could not blame them. Beneath our comfy berths lay rocky mattresses. The end of the trail for most, no matter how many hair-bend turns of misfortune, even with golden dreams of wedding a rich miner. The other choice was saving up. *Hah!* My small amount evaporated with Flint, the nest egg to raise myself up in Frisco, or Orleans. Even start a starvation business—as a laundry or a cook. My cookery skills would merit me the dishwasher's job at the Wylder hotel if I was lucky.

Wed the first man who offered? Or, as Madame said, "Go out on the dusty streets of Wylder to ply my trade"? Until the ghostly tenant appeared one night and took all my options away.

****

"Were you—so *very* wicked?" I drew away, sensing Zachariah doing the same as his phantom body stiffened. I cannot explain it better. It was as if his spectral presence grew colder, and his laugh bitter as headache powder on the tongue.

He answered instead, "*I felt free on the roof. Me. The desperado. Hah! The bandito*"—he curled his hard mouth—"*who galloped the plains like* el huracán, *explored hidden mesas that no man had ever seen before, fought in the war, holed up in caves, was the scourge of big cities…*" He laughed then. "*Hell! Frisco, Chicago—St Louis, Orleans, even New York…*"

"Vandalize, you mean?" I interjected lightly, probing.

"*You ken me well, you irritating colleen. And now it is you, you wanton baggage, that I cannot leave, until I am weighed and balanced to see if I've managed more good than evil in my wretched, useless life.*"

"Wait!" I blurted. "Were you dangerous?"

"*Wicked to the bone.*"

The featherbed depressed behind me. A long hard body pulled my fanny to it, holding me firm. He smiled at me with sadness. "*Not to you, little one…*"

As usual, we managed to get sidetracked.

Chapter Seventeen
Ghost Riders

My wretched phantom strode the confines, rapping walls in brooding agitation. We were both living unnatural lives, and so we went after each other with hammer and tongs, at times, both wanting so much more of each other, of the world—to proclaim we were one proudly, not skulking in shadows. We sniped at each other. Peering out the bays, disquieted and restless, ruminating in the dark place where he often retreated, Zachariah decided to reveal his wicked past. It had been days since he graced me with his presence. Perhaps he was bored. Two could play that game, I decided.

"Really? I find I no longer care…" I bit my lip, recalling his ruined appearance, scars, and bullet wounds. Of course I wished to have that knowledge. I shrugged and rolled my hair in curlers. "Stop. You make me dizzy."

He scowled, plunking down in the red chair, indicating *Come.*

I turned to my dressing table and busied myself.

"You wanted to know all? Now's the time! Come here or never ask again!"

I studied him. He meant it. He could be stubborn as me. We locked each other's eyes like two gunfighters.

"Come," he said softly.

I scowled.

He patted his thigh. "*I won't bite. Much.*" Strong white teeth flashed humor.

I had nothing else to do save sort my undies drawer, mend an old petticoat past saving, my hair washed in rain water, rinsed in vinegar, and tied in rags, and the next man tripping up the stairs was four hours away. I walked over, provocatively slow, and accepted his offer. He wrapped his arms about me. I echoed. "Were you so very bad?"

He looked down at me wistfully. "*Bad?*"

I leaned against his chest, unconsciously listening for a beating heart, hearing his deep rumble vibrate in my ear.

"*It didn't start that way, little one. As all foolhardy, harebrained escapades begin with reckless, arrogant sprats; I was 'bout fifteen or so, after Ma—*" He left the thought unfinished, and I sensed that part of him was a door too dodgy to open again.

"*We were a gang of six.*" He snorted, self-deprecating. "*At the time, I would have laid my life down for any one of them. We were family. Brothers. Most of us homeless punks, the dregs, living off cons and petty theft. One, a mestizo from Guadalajara. A kid who wanted to be me, you ken.*"

He looked down at me again. "*A fearless, fast-drawing, good-looking gunslinger.*"

I jabbed my elbow back and heard a satisfying, "*Ooof!*"

"Si. *That kid!*" He chuckled. "*A baby. Ah! The drubbing he took from us.*"

I nestled closer, sensing he was in a lighter mood. "And then?"

He let out a long sigh. "*We robbed travelers on stagecoaches…*"

"A stagecoach robber," I spoofed. "That's not so very wicked! Some folks fair ask for being robbed." I giggled. "Rings on every finger, fancy watches, and pockets stuffed with cash. Even banks rob you," I muttered darkly.

"*Not toothsome widows and pitiful orphans, though.*"

"You didn't!"

"*I did relieve a few grieving widows of their wedding rings and gewgaws.*"

The way he said it, I envisioned widows weeping crocodile tears behind dainty dry hankies while practically tossing the wedding rings at him.

Suddenly aware of my cherub clock *clunking* away, I yelped, grabbing my rag rollers. "Damnation! I must get ready!"

He cast me a look of annoyance and dumped me to my feet.

"Don't go away," I admonished, racing to my dressing table.

He gave weary acknowledgement. "*Wouldn't dream of it.*"

And promptly vanished.

I glared at the red chair and began hustling into my pink taffeta, wondering if that was it.

****

My pink taffeta was a puddle on the floor.

"Tell me more?" I sat astride his loins so he couldn't get away. Well, he'd have to pass through me. He gazed from my pillows with weary amusement.

"You promised. If we are to—to continue, I must at

least ken who you are, really." I was unreasonable. What good would such knowledge do me?

"*Shhh, I will tell it, but you must not—ah—stir me so. Or leave.*"

I felt his stirring, and not wishing to sidetrack my elusive phantom, I clambered off and sat cross-legged on the bed like a hoyden, not wanting to miss one second of his wicked past, as he regaled me into the night. Raising one hand behind his head, he absently caressed me—like stroking a cat—with the other, all the while studying the ceiling, seeing another place and time.

"*I must tell it all, I suppose. No secrets.*" Zachariah watched me sadly. I stiffened.

What did he mean by that?

Did he ken *my* secrets?

In his other world, could he see all—even my questionable past?

I held my breath. Perhaps this was not a good thing. However, he only crooked a smile, grimly reminiscent in the golden dusk of the oil lamp as he revealed his past inequities.

"*We were a rum lot. One hombre, Frank, I would not trust with anybody's sister—or grandmother, for that matter. Good-looking cuss. Crooked as a broke-back snake.*"

"*There was a black ex-soldier. Old Joe, a creole from Orleans, the quickest draw I ever witnessed.*" He shook his head in wonder. "*My younger cousin. He looked like Ma. Shoshoni. He liked to dress native, too, though he overdid the warpaint when he wished to frighten the ladies. More on that.*" His face darkened.

I knit my brow and opened my mouth to speak.

He placed a finger on my lips. "*And then the Kid. Not Billy—just an aggravating, wet-nosed young'un. Never did hear his real name. Orphaned, he was, trailing after us until we let him in. The last was a Tex/Mex. Alejandro…never got acquainted with his last moniker either. Just called him Jandro.*

"*Thought we were big time, at least heading that way, the six of us. When a poster came out, we snatched as many as we could and took them out of our pockets to admire so much they damned near fell apart.*"

At the mention of a poster, I swallowed hard and kept my face bland as oatmeal. But why had he carped on a damned poster, of all things?

"*The South of the Border Gang! Hah! A piss-poor description, save for Jandro. Not that it made a spit in the wind of difference.*"

"I never heard of you," I said, doubtful.

He chuckled, stroked my hip seductively, gave it a light slap, and out of the blue a cheroot appeared, lit and smoking. He took a pleasurable draw, pluming fragrant smoke, and grinned, his white teeth and turquoise eyes glowing in the dark.

"*Bah! Notorious only in our own* cabeza." He drew and puffed as I stirred restlessly, wanting him to go on.

"*In the beginning, we were* nada *but big-time troublemakers. Had a few successes where we actually made some money rather than lost it. Nobody got hurt too bad. A few bullet holes in our hats, and close calls. We grew older, more ambitious. Cocky, still wet behind the ears, took crazier chances for the next fourteen years or so. Came to believe in our own triumphs—or dumb luck. In our blundering way, we relieved mail trains, unwary travelers, and banks of their legal tender, but the biggest haul that put us on the map was by mistake."*

Zak snorted. *"The South of the Border Gang made off with a shipment of silver headed for the army in Abilene. Had no notion that freight had more guards and soldiers than prickers on cactus. By the skin off our behinds, and one bullet in the arm"*—he winced—*"mine, we got away with seventeen bags of silver and one of gold bar."*

"That benefitted us twenty-four months of high-on-the-hog livin'. You'd have loved it—Chicago, New York, Frisco. Sailed to England to do the grand tour like bigwigs or toffs, as they call 'em over there. The Delmonico. Best hotels, fine dining, aged whiskey… pretty—" He glanced at me. *"Never mind that. The casinos of Europe. Monte Carlo. Biarritz. Hah! Bigwigs! So overdressed and flash, folks pointed at us on the boulevards. Until Joe, the fast draw, stole off with what was left, which was still considerable."*

Zak flicked the cheroot. It vanished, sparking in the distance.

"Looking back, he was the smart one."

"What did you do?"

"Returned on a tramp steamer and bummed back to Wyoming, still crazy as a bag of frogs over Joe's betrayal and our own gullibility. We held up the Wells Fargo stage, first day we hit our old territory. No planning, just raw stupidity. Didn't even appreciate what it carried, or much cared."

Zachariah sighed and lit another cheroot.

"Frank, our ladies' man, though wasn't so pretty anymore, chivied a widow woman. Pretended he was going to carry her off. That he was part Apache,

and she kenned what Apaches did, didn't she?

"*That poor woman. Then she got a gander of my Shoshoni cousin in full native dress with an old tomahawk that wouldn't cut lye soap stuck in his belt. She began screaming. The driver got brave and reached for his Winfield. The Kid shot him, the same time the Winfield discharged. Blew his head off.*"

Zak closed his eyes reliving it.

"*The skies opened up. I remember the rain washing the blood away and Billy kicking until he lay still. But that stirred up some of the other passengers, who decided to be brave. My cousin held them off. We were all wet and cantankerous as a cat down a well. The lady's kid, a pup, might have been all of six, shielded her against us four left, shouting and kicking at us, splashing up mud with the rain drenching him and his ma. 'Stop! My pap just died!'*"

I waited. He turned his head, continuing in a throaty voice.

"*'Stop!' he said. 'Fight me, you bad men.' And that little Buster Brown came flailing away. Frank just stood there with a stupid grin and the rain washing his hair down in his face while this kid kicked his ankles. Not sure I reckoned what to do. What could he do, the dumb galoot?*"

I held my breath, hating what must come next.

"*Then Frank, the* pendejo, *tripped and stumbled back from the woman. His gun went off. She had a bad ticker, I reckon, and what with her husband passing on, she just…fell like a broken doll—lay there all white, lips turning blue. Frank thought he shot her. Might as well have.*"

"Shhhh-shh. No more." *My love.*

"*No.*" He flicked the cigar away. "*This is my penance. Hell on earth. Purgatory, as my Irish pap would swear, drifting in limbo till the earth turns to ashes. I deserve every last infernal year. That lady dead at my feet. An orphaned kid! I dragged Frank off still wanting to rob that damned stage. The* cabrón*! Everyone got an eyeful. Every one of us fixed in their heads clear as a bead on a rifle barrel.*"

He laughed as if he bit a wild persimmon. "*Still want to hear more of my illustrious past?*"

I nodded, mute. He shook his head, tossing a sardonic look at me. "*Bloodthirsty wench.*"

"*One of the passengers, an old soldier who looked like he couldn't lift a slingshot, hauled out this battered, rusty Colt as long as a dog's hind leg while we all stared at the lady, and he shot my cousin straight through the heart. He swung the Colt at Frank. I saw Frank dive out of the way. Last thing I saw was the* pendejo *leaping on his horse and hightailing it out.*" He looked aside as if still seeing it.

And suddenly I did too…in the middle of the room, as if a play were being performed and my room a stage.

Only these were like living creatures…

It seemed I could reach out and touch them, smell the heat and dirt…

An old man with palsied hands, rheumy eyes, thin as a rake. A grizzled beard. Remnants of a Confederate uniform…

The long, lethal Colt thrust out of silver sheets of water. The spit of fire. A woman in a purple traveling dress with a crocheted collar, already crumpled to mucky, churned-up ground clutching her heart… A small boy in his Sunday best, a blue velvet sailor suit darkening with rain… Shots barked, echoing off mountains. Thud of a body hitting muddy ground. The squelch of muck… The rear end of a horse slashing off in the downpour…

Poof! It was my room again.

"Oh!" I gasped, not believing my staring eyes.

"*The last thing I felt was a wildfire blazing in my chest,*" Zak continued, unfazed, as if a vision had not appeared and faded to nothing before my eyes.

His silence told me he ended his tragic story.

"*So now you recognize the black heart of me. Sins heaped on my head heavy as tombstones.*" Zachariah glanced with compassion, warming his changeable eyes. "*You couldn't fathom any of that. You. Soft as a kitten—a spitting, clawing kitten, ofttimes.*" He snorted a laugh. "*What dastardly secret could you harbor in that kissable, plump little bosom? For all your naughty ways, you are innocent as a child. Clean and pure. Why I fancy you so very much. You couldn't hurt a sick flea.*"

Ordinarily, I would spit back at such condescension. I looked away so he could not see my face. If only he kenned. I suppose that would have been the time to tell my own wicked past.

"Don't be silly," I muttered instead, sorely conscious of my sin branded on my forehead with a flaming *S* like poor Hester Prynne.

He watched me with his changeable green-blue eyes for a second and began fading.

"Don't. Please. Don't go. I don't care what happened, or what you did. You have paid. What you said was kind."

No one else had ever stood up for me. Ever.

I nestled on his chest, burrowing my head into the hollow of his neck to hold him there. It seemed to work. Eyes squinched tight, wrapping my arms about his gunslinger hips, never mind the chill metal from his gun belt which astonishingly reappeared with the telling of the tale, as if he readied himself again for the earthly assault of yesteryear, I would never let him go. How hungry I was for a real man, though that is an inaptness. As if reading my mind, with an end of forbearance, my flickering lover picked me up, carrying me to my bed. He rolled me down deep—deep in my feather mattress, like floating on a cloud. I gulped with primitive pleasure as he took me as if he were drowning, and I the air he needed to breath. Perhaps not far from the truth.

I felt a presentiment of doom, however, which I could not shake. I buried myself in him, as he did in me.

From the first touch, as if for the first time, like a falling star crashed to earth, quakes shook the massive bed, then—I was the aggressor in the dark, sensing his hard, rangy muscles, satin-haired massive chest beneath me, as I settled myself down on his almost hurtful length and callously rode his hardness thrust deep. Growling, he rolled me sideways, gripping me head to fanny, pressing me closer still—me wrapping my legs about his lean hips with all my strength, he kissing me ardently, tongue fighting tongue. From a merciless abyss of loneliness, despair, and hunger, we carried on into the night, each desperately needing the other, afraid of losing this fragile chance of redemption and peace.

And so I clung to my rangy paramour, barely hanging on. Zak's clothing had vanished long ago. No more gun belt, chaps, nor shirt. It seemed natural that this being could perform wonders, and I relished the friction of his hard body against my own, melting to quicksilver, bone to bone, until a perfect harmony of thrust and long shuddering withdrawals was attained.

After what seemed hours, I swooned in sleep's blissful surrender. Yet in the middle of the night, my unseen lover led me back from the abyss, stopping for long, slow strokes, slowly building the friction again. I felt the fullness of my tender parts until I was a juddering, quivering mass of heated flesh and bone slick with my own sweat. *Not his,* I wondered, bemused.

Our bodies sleeked across each other in sometimes disharmonic rhythms. So, burning with desire, we two, we savaged each other with need. With each blissful slide, I groaned with an ecstasy denied far too long, no matter my profession. Perhaps he too felt this sense of endings. Somewhere, deep in my primitive brain, I realized our appetite was fueled by fear—of the indecipherable future, our own aloneness—as if banking up coals against an endless, harsh, unforgiving winter.

For now, we did not care.

Care what? I thought upon awakening alone. I was going mad in a handcart straight downhill, infatuated with a thief who caused the death of a helpless woman.

But it wasn't *like* that—and so I warred, glad I did not tell him of my fragile hold on the room. Or that I had a frightening secret of my own…or any notion that my secret would soon show up, like a red-hot penny as a prank on Hallowe'en.

****

As if fates decided to stir the stew, over breakfast the next noon, I choked on my toast when Little Mae returned all agog from the privy, breathlessly relating about a Pinkerton agent "pummeling," as she put it, Mr. Gruenvald out by the wood pile, over Petersen's apparent "French leave" and wantin' ta know how long he bin stayin' at the Longhorn.

Little Mae eyed me in a way I could not translate, but I could feel her cogs turning like a watch. Big Bertha shot me a glance, and as if she'd just recalled her role in Petersen's abduction, changed the conversation to gripes over her cold eggs. Nevertheless, Mae plowed on.

"He snuck off with a year's commissions and left his customers on the fuzzy end of the stick. And he wanted ta know had anyone seen him leave and who with."

It would not be long, I gloomed, until someone remembered Petersen's flight to Paradise, arm in arm with me, though in his case, Paradise was hardly an appropriate description.

Chapter Eighteen
Paradise Lost

I was in a nightgown billowing in a frigid gale. The train barreling toward me, blinding me, I raised helpless hands to ward off the glare of probing lanternlight. Almost upon me. Blotting out the night with its hiss and clank and roar and wicked sharp cowcatcher ready to scoop me up. I couldn't move...my feet were glued to the crossties. Then...I was a child standing before the grinding onslaught of steel and light, noise and the merciless iron locomotive bearing down. It was on me, crushing me under its wheels...

I sprang up, my thin nighty soaked and clamped to my skin. The same nightmare. Something evil, bad, implacable was rushing to me with an unescapable force. I felt it in my skin and bones. I was that child, and my past was almost upon me. I clung to my phantom lover as a savior galloping across the plains. Trembling, I sought him out. Not even a whiff of cigarillo smoke or hint of bay rum scented the air... I sank back in my downy pillow, pulling it around my ears, praying my day of reckoning would not come.

My phantom and I could have gone on half-believing, half-delirious, half-fearing each other. Too many halves... If this be my lot and all we had, I would accept it. He had become more real than any client. I led two lives. Our days began in the evening after clients departed, most times, when he was not teasing or tormenting those who visited my chamber.

I near spoiled it, of course.

After my terrifying dreams and restless night, I was tarting myself up at my dresser for another evening's onslaught of miners and drovers with pay packets just begging to be depleted, plus a few business men satiated with spirits, gambling, and willing girls; I detected Zak watching with ill humor.

Fractious, still upset over Mae's revelations, Madame's tirades, and my own foreboding over a past catching up, and not wishing to go down tonight, I nailed him in my looking glass whilst dabbing the delta of my bosom with carmine.

"How *did* you end up here? How did you…?"

He blew smoke—startled, if the flick of a cat's tail twitch of the eye was any indication, looking testy in return. I had spoken without ceremony, yet the question had haunted me for months.

Was it rude to ask how he died? I doubted any books on etiquette covered that particular subject.

"*Die? Kick the bucket, exit this earthly plain, this vale of tears, croak, perish, leave this mortal coil…? How romantically quaint do you wish it? A queer time to ask!*"

"Why not? We know each other. Biblically—" I wanted it to sound sophisticated. Faltering, I softened my tone. "But not all." I looked at him fully. "Truly, I wish to ken. It will make you more…"

"*Real?*" His mouth quirked a grimace. He tossed the cigar. It vanished midair in a hail of sparks.

"Enough. So you were cheated." I hurled my bristle brush. "Why take your ire out on me?" It bounced off the chair. Maddeningly, his voice hailed from another part of the room. I whirled and found him leaning against the window.

"*Fair enough. This is where I died, as you well ken,*" was spoken as if an anvil dropped. The air turned heavy, sweltering. Obviously, a sore subject. "*And you are tarted up enough! Why the rouge between your…?*" He motioned to my breasts.

"Never you mind."

"*I died here. Isn't that enough?*"

"Not really," I said, flippant, as if distracted by my toilette.

He cast another sour glance, brooding, out at the street. "*Nothing romantic. Nothing like what yellow-dog newssheets spew out as titillation for the gullible.*"

I loosened my peignoir to dab cologne water under my arms and behind my ears.

"*None of that, now. Or you will be sorry,*" he promised.

I sniffed, wandering to the window beside him to catch a lungful of cooler air. We enjoyed an unusual return of Indian summer. Moreover, I accidentally allowed my robe to breeze open. "Must you do that?"

"*What, pray tell?*"

"Heat the room!"

"*Hmmm? I did not ken I owned that talent. Will wonders never cease?*" Said with the sarcasm of any schoolboy. "*You mentioned it was cold last time…your exact words were 'a chill vapor wrapped the room' or some such nonsense. And must* you *do* that?"

He grabbed my waist under my wrap, glaring at my naked body where my robe was now fully open. "*That may work on clients,*" the look said, "*but never on me.*"

Feeling my face redden down to my toes, I was intent on slapping his insults clean to the next territory. He flung my hand down.

"How dare you think I—I… If you were not invading my room, I could parade about any way I wished! I could even stand on the rooftop, starkers! I could—"

He sighed from the deepest pits of forbearance. "*As you wish.*" His teeth flashed. "*I would like to see that public display, however. Alert me whenever you are putting on another brazen show on Longhorn's roof.*"

I flounced back to my dressing table.

I waited. We were having a row.

Our first.

Zachariah did not come to me, merely returned to the red velvet chair in his usual position, brooding and practicing knife-throwing, of all things. Fortunately, the knives vanished before hitting any target, not that they were aimed at me.

Particularly.

****

My client, the last of the night, a plowboy who no doubt had saved up, was booted out the door.

His face said it all.

He felt a foot on his rear.

I strived to look innocent. 'Sides, I was barefoot.

"Whu'? Miss Blossom? Why'd ya kick me?"

"You just tripped is all," I assured him, standing on my toes to buss his cheek, then furthered his journey to the stairs by taking his arm.

I returned rolling up my peignoir sleeves to do battle—

"*Thought that clodhopper would never get through*

164

all his plowing," my phantom grumbled.

I agreed, but rammed both fists on my hips. "Didn't have to be so unkind."

He glared. *"Is he it? Or do you have a line of admirers clear to the stockyards?"*

I scowled back, grudgingly noting he was garbed somberly in black. It looked wonderful on his massive frame, with his sleek licorice hair and bronzy sumac-colored flesh. I think we enjoyed what was called, in some quarters, a Mexican standoff.

He growled, *"All right. I see we will not be friends unless I satisfy your—nosiness."*

"Nosiness! Merely concerned."

"Hah! I was shot! Bullet right through the old lung. I deserved it. That do you?"

I kept a stoic face.

"Another in the shoulder—a piddling thing, but a bleeder, then for good measure, a lucky bullet to my side as I leapt for my horse. It went through my liver—I think. Maybe gizzard, maybe stomach..."

I winced. So that was the long ugly scar low on his right side…

"Oh! My dear," I blurted.

"Never mind that." His bitterness made my toes curl.

"We'd just held up a train. What was left of us. How could I know the cars were bristling with special guards and a gold shipment from Frisco-way. Made it far as here. Better than dying like a distempered coyote with nothing better'n rattlesnakes and vultures for last rites. I was most determined to have one shot of good rye whiskey. One last soft bed. And one—last—lovely— willing gal." He snorted. *"Just like one of those thick-*

as-molasses highwaymen ballads you ladies are so fond of."

"Oh!" I wrinkled my nose. "Don't honor yourself."

However, he continued in mawkish tones like a bad actor in a very bad melodrama.

"*So I rode through the merciless desert heat into the last sunset, barely hanging onto my trusty faithful horse, with a hole as big as a dollar pancake in the side—not the horse's, mine—and bleeding like Old Faithful, hoping for just one last glimpse, just one last tender kiss, from the gal I left behind, my faithful sweetheart, I had so cru-el-ly a-bus-ed, and my gallant horse, who knew where to take me on this last night of earthly plea-sures…*"

"Oh. Do be serious!" I stifled the grin threatening my face and waited through such a long silence I feared he'd vanished.

"*Actually, I was. She was my girl,*" he said quietly.

I assumed feigned indifference.

"*Least, she vowed she was,*" he continued.

"*Least, when I was in town. Mostly. I should not have done that to her. Rachel was with me to the end. I'll give her that, and it wasn't pretty. I lasted three days.*"

"That was—charitable." I was jealous. Stupidly jealous, as Little Mae over her tailor, of an unknown girl who bravely sat with a dying scoundrel, seeing him through what was likely a bloody, messy, painful end.

I was horrid.

"*Shamefully, I died in a featherbed with my boots on, for the record. That featherbed. I figure it's mine as well as yours.*"

His hand hovered negligently in the looking glass,

waving away that statement as if of trifling consequence.

"You died in…?" I blanched, feeling dizzy. I rose too soon.

But it was not that entirely that caused my dizziness.

Once again, I stared into swirling dull gold vapor filling my room like a fading sandstorm, as before…

Out of the mist emerged desperate cries—pleading. The strange glittering dust boiled up, hurting my eyes. Horses' hooves slashed through yellow haze sparking with sunshine too near my face. I felt scorching heat, smelled horse sweat and gunpowder. I heard a train's pistons, the hiss of steam, felt hot vapor and the wheel's *clackety-clack* rhythm, iron on iron…

I jumped back, colliding with my dresser as the train ground past me and a horse raced from nowhere. Rifle and pistol shots seemed muted, as if I wore earmuffs—horses neighing, screaming. A *thud* of a huge body to the ground—or my carpet, rather. I gaped at the poor horse lying there, writhing, striving to get its footing. I could see the carpet pattern through the horse. Very confusing. More gold fog-dust billowed. I envisaged a man in a uniform with epaulets, gold buttons glittering in the sun, and some sort of insignia, aiming a long-barreled rifle from an open boxcar…

A man-shape crumpled to earth, twisting, as if screwing himself into the dust, where he lay prone and broken. He tried to rise… *It was him. Zachariah.*

I stared at the being, both in my room and on my carpet.

Riders galloped off.

I cried out and, merging with swirling dust, tried to

go to him. I walked through the horse's body, I realized, gagging, wanting to withdraw. A bullet whipped past my head with a hot *sizzle*, vanishing where glittering dust ended. I waded about desperately as the fog grew thicker. I felt trapped in this otherworld… *Was I on the other side?* The fog thinned till I once again detected the carpet's bluebells at my feet and the shape of my dresser…

I saw Zachariah once more as he diminished, and something more ominous than silver medallions appeared. Sin-ugly bloody splotches ringed in hellish black drenched his vest with port-wine stains. I recognized gunshot wounds, the crusted, singed hole close to his heart, or where I imagined it would lie—far too close for life…

I screamed.

Abruptly as it began, the golden, sunlit dust receded. Shrieking horses and shots dissolved…

I sat stunned. "Always wondered about that stain," I managed.

"*What, pray tell? I was right in the midst of relating a very thrilling and tragic drama, and…*"

He hadn't seen a thing.

I must have been white as whey milk.

"I saw it," I whispered.

"*Did I present myself well?*" His grave face told me he considered that question important, but not for vanity's sake.

"Very."

"*What was I wearing?*"

I wrinkled my nose, showing my confusion. His garb had changed, I realized, as he told his grisly tale.

"What does it matter? I couldn't tell… Oh, all

right, if you must. It's what you wear now, the same jacket—or vest?—with the silver medallions. It—it had blood stains. *Huge* stains—wet, soaking your shirt through, running down your side, past your gun belt. A scorched tear in your shirt, blood leaking down your leg, making your trousers sodden with blood— You were in pain!" I clutched my arms, shaking, reliving the horrific scene.

"*I…regret that…unwelcome show. I wish it had not happened.*"

"Oh, couldn't you try? That was horrible—I saw you die!"

"*No, not then, not quite—that honor lay before me, as I said.*" His face, so grave I forgave him, paining me to think of his desperate dash on an off-stride, jouncing, dying horse. The agony of his wounds was now so real.

Then I heard… "*I lied. I did not expire in that bed. It was in this chair…though I lay there while—she tended me. I tried to leave. I got this far.*"

"I am sure I don't care a tinker's dam where you died! Don't show me again." I ached with pain for him. I could do nothing to ease it, yearning to swallow those mean words. I wanted to say I was sorry. Pride stoppered my lips.

****

Not that I am complaining, Dear Reader. Nevertheless, that is what swirled about me like a prairie duster that winter of 1885. But the real storm to come would steal my breath away, involving men in black-and-white tweed suits with badges, derby hats, snooping friends, a Madame hardboiled as a fifteen-minute egg, and a phantom who drove me to lunacy in more ways than one.

It looked to be a barn-burner of a night, yet my innards were a prairie twister.

I heard little. Saw nothing.

Guffawed like a stupid donkey toward a leering face. Smiled like a doll. Nodded at pauses. Chuckled emptily at lewd gibes from chapped, weathered cowhands who designed to impress or enflame, when all I saw was a dark, hard-ridden face.

I got through the evening with no one selecting me after all. Spying myself in the blotchy bar mirror, I knew they picked up my underlying pandemonium. It returned no favors. I told myself the murky, smoke-veiled air caused the purple smudges beneath my eyes and abraded my cheeks.

Madame was not through with me. Coming up behind, as I was belatedly choosing which admirer to approach with smiles and repartee, she hissed, "You look like you've been ridden hard and put away wet!" She chopped her hand like a meat cleaver when I opened my mouth. "My dressmaker informed me you were out on the roof a few nights ago, caterwauling. *Caterwauling!* All by yourself." She said "roof" like it was an opium den in a steamy stewpot down by Wylder stockyards. "Drunk as a lord, talking to yourself. What sort of establishment do you suppose I aspire to? A cheap crib with girls fond of drink and—and opium?"

I started to protest. She rolled over me like a sow on her litter. "My girls must at least *seem* sweet, clean, and most of all *sober*."

"Yessum," I demurred. "Won't happen again..." *Where your dressmaker can see us.*

Raising brows at my docility, she noised a "*Humph*!" and marched off, birdcage bustle swaying with outrage. My heart fluttered as I caught who she returned to—the toothsome girl with scorching red hair in bouncy ringlets brushing creamy, lightly freckled shoulders. Sly eyes, bright and hard as onyx, assessed my bedraggled state from across the mob. Madame and she put their heads together, chuckling. Didn't take much to imagine it was over me. Even timid Flora smiled as the redhead included her.

It wasn't the redhead I needed to fear, however. It was the broad-shouldered man clad in salt-and-pepper tweed and a brown derby.

His back was to me, and he seemed to be showing a picture to a miner at the bar.

I slipped out the back way.

Chapter Nineteen
The Devil's Dance

The next few days lightened my frame of mind. I put the Pinkerton agent's image firmly behind me. Down in the Longhorn, fueled by pre-Christmas cheer and still decorated from the Harvest Festival, gambling tables were shoved aside for a hoe-down—fiddlers, a banjo, a straw-haired, gap-toothed blacksmith named Sparks, renowned for his ribald calling in a foghorn voice, plus free-flowing whiskey, syllabub for venturesome ladies, beer, and a bounty of goodies: spoon corn bread, fruitcake soaked in rum, wild blackberry cobbler, buttermilk, hard-boiled eggs, buttered scones, sweet watermelon-rind pickles, wheels of butcher's cheese, oatmeal raisin cookies, and platters of thick ham sandwiches slathered with onions and mustard.

We girls looked mightily forward to the Longhorn's yearly celebration as a chance to show off new or reworked finery and act like normal dancehall girls, or maybe even sweethearts, for the night. Subconsciously, I raked the floor for sightings of salt-and-pepper tweed before stepping off the last step. Truth, I wished with all my soul that only one wretched scoundrel accompanied me. Nevertheless, I plastered on my brightest smile, laughed the loudest, flirted to beat the band, danced with whoever fancied a jig, told a few farmer's daughter jokes I got from travelers, and strove to be the gayest, pluckiest, most audacious doxy Madame Solange could ever wish for.

I saw her gimlet eye—she looked not with favor, not with approbation.

Assessing.

I avoided her nevertheless and plunged back into the ever-rowdier mob—after a paltry admittance fee, thanks to Longhorn's generosity with the spirits bar, groaning with platters of comestibles. As I spun round to chivvy some trapper in from the hills, I sucked a breath, struck still as a Frozen Charlotte doll—doxies and men stamping about me, heedless, flounces and faces in a blinding blur. The smell of sweat, tobacco, jasmine perfume, whiskey breath, the sight of gleaming wet teeth, and jaw-splitting grins might as well have been in another time and place.

I only had eyes fixed on the apparition at the top of the stairs, as if Zachariah's longings had turned to flesh. Deliberately descending as if on ice, or the steps were melting, or missing altogether, Zachariah seemed to test each tread. With a grin of intense satisfaction, he stood at the bottom, savoring an effort that lit his face from within, like a Chinese lantern.

Zachariah had "dressed" for the occasion, head to toe in black except for a red silk neckerchief—black leather trousers, black side-buttoned, bib-front shirt, glossy black boots with silver toes, his licorice black hair hanging free, framing a square-jawed, fiercely mustachioed and browed face. He made my knees weak.

A head taller than most, my phantom raked the crowd. I darted furtive looks about. No one else noted him, or if they did, supposed he, though a stranger in town, was just another merrymaker.

I wended through the jigging mob to rescue him—then halted.

He must come to me.

I recognized that.

Zak eyed the floor as if it was a bottomless pit writhing with snakes. Flashing a hungry look for the chance to be part of this disorderly joyous life, he closed his eyes and placed boots on the thumping dance floor. Grinning like a boy stealing a cherry pie off the cooling ledge, I watched him pass through a body without complaint from the host regarding his momentary habitation.

Beyond a "pardon-me" grin, my lover boldly crossed the crowded floor, slicing whirling bodies performing the Alabama Jubilee without hinder.

Raking the throng whipping about him with jubilation, he bent his head to mine and placed two great hands spanning my waist.

"*How do I do this?*" He meant, "*How do I go about this dancing thing?*"

"Mind if I lead?" I answered instead.

A couple knocked me aside as they do-si-doed down the line. I edged us to the end of the bar. Nevertheless, the reel stopped. "How?" I queried back, my voice overloud in the hiatus. A few celebrators laughed amiably, thinking me drunk. At the same time, I was discombobulated when a farmer reached through him for a tumbler of whiskey—the farmer winced slightly, then shrugged. I lowered my voice. "How did you manage this?"

Zachariah looked happily over the mob. "*The will*

was especially strong. The yearning to be here among all this! I could hear music. The noise! I kenned you were here. How could I stay away?"

I smiled, tremulous. He waved an arm, whipping through Big Bertha as she whirligigged past at the commencement of a new reel that I recognized as Flowers of Edinburgh, with her enormous skirts flying, exposing crochet-trimmed knickers.

"Get yourself in here and have some fun!" Big Bertha giggled, taking hold of her partner, a scrawny farmer, and swinging him off his feet.

My phantom, bemused at the sight of those crocheted bloomers, gave a lopsided grin. Looking over the heads of men imbibing at the bar, he exploded. "Damn! Give my eyeteeth to have a taste of that whiskey."

"Never mind. You are here!" *Among the living,* I almost voiced. I did not want to wonder if now he could go far afield. If he would leave…

With green-fire eyes ferociously blazing, Zachariah set his mouth, held one arm formally out, encircled my waist with the other, and rushed me to the midst of the thrashing mob in full bloom of the Flowers of Edinburgh. "*Never done this before, but let the devil watch out!*" And plunged into the square dance lines with a vigor that would have knocked half the dancers over like bowling pins had he been flesh.

I noted giggling and pointing, behind fans, at my apparent clumsiness. So let them think I was sozzled as I twirled madly alone among them, in defiance gleefully lifting my skirts higher like a French dancer as we spun and reeled, kicked and pranced down the line, for all the world as if I had a partner. He was careful to have me avoid others, though he had no such compunction as they whipped through *him*.

Through a daze of happiness, I noted revelers eyeing me with humor, a few chuckling derision. I cared little. Then, young girls skipped out and copied what they supposed my solitary dancing, followed by a few women, dancing together. Giggling, I spied one male as I twirled about, strutting his stuff alone at the end of the line. I did not care. My lover and I were in each other's arms, back together, giddily happy being ordinary.

With a final squeal, fiddlers halted their bow arms' energetic ins and outs.

I bounced on my toes, waiting for the next reel. It melted into a lone fiddler's romantic waltz. We danced lingeringly, bodies clamped, gazing deep as if making vows. I could tell, too, that freedom overwhelmed him, unsure as he was on how long that state would last. For now, it was enough. The waltz finished, merging into a frantic jig.

As I spun with a manic smile, arms lifted in the air around seemingly nothing, Madame's outraged face came to view. My mood extinguished like a wet lucifer match. At her side, the young woman eyed me as if I were a gravy spot on her gown, she with the saucy ringlets like red-hot embers cascading over a lush bosom reminding me of two ripe pears. Glancing down at my own modest bosom I jerked my bodice lower.

She smirked and hooked Solange's arm, bending her head, intimately sharing a joke. I thought little other than pitchforks of envy over her tiny waist and flaming hair. "Those milk-pale cheeks will crack like a dried-out crick-bed in two years," I scorned when I had wended my way to Big Bertha to fill a cider mug. Mostly, I wanted to hear her agree. *Oh-oh, too late.* Madame's voice brayed over the raucous throng.

"Miss Cherry! We shall speak on the morrow. This is unseemly!"

The redhead, elbow on bar, lily hand propping her chin, watched, demure as a cat with a mouse tail dangling from her cherry-red lips, as Madame sailed like a juggernaut through the crowd, inadvertently passing through my lover. He grimaced. She snapped her fan on my cheek. "You make me a fool! Right along with you."

Bertha raised shaggy brows and jigged out of the range of fire.

"But it is yet early," I reminded her tartly and spun off, in a reckless mood. But I was making it worse.

Grabbing Zak's hand, I attempted to steer him out the side door into the crisp night, drunk on possibilities and hard cider—that is, until Zachariah rammed into an invisible wall. I looked back as his hand jerked from mine.

He faded helplessly back into the gaiety, gazing hapless with intense yearning out into the night, festive with pea-sized snow placing rhinestones in my hair and melting on my warm eager lips. He might as well have been on the moon. Even as I watched he grew fainter, until the stomping, twirling mob closed over him. A small detestable part of me was thankful he could not go out into the night…and leave me.

I was horrible.

The one I did not see was the man in the salt-and-pepper suit, handlebar mustache, derby hat, and Pinkerton badge pinned to his vest concealed under his coat. At least not until I turned desolate back into the dance, making my evening complete.

****

I tossed in bed, the worse for drunkenness. Not the cider kind, my own disquiet—the thrill of the rare party, my otherworldly dance, dulled by the clash with Madame, the red-haired girl, and lastly, the Pinkerton agent warring with myself it might not have been me he was after. I flung about, frantically humming "Sweet Nelly Bly," one of the fiddler's tunes ringing through my head, to keep ill thoughts, like rabid wolves, at bay.

****

With a thumping heart, I crept down to breakfast, bracing myself. Surely, I dramatized the day of reckoning.

So I seemed rather giddy and silly last evening. I drank too much cider and feigned to dance with a lover, I would trill. Or some such, stifling my grin, when I caught her sourdough face.

"Miss Cherry! We may speak here." She shot a telling glance at the rest. "Or in private."

I cocked my head as if puzzled, then shrugged, rolling my eyes at the girls. "Why, here, Madame. I've nothing the gals can't hear." I crossed fingers behind my back, while the girls did not attempt to hide their curiosity, interrupted when Mr. Gruenvald stuck his head in.

"So-So?" His pet name for Madame. "You be needin' this room for long? Gotta bunch of miner bosses comin' in, wanting a place to confab."

And save me from the disgrace to come.

"Oh, and there's a Pinkerton feller wants ta palaver with you some, mebbe the gals, too." He shrugged grumpily.

My breath stopped. I stared blank-faced, my mind racing like a rabbit chased by a fox.

"This won't take long," she said, too grim for my liking. "Though I don't ken what a *Pinkerton* agent has to do with *me*."

Bertha, Little Mae, and even Flora pinned me like stitches to a quilt. Titillation to lighten the day, from the looks of them—all hungover as dishrags on a line, they welcomed this bit of speculation, but I didn't cotton to Bertha and Mae's calculating stares.

Hastening back, trailing importance, Madame nodded archly at the empty doorway. "Mr. Gruenvald revealed last evening during the festivities that one of your guests, Miss Cherry, left in a decidedly rumpled and ill-treated manner some nights ago. *And,* I just spoke with a Pinkerton agent. It seems a man is missing. A Mr. Peters…or Robertson…? Oh!" She snapped fingers, clucking. "What was that name? At any rate, he was last seen here by a fellow salesman he met on the train. They were to meet the next day for some folderol."

"A guest of mine?" I asked feebly. I had supposed she meant to comment on my solitary twirling about with a nonexistent partner.

"Indeed, one of yours. Jake saw his shocking departure also, it seems. Not a rough, untrained cowhand, but a *gentleman*. The sort we strive to promote. He even shelled out for the entire night."

I smiled inwardly. Even before he kenned which one he'd choose, not caring who his evil intentions were satisfied by. Once more, I thought of Little Flora. Petersen would not have taken on Mae or Bertha.

Thank heavens Flora had not come down till later.

"What was that name?"

I threw a shrugged, *Sure I don't know* look. "If they aren't regulars, it's silly to catch a name," I offered.

She glared at me as if it were my fault, slashing saber glints toward Big Bertha. "Bertha, you were helping this man down too, I believe, if I recall Jake correctly."

Bertha shot me a look. "Yessum. Maybe I did. Can't hardly believe nuthin' Jake sez, though."

Madame frowned, considering pros and cons. Hoping desperately no mud would be slung on her fledgling establishment, or on Levi by proximity, and wanting to stay on the right side of the law.

She nodded. "Yes, that's true. Jake would say most anything he thought you wanted him to say. *Or* the exact opposite, if feeling ratty. I do wish Levi would— never mind."

"He tied one on, all right." Bertha offered.

"That's true," I broke in. "The gentleman, whoever he was, was drunk as a lord. May have tussled some. When he stepped out of his britches, he stumbled against the washstand. My! Took forever to clean that up! He hit his head. Didn't want to bother you none, but Bertha, she—she helped me."

I was babbling too much. I shot an appeal to Bertha, in as deep as me. "Didn't you, Bertie?"

Bertha nodded, glum. Madame arched a brow. "Is that so? His calamitous appearance seemed more than a mere falling down. Jake said he looked like he'd been through a mangle and tied up in a sack of bobcats."

How had we missed Jake? All-seeing Rattlesnake

Jake.

She frowned, unsure how to continue her tirade, while I fretted where the Pinkerton was. Outside, ready to spring? I gripped the chairback, watching the door until my knuckles screamed. Wondered if Little Mae still had Petersen's case or would have sold it by now. Later, I discovered she'd given it to her little tailor. Not that that helped.

"Fortunate for you, we have not had repercussions." My shoulders drooped in relief.

Unless it was from the pigs. Maybe they didn't fancy him either.

She looked disappointed Petersen had not come forth filing a grievous complaint against me, but then Mr. Gruenvald, checking his watch, stuck his head back in.

"A last warning!" she hissed, then trilled, "Coming, Levi!" A blush rose from her neck, pinking blotches on sallow cheeks. She gritted her teeth in passing, and I could hear them crunch before she said, "The john is always right! And I still want a word over your hoydenish behavior at the dance!"

"Yes'm." *I'll just let them use me as a punching bag, or a rug to clean their boots on, next time.*

****

I should have paid better attention.

Been more alert. I might have been prepared.

I got through the evening with no one selecting me after all. Again, I spied myself in the blotchy bar mirror.

The girl with hair like burning embers was here again, or maybe never left, chumming up to Madame, giggling, sipping bourbon, even as Madame kept hawk

eyes soaring over the Saturday crowd.
    I tensed, awaiting the next mishap.
    I should not have wished so hard.

Chapter Twenty
Innocence Has Nothing to Dread

I had good reason to fear. In the end, it was not Madame but Little Mae who tripped me up.

Next evening, I swept into my room to scrub a liquor stain from my maroon velvet before it set in—a mining owner, no worse for wear, had drunkenly sloshed on me. Dresses were dear, even if the maroon velvet was not a favorite, nor was maroon a particularly advantageous color for a goldy-haired female with hints of strawberry.

I stopped dead.

There stood Little Mae in the middle of my room, cheeky, sheepish, defiant, all at once clutching a handful of stiff paper she swept behind her back.

"What are *you* doing?" I checked the room with fleeting eye glances to see if anything, or, most important, any specter-outlaw lounged about.

If Little Mae's chest was a fall harvest, the entire West would have a windfall. She lifted that chest now, near shoving me out the door, snorting, "Hunh! You gotta right to talk all high and mighty! You was snoopin' in *my* room! Why shouldn't I have a look-see in yours? 'Sides…" She narrowed small eyes into sideways commas, raking my room and wrinkling her pug nose as if she smelled something bad.

Only Zachariah's hellfire and brimstone trailing

him. I needed to giggle from sudden nerves.

I did not see that yellow scrap sticking from her fist!

I did not see that yellow scrap sticking from her fist.

I did not *see that yellow scrap sticking from her fist.*

I won't look down.

Mayhap, she will forget.

Or drop it.

In a pig's eye.

I changed the subject.

"Now you are here, Mazie," I twittered inanely, "why not tell me what you think of my new"—I wildly searched for something novel, stupidly alighting on the maroon velvet—"dress?" Babbling, I added, "Does the color suit?"

Mae surveyed me with derision reserved for a lunatic. "Hunh, that ol' thing? I seen that old purple rag a *hunerd* times!"

Then my eyes cast swiftly down as if dragged to the yellow wad in her hand. I could not help it. The smidgeon of pale-yellow peeking from her fist was horribly familiar. Sweat trickled between my shoulder blades, down my forehead, between my breasts.

I felt Zak's answering mood by a feathery touch on my hand and kenned he was beside me. He made a breeze maneuvering around Mae, fanning her neck frizz, and lifting more papers—letters mostly, that Mae had left scrubbled up carelessly on my dresser. Little Mae blinked, absently rubbing her neck, then brought her eyes trained on me like twin rifle barrels.

"I *hear* things," she accused. "I *know* you got men

in here *witho*ut Madame Solange's by-your-leave."

I slumped, relieved. *That old saw.*

"She ain't a notion what goes on in here. I hear them through the wall. You got men in here!" As if that fact were the vilest thing on earth, and one she did not have truck with herself, daily and vigorously, judging from her headboard pounding till I thought the plaster would surely crack.

I tried on a sneer. "So. You go through my things, looking for a man hiding in my dresser drawer?" She was unimpressed.

"But that ain't *all*!" She raised the fatal yellow pasteboard, triumphant. I recognized with a fluttering heart what that battered poster crumpled in her fist was. I hid the blasted things, cleverly stuck to the bottom of the dresser drawer with cowhide glue. Why had I kept those damning posters?

'Sides, they didn't favor me.

Little Mae opened her fist. Smoothing creases on her bosom, she waved the frayed yellow cardboard with the nail holes in the corners at me. I snatched at it. She held it above her head.

"I can *read*," she proclaimed. "Didn't know that, did ya? Sez right here…"

She waved the stiff grubby paper with a face alive with self-righteousness. "And that there's *you*!" And she stabbed her stubby finger at the black etching of a female.

I blanched like a sack of flour, before my cheeks flooded with heat matching my maroon gown as I beheld the damning too-familiar portrait.

"What are you going to do with that," I whispered with a throat choked with dust.

Little Mae made a great show of assessing my room. "Wouldn't you like to know?"

My knees turned to custard. I tried not to grab the four-poster to stay upright as Little Mae swept triumphant from the room, still clutching the wanted poster.

****

I perched on the veranda roof after midnight, brooding. It seemed Zachariah had a longing to hear of mundane things. Tonight, I scarce had an appetite for cozy chat. Gossip or news that in his former life of mayhem he would have groaned at, and swiftly retreated from, now he was hungry for. Wylder news, such as it was, and newspapers of the goings on in Washington that trickled in on the wires. *What did you ladies dine on tonight? I've sampled everything from armadillo to rattlesnake, but…*" His voice trailed off as he watched sparks from his cigarro sail away like fireflies. *"How many are in town now? Have they finished the new stable down on…?"*

"Yes, there's only one." With choking fullness, I did not say it was built fifteen years ago.

Tonight, he ventured, *"Does Miss Solange, the old bat, make the coffee so strong a spoon would sit up and beg, or so weak one could read a newspaper?"* He continued with tales of his gang making campfire coffee like it was stewed from tarred rope. I heard a searing wistfulness. *"Miss coffee almost as much as whiskey."*

However, my mind was spinning like a whirligig over Little Mae's treacherous find, evidence of a happening left behind me, in another time and place, and I dreaded the devastation it would bring if she chose to tattle. Not only would I be kicked out of Madame Solange's employ, but perhaps out of life itself. *Brought to justice*, I thought bitterly. There was none. The most to hope for was a shaming stay in Wylder's jailhouse, at least until the circuit judge arrived, or until I was returned in manacles to Indiana.

There, I would hang.

Even if I could prove Petersen had not died from pestilent-ridden tines, they would say I vindictively murdered him here, in this room, when I failed the first time. I pondered morbidly what it would be like—*to be dead.*

Would I join Zachariah?

I felt sudden joy. My heart lightened as if it developed wings.

Idiotic! Most likely, it did not work that way. Heaven did not reward folks like me. And I was not on the side of the angels.

Zachariah could not even see his own ma.

Besides, I did not want to be dead.

New suspicions arrived uninvited, like a pig to a party.

Just what *had* happened to Petersen's body?

Bones, if there were any, did not stay buried when bloodhounds nosed the ground. I had an overwhelming compulsion to visit the noisome stockyards and pens, only half listening to Zak.

I sensed his strange eyes on me. "Little one? So quiet?"

"My turn," I said simply. I gazed somberly in his face. *Understand,* I pleaded.

"I have something to tell you. It—it might change things…"

I dug in my pocket and revealed a copy of the wadded pasteboard Little Mae had ferreted out. How many times had she snooped about my room? I yearned to query Zachariah, yet felt he did not show himself when I was not present, or retreated to the mysterious unknown while anybody happened there.

I unfolded the damning yellow poster, a raw black-and-yellow rendering of a face—*my face*—in a frame over the stark, damning lines:

W A N T E D
for
Murder
REWARD
$1000.00 for the whereabouts and apprehension of
Beulah Anne Creighton
Reddish-gold hair, green eyes. Height unknown.

I recalled Little Mae's triumphant gleam as she displayed it, scuffed and grubby with time and weather.

" 'WANTED' sez here! You're wanted in Indianer! Sez right here!" She had pointed. "For killin' some fella—a drummer in Indianer hawkin' seed stock. Queer thing. That feller Big Bertha hauled to the pig lot had one a these-here poster things a lining his sample case. I snuck a peek in your room. Danged case was left behind. Didn't think I saw it, did ya. I cottoned on to it." She studied the poster. "Din't recka-nize you at first."

Leave it to Little Mae to stumble on information to get a leg up. I'd forgot the sample case, until then. She must have cabbaged on to it while I slept like the dead.

What happened to it? I dreaded to think. The case was a fancy number, with brass corners. A thing she could sell. I hoped so. I hoped it was in Alaska by now with some miner.

"And here you had one a them posters too," Little Mae had crowed. "Jus' like it. More'n one. Why? Wuz you proud of it? Now, Ma don't raise no dumbbells. I call that a co-in-cer-dent."

I had hugged my knees. I watched her smooth the yellow poster like a page from a rare Bible, yearning to scream at her, *Because I snatched down every one I could find! Five of the blasted things.*

"Queer sorta thing to hang on to." She had looked slyly at me. "Less you 'as proud of it."

No, just a reminder to keep low.

"Not what you think, Little Mae," I had lied. "See here? Doesn't even look like me."

In my favor, that damning poster *was* badly done.

Stark thick black ink on sickly yellow.

My eyebrows resembled caterpillars, teeth with black spaces between them from the heavy inking. Eyes like black holes. I looked like a badger.

Little Mae rolled over me like a plowing machine. "Nah! Sez Indianer. *Yer* from Indianer. I *know* it's you."

How? I wanted to protest. I opened my mouth to deny it. Nevertheless, she saw veracity in my anguished face. An inked drawing of a girl taken from a tintype that, beyond a birthmark on my left cheek the artist had enlarged to an elephant-shaped mole, resembling me as much as it did Queen Victoria.

Would any soul here in Wylder believe it?

Could I risk it?

Rumors alone would set Pinkerton bloodhounds sniffing in earnest, ending in dragging me back to Indiana—back to a hangman. Well, it would be one of those places, either here—or there. The salesman's wife would want vengeance, too, after thinking him dead these years, or an absconder.

Thoughts racing, I despaired. My knees wobbled with a life of their own, kenning soon Little Mae'd hear them knock like Spanish castanets.

"Right here, in black and white in big letters." She kept on pounding, waiting to see my reaction. Not wanting to end a self-righteous confrontation, she punched the stiff poster again with her nail. "You're wanted for killin' a man, I said! Don't you got *nuthin'* to say? Sez right here, he 'as married. Didn't he want any truck with you? That why you kilt him?"

"No! It wasn't that way."

I clamped my mouth shut at her smug look.

"I'm certain-sure you got some tall tale covering your skinny fanny!"

Not true! I wanted to scream. It would not matter. I caught envy plain on her pudgy spotted face. Her yearning for the prize room. Funny how much it meant to me at one time.

"Clearly, I did not kill him," I snapped at her. *Then,* my angel chided. "He was here! Bertha saw him." I groaned, worn down from the incident that had changed my life.

I motioned her to sit on the bed. "I'll tell you."

She made the mattress heave, her face alive with prying interest.

****

"He wanted to interfere with me," I reported dully to Zachariah.

Interfere! Hah! I could still see Petersen, only I did not know his name at the time, only his red moon face with the smug lust-filled eyes.

...the salesman, Petersen's sweating face—his slippery hands. Foul, liquor-soaked breath.

And me running for my life with a torn pinafore and ripped knickers, a hank of hair still in Petersen's hands, my head smarting and knees skinned from where I tripped, and his ugly hurtful words raging after me like a ripped filthy rag...

"*You little tramp. Slut! All alike, flirting, leading a man on! Throwing your legs around...!*"

Even now I still felt the shame of his fingers where they should not have been.

I was up in the loft again, playing with new kittens the mama cat had stashed away from my eager hands and eyes.

I jumped down with one of the kitties, to fit it into a doll dress. My skirts blew over my head, and before I could pull them down, felt my arms gripped and bound in one huge fist, with my head hooded and wrapped in my skirts while I struggled to get free.

Muffled in thick burlap, I shrieked for Ma. I couldn't see through the coarse weave—could hardly breathe, sucking in chaff... I could still feel his fingers...hear the kitten squalling and skittering off on stiff little legs through the straw.

"And he said he knew my ma was in the back gardens and couldn't hear, and he had switched back, so no one kenned he was anywhere near, and what was I gonna do about it?"

I had stared in the air, unseeing, so Little Mae could not feed off of my wretchedness as I related the rest in a rush to get it over.

"Going on thirteen. Didn't even have my first

monthly. Ma never told me anything. Just that it was painful woman business." I raised my head to glare at her. "I scratched him good! He let go. I grabbed a hayfork. When he wouldn't stop—he just kept—*comin'*, I held that hayfork in front of me. He ran into the tines. I swear. It scarce pricked his coat at first, but he couldn't stop in time, and the kitten ran in front of him. I guess he tripped a bit. The tines went through his coat and vest. The hayfork slid on in. He bellowed and bled like the pig he was!"

"So? What did he do then?'

"He went to the sheriff. Said I tried to kill him! Maybe I did, but I was so afraid and mad, and he just kept comin'."

Mae looked troubled at that. The poster drooped in her hands, yet I could not stop the flood of words held back for so long.

"I s'pose to get me in trouble and make up some story to his wife, he told her I tried to kill him too. Later—" I hitched my shoulders in an angry shrug. "He ran off. But not for good." I spoke with the bitterness of a green persimmon. "He showed up here like a Confederate note."

"Well go on. You got my attention," she said, without a trace of humility.

"His wife said he went all feverish—infected, I guess, from the muck on the hayfork. He kept mumbling about a demon girl attacking him as he came to the barn door to catch the farmer and make a sale.

"The wife called the sheriff. Petersen vowed I ran after him with the hayfork when he caught me with a boy. That I had kept on stabbing him, even as he shouted for mercy and tried to get away. Or some such lie."

"Well, what happened?"

"Later, he got out of bed and wandered off in a delirium, *they said.*"

I wondered about that later. It was winter, by then. They found his clothes by the Scottsburg mill pond. The sheriff and some men and a matron from an asylum, came out again—stayed for hours pounding at me, saying I was wayward and unstable. Telling parents, I was accountable for Petersen's death and probably criminally insane and would do others harm. I saw Ma look at my little sister and then at me. I found out later, too, that was a popular new notion…some alienist from Germany thought it up…

I saw Mae looked bored to tears and hurried on.

"How they kenned *where* to come, I don't to this day comprehend. Maybe he told his wife while he was feverish. Maybe she witnessed the fork pricks and asked. Or read his accounts book. I often wondered. Ma wouldn't speak to me. Step-Pa gave me a thrashing for leading a man on…"

"I overheard them in the kitchen, the sheriff deciding whether to send me to a home for wayward girls first, then something about a trial, then prison or an asylum." I looked down at my twisting hands. "And that he was coming back in the morning with a matron…so I ran off."

"Hu—*nnnh?*" The skepticism on her face would curdle fresh cream. "So? Did he *die* or not?" she demanded as if I had cheated her.

"No. It was *him!*"

"Him? Him, who?"

A sluggish dawn murkily lit her face.

"Petersen? So why didn't he—?"

"Recognize me? I kenned *him* all right! After a time. He changed some—he grew a mustache, gained weight, and got a lot grayer and wore thick glasses. Wasn't till we got to my room that night and I got a good look at his eyes."

The same pale, mean, yellow eyes.

"They didn't change. He didn't even remember me." I spoke bitterly. "Seven years ago. He never thought he'd run into me again, probably. I always wondered how many others he…"

Mae heaved impatient.

"It's a wonder I like men at all…but I do. The right kind."

She nodded wisely. "Prob'ly run off from his wife. Anyway, makes me no nevermind. I want this-here room. If you don't let me have it, I'm gonna tell Madame Solange, an' if she don't let me have it, I'll march right on down to the sheriff."

I narrowed my eyes and threw her a stare with icicles in it. "I doubt Madame will thank you. I'm one of the best draws she has." *Though I wondered about that.*

I hated bragging, and the scalp-hunting looks Mae threw warned me not to be so puffed up. We aren't responsible, as Zak said, for how the cards are dealt, or where the spin of the roulette wheel stops. Large nose or small, wits of a gnat, or donkey-stubborn…freckled and kinky carrot-haired, or silky brunette. I could not be proud of my looks when I had no say or choice of parentage.

What she said next jolted me out of all vanity.

" 'at's what you know. Favorite? I seen her and

Mirabella down at the Vincent Hotel when I was on my half day. Cozy as two ticks on a dawg!"

The redhead. "I have money." I tried not to show desperation.

"Hunh! Let's see it."

"It's in the bank." *No longer.*

"You better hope…"

Then Mae had surprised me. She grinned. "Hell's bells, Blossom, I won't say nothin'. No skin off my nose. Don't like that Mirabella's fancy-schmancy ways no how." She rolled her eyes. "An *sure* don't wanna get on a wrong side of Bertha! But I *do* want that mother-a-pearl brooch, and *that* doodad, too."

She snatched the small cameo off my gown, tearing a jagged hole. Seems it was my lot to lose Ma's gimcracks twice. I doubled over, clutching my chest, my heart, and fear of discovery, to myself. A small price to pay.

Mae gave me a sideways scared look and swept out, pug nose in the air as if a major victory was won, still clutching the cameo and that creased, folded-up, damning poster.

****

"I am a killer—at heart."

I related all of that—and about Bertha and the pig lots, awaiting Zachariah's reaction.

"I wanted to kill that man, Zak. I meant to jab him good. I wanted to feel the tines go into that soft belly! I wanted to see blood like at a hog slaughter. Don't you see? It wasn't an accident. I wanted that—I am as guilty as if I ran him through!" I felt my face fall into savage planes. "I was so—so shamed, mad, and scared. Ma would have blamed me, and Dad would've give me a hiding. Ma always said I led a boy on. It would have been the same. I kenned all that when I ran at him with the pitchfork."

I heard my remorseless voice but would not take it back—once again a thirteen-year-old girl suffering humiliation, fright, and helplessness at the hands of an older man three times her size, with no one to hear or help.

He threw his head back, staring at the merciless star-studded sky.

Did he think differently about me?

I recalled my stumbling sidewinder path to Wylder, when I scarce kenned where Wyoming was on a map. I did not plan on becoming a doxy, when I was a girl of almost fourteen tumbling off the mail train, straw in her hair and bedraggled dress, no matter her partiality to men. It seemed another girl.

"*I think, now, he is truly dead.*"

A deep cleft working in his jaw, made it a jest.

"It isn't a jest. I am guilty."

"*You say there is a Pinkerton after you?*"

I widened my eyes. "You can't! *Say* you won't do anything. They will only send more, and it will be worse for me…if all they see as a—a culprit *is me*."

Zak studied through me a long time, finally nodding. "*So—now we are compadres. Aiming to join my gang of thieves?*"

"And murderers," I said dismally.

"*No, little one, no matter your intent, your rage, you pulled back at the last second. It is I who put that woman in harm's way and stopped her heart. Be glad. You always see their faces.*"

I had nothing to say to that.

Chapter Twenty-One
Appeasement

My peace of mind was not to last. As I skimmed through the back door for use of the privy, a backward glance allowed me a glimpse of salt-and-pepper tweed and the now-familiar figure in earnest confab with Rattlesnake Jake. I saw what I feared seemed a poster lying flat on the bar. Mr. Gruenvald was in attendance, too, shaking his grizzled head first one way, then the other.

The door swung shut.

In agony, I peeked over the gallery, after skirting the building, coming up the back way. The agent was not in sight. I spied Jake indolently mopping the floor—then pointing up, to someone concealed beneath the gallery. I leaned and saw the blasted Pinkerton nod and approach the stairs with a manly, forceful stride. I bit my lip—my fingernails. Felt my wrists weighted with cold hard manacles.

As bad luck would have it, I met Little Mae on her way up, ahead of the plodding Pinkerton.

"Don't think I ain't forgot," she simpered. "I could tell that Pinkerton snoop anything!" She nodded behind her.

"Why haven't you?" I hissed.

"What good would that do? Still might not get me that room. Better I save it for Madame."

I couldn't tell if she were taunting. Little Mae had a cat's-paw way of teasing.

"Please, Mae!" I struck a humble pose, keeping a frantic eye on the Pinkerton, still lumbering his way up, as I backed her to my door.

"Yer dessert for a week? Less'en it's bread puddin'. Don't fancy bread puddin'. All it is is leftover dried-up old bread that other folks have prob'ly already chawed on. Not a *proper* dessert."

"Yes!" I agreed, one eye on the agent, near the top now, huffing, head down. "For a year!" This was not real. *Alice in Wonderland talking to the rabbit.* The Pinkerton was right behind her now.

"Or tapioca. Hate that slimy stuff like little eyeballs." Mae made a face.

"Yes, yes." I'd already turned away, ready to bolt before he saw my face.

Mae looked triumphant, as if she'd just won the biggest poker pot in Longhorn's memory. She about-faced, knocking the Pinkerton aside, and jounced down the steps, glancing back with a wink before I nipped into my room and clumsily locked it. *Mindless.* What good would that do? Reluctantly, I twisted the big iron skeleton key, clicking the lock open. At least look innocent.

I heard the agent's confident steps of serviceable hobnailed boots clomping closer. *Closer.* They stopped and thumped on past. Grew fainter. I heard knocking on Big Bertha's door. Her opening it. Murmured voices, hers an earthy growl. Forgetting to breathe, my back to the door, I held my sex to keep from peeing. That's how tremulous I was. How convinced.

I couldn't stop dreading. Was he probing Bertha, in

place of Mae? Realizing I looked odd plastered against the door, I glanced over. My phantom paced the room practicing quick draws. Still holding the pistol, he was beside me without seeming to move.

"*What is wrong, little one? Pale as a—forgive me—a ghost.*"

"Don't call me 'little one.' "

He raised his scarred brow and aimed his pistol at my painted oil lamp, pressing the trigger. "*Take that, she said.*"

Still fretting, I ignored his attempt at ill humor as I furiously fitted the pieces together. Big Bertha had avoided my worried looks, casting her eyes aside, earlier. Or was it imagination? Never a chatty type. Surly rejoinders mostly. Some men liked that. Yet it would not take much for Bertha or Little Mae to curry favor with Madame, the dratted Pinkerton, or *even,* though Madame strives to stay low, the sheriff himself.

My mind was like Rattlesnake's pet rat he kept in a cage, clawing to get out.

Bertha would cover her own fanny, *wouldn't she*? And Little Mae? Did she still have that damned poster? *Plus,* the one from Petersen's briefcase?

****

The man's eyes were cold steel bullets as he studied me, a warming in them that did not touch his lips. "Madam."

I gazed up at the Pinkerton agent.

"Name's Mullet. Seems I've overlooked you. Don't want to seem uncivil to a lady, but you never seem to be around when I am. May I?" Without invitation he thrust on past, appraising my room with interest. "Hmmm. My wife would take kindly to this.

She likes frippery."

I stared at him coldly. I would not beg.

He sat in the red chair and, after a moment's appraisal of me, dug in his briefcase. "You ever see this gal around here? It's old, grant you." He studied the faded, familiar poster, now more a dirty cream than pale yellow, folded many times over and frayed at the corners. The image was missing an eye from the creasing, showing only a ragged line through the left side of the image.

"Ya know," he said conversationally, holding his palm over the offended part, "if I had to swear in court, I'd say this might be you?" His eyes never left my face. I revealed nothing, but my clenching hands itched to do *something*—throw—hit— My mouth clenched to keep from screaming.

"Really?" I spoke. "How exciting! Me?" I pretended to study the poster. "Was she *awfully* wicked? What did she— *oh!* Murder! Oh, my! How *dreadful*," I enthused, as if the deed were anything but. "I must tell the girls!"

Then bullet eyes were shooting me again. "They've already been informed. Still"—he regarded the sad poster once more before folding and tucking it back into his valise, where I saw a Colt revolver and manacles among the papers—"funny how much this favors you. Where did you say you were from?" He blindsided me, like a snake striking from behind. "Beg pardon?" I stammered stupidly.

"Your hometown. Surely you got one?"

It would be easy to discover that. Better not prevaricate. "Why, Indiana," I said with all the candor and innocence I could muster. "Why? Is she from there?" I jabbed a thumb at his case. "How wonderful! I s'pose some of us Indiana gals look the same. Probably from the same pa," I grinned like a brazen doxy.

"You seem to find this exciting, even cold-blooded, I might say, Miss—?"

"Blossom Cherry!" I winked and bobbed a curtsey low enough to show my bosom. He did not ken my real name, I exulted.

He curled his lip under his mustache and rose. "You planning on going anywhere, Miss Blossom?" He blinked once and leaned close to my ear and snatched my hand. I did not flinch, expecting the snap of cuffs.

"Might want to hang around, might have some more questions." He gave my arm a shake.

I pressed the door closed behind him. I was trembling inside.

I looked up at Zak's questioning face, dropping my head against his chest to stay hidden.

Nothing. There's a Pinkerton agent asking questions and pumping Big Bertha like a cistern. I need to give Little Mae my dessert for a year to buy her silence, and I am going to jail. I will be taken away from you and hanged somewhere. A maddened, bloodthirsty shrew—they will say I had my revenge at last…

I choked back a panic-stricken laugh and smiled up. "Naught…just a silly fuss with Little Mae and Miss Nibs riding her high horse…"

He looked at me, growing, ebbing, watching, his long, slanted eyes blazing doubt like St. Elmo's Fire in the dimness. He bit his lip. His scar showed white as he pinched his wings of brows together. "*I have something I must—talk to you about. It's time.*"

My heart thumped. *You too?* That giddy laugh threatening to overwhelm my lips was saved by Jake banging on the door. "Miss Solange wants yer all downstairs, lickety-split," he bellered, passing on to the next door with the same summons.

"*Damnation! I need to talk to you! Pound some sense—*"

"I must go." I gripped the brown china knob.

His eyes glowed green fire. He nodded, finally, with pinched lips. "*Until then.*"

I hoped there was a "then."

****

I could tell, when I met the girls galloping down, that Little Mae had not kept her promise. The shamed, half-gleeful look she shot me, scuttling ahead to keep out of my swatting hands, gave her away. I wanted to yank her frizzy hair, snatch her baldheaded.

Big Bertha couldn't help allowing meaty gossip chewed to the gristle either. "Hear tell you gotta new portrait. Gonna let me see it? Though I don't think yeller's yer color."

Madame would rather give up old Levi than demean herself asking what it was about. Still, I froze when Little Mae sassily called, "Heard your new beau likes pork!" Bracing, I marched into the lean-to, expecting the sheriff, his bully-boy deputy, and the Pinkerton, already feeling the chafing of cold rough steel scraping my wrists, imagining them dragging me before everyone to a dreary cell, until my future writ by cold-blooded strangers.

I couldn't blame the girls. It was their future too. They'd be collaborators, I thought bitterly. What a hornet's nest Petersen stirred up when he stopped off at the isolated Indiana farm so many years ago. I looked around the back room as if for the last time. I had not said goodbye to Zak. I bit my cheek to keep from wailing.

Madame seemed oddly high-spirited, as if any previous storms were mere cotton balls in a bluebonnet sky. Probably winding up for the kill, I thought miserably. Why else would my two sisters in sin be dragged down?

"We are expecting a *special* arrival," she trilled. "My friend at the station received a wireless this morning!"

More Pinkertons!

I shot a glance at the door, expecting burly males in salt-and-pepper suits and brown derbies clinking hefty manacles, eyeing me like a wolf does a quivering rabbit. The doorway was still empty. I breathed again, in time to hear…

"Seems we are to have prestigious thespians. From London!" Madame gurgled with delight. "And right here in Wylder. They are sojourning here on their way to San Francisco to perform Christmas pantomimes," she crowed. "We are certainly on the map now!" No doubt already mentally hosting them in her rooms, enticing them to put on "a little show" to draw clients like bears to fermented honey. We had a small stage in the back of the saloon, I mused, feeling my shoulders slump in relief, yet oddly disappointed. My trial was not to be over, merely delayed.

"I want you *all* refreshed, *clean…*!" She shot a glance at Big Bertha's trailing, half-buttoned, petticoats. "And *more* than presentable. *Dazzling!* Flora?" Shooting her a stern look. "Your favorite dress, the one that makes you seem like a bloodless pre-Raphaelite painting, needs sprucing up. Last I saw, it looked more like a bedraggled nightgown than an alluring peignoir."

"And Mae. I like the ruffled slit in your red satin gown and new garter belt."

I groaned. *The garter belt resembled a string tied around a sausage.*

"And you, Bertha, show a hint of nipple. Let us shock the sybarites for a change." Madame smirked, clapping hands as if that were the most daring suggestion since handmaidens sent Moses down the river, as if we had not already employed *that* bit of seduction many times over, albeit *not* down in the saloon.

How could I ken this coveted diversion was one more nail in my coffin?

****

"Little one. I must stay firm for what I am to say."

In a blink, my phantom hovered midway between the red chair and me. He forgot it unnerved me to see his boots drift-walking inches above the carpet. A worm of unease wriggled in my belly. I busied with my rouges and lip paste.

"You must leave!"

"What? Now? What nonsense." I quavered. The specter of fear wafted over me like the angel of death marking doors with blood.

His voice was strange, as if he had a rope about his neck. Strangled. *"You must leave this place—for good."*

"I must *leave?"* I over-tipped my chair, wrapping my arms about his knees as he still hovered above me. He came down through my arms as if he had weight. I

204

hugged his waist, my head beneath his chin.

"Paloma. *Little Dove, I want to keep you. Trapped in this hellish room where evil visits any time the devil gets past your greedy Madame. Where the next hombre up those stairs might murder you as that last* cabrón *would have. I'm helpless, kenning whatever I do puts you in danger. And you are. I'm not blind. You keep things from me when I am—not here.*"

He thrust me from him, raking me with his strange eyes like stained glass with the sun shining through, with me scarcely listening, so caught was I in his stunning, rough beauty.

"*Darling one. I have a bloody treasure! The wealth of small nations.*" He chuckled self-deprecatingly. "*Or kings in tinpot countries. It's doing not a tinker's dam for anyone. Least of all me. Money, more money than you've ever seen. I can't give it back. It molders beneath the earth. Gold, jewels… All I have to do is…*"

He scowled, thinking furiously.

"That's crazy! How would I explain a sudden fortune, even if it is true? I'd look even more guilty if I ran. I'd never be safe. No! I must ride this out. Would you run? I took care of myself before you—*you* came into my life. I will stay!" *I kenned I was mad.* He spoke sense even without the damned Pinkertons sniffing about my heels, yet never having to worry again about money was the Devil's lure.

"*You must go! Take my—*"

I swatted. This time my arm sailed right through him. "Oh! *Oh*!" I stamped my foot. "Stay still, will you? Not going anywhere, so keep your dad-blasted money!" My makeup ran. I smeared my face with the back of my hand. "Now look what you made me do!"

"*Beloved...*" Savagely snatching my hands in his, he kissed my fingers, effectively trapping me. I yanked my hands away. I beat his chest, this time contacting solid—or near solid—flesh. "This can go on as long as we can. *You* will keep me safe," I pleaded.

"I can fight bad hombres, but not the law. Not forever." He looked down, eyes blazing as the first green flame in a lit lamp. The flame lowered, grew softer. "*What am I to do with you?*" he whispered hoarsely.

"Love—love me, as long as we have…"

He groaned into my hair, sweet-smelling of the fresh rain and rose water in which I had washed it. "*That I can do.*"

And he took me in his arms as if we had sealed a bargain.

He lifted me.

I looked down.

Heavenly! I have wings! Not real wings. But as if… Nothing beneath me? Floating. Dancing in air! Wafting as a zephyr…

I touched the ceiling. Looked down at my room.

I giggled like a girl as we drifted to the floor.

"Oh! Do it again."

He laughed and sailed me up, caught again by the imperceptible barrier of his arms. We circled the room. In too short a time, we came down, gently—a feathering to earth, safe, where my phantom lover cradled me, rocking me all the way to the bed.

We only had a few moments, but that was all it took to seal our devil's pact.

Chapter Twenty-Two
All the World's a Stage/the Overwrought Thespian

Looking back, I should not have been lulled by pre-Christmas spirit invading even the Longhorn, by a false sense of warmth and safety. I had made presents for everyone, even Jake, though my heart wasn't entirely in it. Pillowcases embroidered with their names for the girls, orange-and-clove-spiced tea for Madame. I had nothing to give Zak, save myself, and that I gave generously and he in turn. Nothing seemed imminent— the warmth of the season sidetracked me.

I almost believed the worst had passed over me, like the angel of death did the Israelites, especially after fear of the Pinkerton agents lessened by their apparent nonappearance. Even Pinkertons go home for Christmas, I reasoned, though I had become wary of illustrious clients and was still goosey over my encounter with the oily detective, worriedly absent. Give me an honest cowboy any day.

Then the diversion arrived in Wylder, clanking in on the morning train and lowering my guard even more. The grand event was here.

The actors descended from the train as if they were visiting royalty, with considerable cape-tossing, arm-gesturing, and bow-sweeping to us girls, even while openly sneering at Wylder's main streets. Since we were across from the station, we girls had front row seats to the performance, especially scrutinizing the two actresses gussied up in Eastern clothes and hairdos, with charming little cupcakes perched over one brow, or huge dinnerplates weighted with roses and velvet ribbons.

I took special care dressing myself to please Madame, knotting a bracelet in my hair, which I thought resembled a tiara, for my own performance. As I left, I looked back in. The lamp was low, bedcovers temptingly back, pillows plumped. An inviting love bower. *"Come back later,"* I whispered to the red chair.

Plastering on my best come-hither smile, I sashayed, hips swaying, bosom jiggling like cream custard above overflowing cups of my best pink velvet bustier (decorated with satin rosebuds and lace), when Madame bustled up, hissing in my ear, "About time! I could not keep him much longer." I flashed a glance at Big Bertha languishing against a potted fern designed to give the saloon class, while a flashy thespian tried to ignore her, moreover, glancing desperately toward the streets as if he wished to skedaddle.

I kenned I was kept for special, vain that I was, despite Madame's condemnation, as well as Flora, who had her own unspoken delicate appeal. I nodded archly and did my grandest imitation of either a grand duchess or Salome wrapped in veils and musk, gliding over to the actor in question, knuckling his mustache and making a great show of looking broodily about under heavy-lidded eyes.

Dashingly handsome, I think they say in places more sophisticated than Wylder. Jet-black ruffled hair, a cowlick drooping over one eye gazing blue as crystal and just as hard…lips red, skin pale and romantic.

Madame, all aflutter, batted lashes like a fan—the breeze alone would knock you down. She gushed, simpered, and offered her best cordial. He demurred with a wave of a weary hand. She performed a sort of clumsy curtsey and, with a frozen rictus smile, left him to his devices.

I raised a brow, pretending indifference, yet cringed when she approached with his cohort, a skinny, spotted character with a river of red hair surrounding an island of freckled dome—the comedy relief, no doubt, in any play they cared to perform. To my relief, the first actor, shouldering ginger-hair aside, indicated me. "Guess you'll do," was not designed to make me swoon with rapture.

Madame shunted off the redhead thespian to Big Bertha. I saw him swallow hard as she hooked his arm and swept him off his tiny feet, yanking him up to Paradise. I turned, bemused.

"Cranford St. James," he announced, pausing for recognition to overwhelm me. Me, who'd never been to a town bigger than Kansas City. Overdressed in as flamboyant a manner as another traveling troupe breezing through Wylder by providence of the odd August blizzard of 1878 blowing them off-course. They had put on a play called *Taming of the Shrew*, which had a lot of whipping on women's backsides—men loved that part, though womenfolk bridled—and fancy velvet gowns and turbans. The other was a thing called *Hamlet*, with a fellow in tights talking to a skull.

I didn't fancy it.

Cranford was fine-looking in the gaudy manner of riverboat gamblers and drummers of cure-alls but dressed for the stage, not brutal Wyoming winters.

Scarlet satin waistcoat. Mustard brocade gentleman's smoking jacket with a fur collar. Muskrat, I believe. Tight buff breeches ending in shiny, high-heeled, Spanish-style boots with silver toes and heels affording him two more inches of height, hair pomaded with attar of roses—just on their way to the compost heap.

I wrinkled my nose, but had smelt worse, as he bent to devour my hand with kisses designed to make me faint away. He wasn't near as flash—or as flush as Madame hoped—the closer he neared, his clothes showed signs of hard travel with discreet darning and rubbed-out sauce spots. But at least he smelt clean, with a natty trimmed mustache shaped to enhance cupid bow lips. His eyes were dark-lined as if he, too, had a dab hand with burnt cork, on or off stage. Pink smooth hands with a hint of green grease paint under one nail matched a smudge over one eye.

He indicated, waving a limp wrist, that he endeavored to finish his rum before ascending. I tossed back one too and waggled my rear like a good little doxy all the way up, nevertheless fuming like an extinguished candle at his careless attitude.

He posed at the door as I entered ahead, one arm braced on the lintel, smoldering looks at me and pursing lips until I acknowledged him, then swept in, tossing his feathered hat on the red chair.

I winced.

The hat remained un-flattened.

I glanced furtively about—no depression on the bed, pillows, carpet…no cigarillo smoke, or brimstone. *He has to be here.* I kenned him. Zak would not miss this juicy morsel of entertainment!

The actor gave a swirl to the short cape slung

behind him, and it landed on my best oil lamp with the glass Tiffany shade. I yanked it off before it began smoking. Then, Cranford stalked me with a burning gaze intended to disable me with lust.

I noted he was not youthlike, either, as he might appear onstage. Powder tinted pinkish-ocher coated lines radiating from his eyes. His brows seemed both plucked and blackened. *I must ask him where he obtained that powder.* While taking stock, of a sudden Cranford leapt, sweeping a hand in dramatic gesture and near knocking off my bedside clock, the other hand wrapped snakelike about my waist. He crushed me to his concave chest in one abrupt clamp, bending me over his arm, looking limpidly into my eyes.

Nose to nose, with a gaze like melting blue ice, the actor pursed ruby lips and intoned with organ-like vibrations, " *'Did my heart love, foreswear it now? Foreswear it sight, for I never saw true beauty, till this night!'* "

Cranford looked heavenward—well, to the ceiling—and taking a breath, clamped me closer. When I appeared to swoon…actually aided by the tight bustier, he bellowed sonorously,

" *'Ah! Love is a smoke made with the perfume of sighs… Being purged, a fire sparkling in lovers' eyes; Being vexed, a sea nourished with loving tears. What is it else? A madness most discreet, A choking gall, and a preserving sweet…'* "

As I struggled up, to my giddy delight—giddy because I had little to laugh about lately—a familiar roar of laughter tolled like an unhallowed bell, rattling picture frames, subsiding into strangling fits. "*Hoho hohohoh, hahahaheh…where'd you pick* up this *fine specimen? In a ladies' dress shop? A hen party? Haha-HAH...!"*

"No!" I hissed helplessly. Only a wall of teeth held back my own wave of giggles.

My thespian dropped me as if I were a burning bush. He looked at sea for an instant, then... "You dare to laugh at—*me*? Do you not recognize who I *am*?"

"But I—"

"How *privileged* you are to meet my *person* in the flesh—and in *private*! And you *laugh*!"

I detected helpless chuckles from behind him.

The actor struck an injured pose, blue eyes icing over. *Should I respond, or throw cold water on him before he sets his ego on fire?*

"I do not grant audiences to just *any*one! You *trull*! Demeaning little *slut*! You *gutter*snipe!"

"*Really, sir! She is not a guttersnipe, merely a hoyden,*" offered my phantom pest.

In such high dudgeon, the actor did not appear to hear Zachariah's protest. "My public, my *fans,* my *adherents, constantly* swamp me with entreaties to *engage* with them, and I—*I,* seeking an evening of *privacy* and delights of the *flesh,* so *rarely* granted, given my *notoriety*..."

"But sir! I did not laugh at you, sir!"

His artificial brows rose to his low hairline as if a homeless cur had suddenly taken to speech. I suspected his wig had slipped, too. "How *dare* you contradict—*me*!"

The chuckles renewed, from all over the room now, as if my phantom, following the actor, tweaked him, for at times Cranford smoothed his hair as if a fly had landed, or plucked at his sleeve, or he strived to reach his back, until he resembled a man with St. Vitus Dance.

"Stop it!"

"*I cannot,*" came the disembodied voice. "*I—'m trying! Truly! HEEEHEEEHEE—HA-HA-HAH-HO-HO HO-HO. He is just so…so damnably—!*"

"Oh, for Pete's sakes! Don't *do* anything!" I feared what would happen. *Oh, no!* Out of the corner of my eye, I caught the peacock's cape spinning, and plumes from Cranford's hat floating like plucked chicken feathers. I winced. Cranford's wig tilted over one eye. He grabbed at it. His voice changed timbre to guttural slang. "Who's that? See 'ere, you *slag*," he snarled. "Where's 'e hidden? I don' know wha' tricks're up yer sleeve, but…?"

I covertly darted looks.

A disturbance in the corner—the chair shifted by itself. I raced to sit on it. My snow globe rose from my dresser, floating toward the actor while his back was turned. I dashed after it, slamming it down as Cranford checked behind pictures on the wall.

"Come, sir! Perhaps it's ghosts," I trilled hysterically. "This room is haunted, they say, by a doddering sort of toothless old spirit. He's harmless."

Cranford cast a scathing glance. "A *ghost*? Really? This is not a *play*, my dear deluded *frump*!"

Frump? I'll show you frump! I began unlacing my bustier, shimmying out of voluminous skirts to distract him, until I stood, clad in knickers and a half-bosomed camisole guaranteed to sidetrack the most weak-blooded male, wanting him satisfied and gone before something very bad happened.

He cast another withering look, as if to say, *Can't

fool me! and flung out an arm. "All is not well! *Something* is rotten in Denmark," he intoned. "There *is* someone in here, some *varlet!* Some spineless *knave* in this very *room*. Come out, I say, cowardly *cur*! Show yourself, you puling blaggart! I am on to you *and* your strumpet!" Leaping histrionically past me, the actor ran hands along the wallpaper. "*Nothing*," he snarled. "Yet I vow you 'ave secret spy holes 'ere, you low-rent baggage!"

Oddly, he studied me with admiration.

"Take pictures an' hawk 'em, or for blackmail, do ya? You clever *wench*!" He leered, giving me a broad wink.

"None of that, sir! No one is taking photographs. For one thing, you'd see a smoke-flash." That was desperation speaking. I had no such kennage of taking daguerreotypes.

That stoppered him, as he mused it over, then smirked. "We'll see what calumny I can ferret out," and showily checked behind the chair in increasing frustration and embarrassment.

Abruptly his attitude changed.

Half-closed eyes flared to smoldering embers in imitation of seduction, his passion rehearsed, designed to make a female, *any* female collapse in a puddle of helplessness. Again, it did not work.

"All right, let's get on with it," he sneered.

He went about taking me, as if mining coal or thrashing wheat. Beyond the actor's grunts and groans, snuffling like a pig in my bosom, the room became leaden with brooding silence.

"*Don't!*" I whispered to the room.

"Too late for *that*!" My client smirked.

And indeed, it was.

At the door, he paused. Re-entering, to my dismay, Cranford stroked his chin thoughtfully, circling my room. He cocked a pose. "Those racy pictures? You fetch a pretty copper for them, I'd venture? I might…" He was all business now. "I might be interested in a little proposition. I 'ave a friend. Actually, another actor. Not as first-class as I, naturally. However, he might be well able to imitate a bit of lusty rumpy-pumpy for the camera's eye. In fact, I hear they make pictures that actually move! Imagine!" He became lost in the erotic possibilities of pictures that moved.

I too had heard of such a far-fetched notion. Moving pictures, indeed!

"A redheaded fellow. You might have met him…" He maundered on.

In actual fact, I had. The pimply-faced, slat-thin thespian being pummeled by Big Bertha.

"Just leave, you—you overcooked *ham*!" I chucked my bed pillow at him. Might as well have tossed mushmellows.

"Huhn!" He sneered. "Don't want to share the coin, eh? We'll see about that! Or is that frump of a harpy down below not in on your little con?"

With that he swept out with a final *You'll regret this, now* look.

Hot tears wet the pillow. I hated him. What next? Any hint of such disgusting enterprises tarnishing Madame's reputation would finish me at last.

I heard soft chuckles. "No!" I shouted to the room. "I do not wish to see you either!"

****

Over breakfast, Madame seemed miffed over their

hasty departures. "Thespians have no more manners than common ruffians," she announced. "No wonder they have soiled reputations." She did not blame us explicitly, but, tight-lipped, doled dollops of cold oatmeal in place of ham and eggs, showing her temperament as nothing else.

Yet I could not miss Madame Solange's stern looks. If bullets, I'd be shot. She veered behind the woodpile and stood tapping her toe as I headed for the washing shed.

"Oh, no, you don't, Miss Creighton!"

"Ohhhhh!" I let out a long breath. She meant business when she used my old name. I'd left Beulah Anne Creighton a long way back when jumping off the empty mail train here in Wylder, hungry and at the end of the line, at least for me.

I stuck out my chin. "Why, Madame, just on my way to do some washing up. I could do yours…"

"Enough. I know all about your sweet ways. What was all that ruckus? The girls won't tell me. Their lips are buttoned tight as their twats. But you will! What was all that to-do? If I hadn't been…" Her sallow cheeks pinked, "*conferring* with Levi…*Mr. Gruenvald,* I would have heard for myself!"

I knew all about her 'conferring' with Mr. Gruenvald. "Sure I don't ken what you are talking about."

"Butter wouldn't melt in your mouth. I've heard the gossip. I *know* you are entertaining out of *my* pocket and sneaking in clients. How they get past me is what I want to get to the bottom of." She narrowed her eyes. "Do they shinny up over the roof, like prowling tomcats? And that actor left like a scalded cat! What did you do to him?"

My mirth was so genuine, she reddened. Grinding her teeth, she huffed off, then swiveled and stuck her finger in my face. "This is a warning. There's *something* going on. I can smell it like cheap perfume covering sweat! Any more shenanigans, *you* are plying your talents down by the stockyards. Won't smell so sweet then!"

That chilled me. She hadn't heard about the poster, my wanted state, or the salesman.

Yet.

Little Mae still hankered over the best room, and the saucy witch, Mirabella, breathed down my neck and eyed my wardrobe. It wasn't an even race. She was juicy like a crisp apple. No more than seventeen. I detected my first wrinkle, no bigger than an eyelash on the bridge of my nose, but it foretold my future, written in spider lines, and I determined to paste a postage stamp on the offending spot whilst I slept.

I must keep out of sight a few days. I *must* be on my best behavior!

The sight of a new Pinkerton took on a whole new meaning.

****

"*I'm bored to—well, death,*" came the dry reply. "*What else? When your clients afford me my only amusement.*" He was endearingly sulky, yet I was in no mood. I breathed deep, trying to rein in my vile temper. "You don't understand…" I began. I—*we* are in danger!"

"*Accepted, wicked Circe, witch of Wylder. That is why I wanted to pound some sense into your—*"

He sounded too much like the despicable actor.

"Talk to me then." I glanced at my cherub clock he so disparaged. "I have a few minutes."

"*Hah! Next to eternity? But continue. What shall we speak of? Your turn, since you are affording me so little of your time.*"

"You ken very well. That mischief you pulled on that poor actor could get me tossed out with my portmanteau and a nickel's worth of pay," I tried lightly.

"*I wish I did not need to live through you. I wish I lived with you.*"

His melancholy voice and then his shape shimmered by the bay windows as Zachariah moodily studied the streets. Tonight, I noted, he wore the tight leather gaucho-style trousers, with silver medallions down the seam, encasing neat buttocks and muscular thighs as second skin. That was all. Bare chested. Wide shoulders. A strapping back with the deep cleft of spine dipping below his low-slung waistband. One ear sported a gold hoop. A thick, shining, tarry plait hung below his shoulders.

I yearned to stand behind him and run my fingers down his satiny bronze skin. To feel him as he turned and pressed me to him, hip to hip, mouth to mouth.

"I must go now," is all I said, not trusting myself.

As I was leaving, I felt a touch. My hand fled to the side of my head and encountered silky petals. I smelled the wild lavender iris tucked behind my ear. Long grown used to his legerdemain, I refused to wonder where he'd plucked wild irises in the icy hand of winter. The flower shifted higher, with a glimpse of ghostly fingers tucking it in more firmly.

"*Yes, much better.*" I heard the low murmur. "*Adds*

perfection to one already lovely, though rough with her cat's tongue." My phantom tempted me like a serpent with a poison apple.

There he was when I returned with the blacksmith's youngest son in tow, the handsome bastard dwarfing my poor fireplace mantel, where he stood garbed in dusty, hard-ridden Levi's this time; grime obliterating any colors, sweat stains under the arms, boots scuffed and down-trodden. I was flustered. Flame flickered orange through him. The clefts in his jaw winked as he polished a long-handled pistol and rolled his eyes at my latest client.

"What, pray tell, does that represent?" I hissed in passing, indicating his garb.

He looked down unsurprised. "*A chapter in my book of tattered pages, and one I will not share at present whilst you are in this mood.*" I swatted him away. When I glanced back, Zachariah had vanished.

"Probably up the chimney," I muttered.

After my young charge left, with worshipful eyes and vowing he wanted to make an honest woman of me and marry me anyway, even if I was a soiled dove, "just like the pastor sez," I stabbed at my pot of carmine, dabbing roses on newly sallow cheeks until they bloomed rather too much, and I resembled a painted doll. I rubbed most off and desperately dusted the smudge under my eyes with the crushed pearl powder saved for special occasions.

I savagely wiped more smudges, feeling Mirabella's breath ever stronger on my neck.

****

He came to me that night.

I questioned nothing, yet by a warm stir of air, a

velvety smoothness to the dark, I kenned he was beside me. His hand on my breast, then his lips. The hunger was on both sides; my appetite whetted by repentance, his by what forces of denials I could not fathom, as I was pleasantly weary from my evening's exertions, which had left me unfulfilled. Zachariah entered me as in a dream, but nevertheless I was yearning for release from accumulated, unrequited cravings.

"What was it you wanted to tell me?" I murmured later.

"*Almost light, little one. I am selfish, wanting more of you than reasonable.*"

"I am quite awake now," I demanded.

He gazed at my canopy. "*Not sure what Heaven allows. Maybe part of Hell is to let one wander earthly pleasure without partaking. After the other evening. Our dance?*" His eyes glowed like Saint Elmo's Fire, always a bit off-putting. "*I found I could venture almost at will. Well, not quite—but...*"

My heart stuttered.

"*I sat in on the gambling and fooled with the cards.*" His grin was wicked. "*Made a fortune for some clodhopping farmer from Wisconsin who'd lost his ranch stake after a tinhorn hustler robbed him blind.*"

I had heard tell of the phenomenal luck of a certain young greenhorn from the East.

He chuckled. "*He had to fight off a few to reclaim it. He and his wife have the prettiest little spread in all Wylder now, I expect.*"

"So now you can leave?" My heart squeezed to a cold knot.

"*Not sure, little one. A cold wind is coming. It is not me that must leave...*"

"It is winter. Of course it is cold."

"*Not that sort. A…warning. Danger is close. Don't ask how I ken this. I feel it creeping up like stinking swamp mist.*"

"What are you? A gypsy now?" I kissed him to keep him from talking. He rolled me over, scrutinizing with his arresting eyes.

"*Leave. Take the money. Take it! You damned fool, if nothing good ever came of my wickedness, this will make up for some of it. You can't deny me.*"

I felt unreasoning anger boil up. I had much to worry me, and he wanted me to search for buried loot in some godforsaken wilderness. I had no clue where he did "bury" it. Could be under Longhorn's crawlspace or stuffed between attic joists, for all I was aware.

We both turned to the door, him before me, at a vibration only he could detect, followed by a flurry of raps, piercing as raven's beaks. I had a sickening foreboding. The door crashed open. Madame barged in. All I took in was her grim death's-head face and the despised yellow poster gripped in her fist waving at me.

"Miss *Creighton*!" *Not Miss Cherry*. "How *dare* you!" Her face blotched with high color; her eyes narrowed to slits. "Don't play the innocent! How *dare* you besmirch my establishment?"

She poked a bony finger in my chest, pushing me back. "Not in the hall, you—you *murderess*," she hissed. "You make mockery of God-fearing folk with a face like an angel and spun-sugar lies. To think I harbored a *viper* at my bosom, a dangerous *fugitive*. We *all* could have been murdered in our beds!" She smashed the poster to her chest. "I shudder to think."

"Who is *that* creature?" I cast aspersions at the

ugly inked face. I backed, mind racing fast as a slog through a swamp. "Aren't you afraid to be alone with me?" I insinuated. *That wasn't smart.*

"The Pinkerton agent showed this to the girls, even Levi. Only *I* saw it for what it was! He nailed it on the wall of the train station."

"Good for you," I said sourly. "But that isn't me."

"Hah! Little Mae broke down when he confronted her with this vile thing. She told them everything. Poor soul was petrified to be next to you!" *Probably.* "Frightened into silence, she was. The Pinkerton told her what would happen if she didn't confess. Lord kens what Bertha told him."

I did. Pig lots, bloody bones, shreds of rusty tweed swam before my face.

I seemed to shrivel inside my dressing gown. If I looked at my face, would I see an old woman or one with a rope about her neck? She saw it too.

"So! It's true. I want you out of here! Gone! Won't have the whole posse parading in, leading you off in cuffs. I'll hold them off that long. I already warned Mae and Bertha. Flora, sweet lamb, is innocent."

I envisaged the sheriff—the manacles, the parade through the Longhorn in ignominy, past Rattlesnake Jake and the girls—my former clients—most of all Zachariah, for the long train ride for my Indiana execution, or perhaps it awaited at the end of a short trial in Wylder. I kenned my phantom, my only friend, could do little to stop the dead-head train rushing me to the end of my personal line.

I jerked my head up as her words penetrated the mist. "What?"

"Now, Miss Creighton!"

"But it is not what you think, Madame!"

She jabbed her finger repeatedly in my chest. "I don't *care* if you are *innocent* as a new born baby *lamb*. I want you *out*. Out, or I *will* hail the sheriff, bedamned with scandal. Hah! It just might heighten the interest of this place."

Instinctively, I kenned she wouldn't. She had old Levi to please. He would not welcome news that he harbored a "murdering doxy" upstairs servicing his drinkers and gamblers, or the sheriff's interest in such a person. Moreover, Solange's aspirations would be sunk in the deepest, driest well.

"What are you waiting for? Christmas?"

My face must have shown a mix of confusion and downright terror. "*Now?* But I can't! If only…you'd…" I despised begging. I wouldn't.

"Of course! More vile fabrications."

Zachariah, where are you? I searched the room frantically over my shoulder.

"Miss Creighton? Are you *listening*? Do I need send Jake to pitch you and your unmentionables out into the street?"

Gritting my teeth, I pleaded, "For the love of God, Madame, please. I have been good for you. If you would spare one minute, I will tell you a story."

Poor choice of words.

"Of that I'm sure. Only truthful word out of your mouth!" The sneer washed her face in ugly blotches. She barged in, yanked at my dresser drawers, and began hurling my things to the floor. "You have nothing to tell that would interest me as much as you could put in a thimble. Mirabella, that sweet girl, is more than ready to take this room." *Poor Little Mae!* I had time to think.

She flung open my wardrobe, slamming it shut as if denying me my lovely gowns.

She whipped round. "A fresh young vivacious gal—not a brooder and sly puss with all your airs, and Lord kens what else went on up here! I will give you an *hour.* I am being *generous.*"

She flounced out, clutching the bit of yellow shame with her.

One hour!

I clutched at her arm, all pretense of pluck and righteousness gone.

"Madame, it is night." I indicated the windows. It was raining. The dreary chill rain of Wyoming winters. "Allow me one night to collect my things and leave at dawn. *Before* dawn!"

Buy time. I have to say goodbye. I must think! Where is he now?

I could not bear it. Tears sprang unheeded, pouring down my face. I sobbed and dropped my forehead on her meager breast. For a wicked flash, I saw Madame relished such ultimate mortification. With a last act of humanity, Madame Solange patted me on my back, looking unsettled at my contrition as I raised my face in a final humiliation.

Thrusting me away, her gaze dropped. She worked her mouth. "Very well," she grated with a voice like dust. "Don't ken why I am being charitable. One night, mind you. Dawn it is! I want to see those bags packed, and the backside of you." Setting her jaw, averting her face, she swept out. Perhaps with tears of her own, or so I would like to believe.

"Oh, Zachariah!" My voice held all the anguish I felt inside. I was lost. There was no place to go. And investigators hot on my trail.

"*How long do you suppose their loyalties will last?*" Zachariah's comments matched my fears like two dirty spoons in a drawer, making it real.

"*Now will you listen to me? Obey me, you stubborn, willful—beautiful...*" His words caught on a barbed wire, tearing his voice to rags. "*—loving...*" His deep breaking cry caught me up in its misery. We clung to each other. It lasted a lifetime of missed opportunities, regrets, heartache, and love.

"*I must let you go. Live long. Live your life. You are so young. A world out there is yet waiting for you. Go now, before it is too late. It is dangerous, from what I have picked up. Why have you not told me all?*" He hesitated, holding me fast in his embracing arms for the last time, kissing my hair, my ears, my mouth, then thrust me rudely from him and sank backward in the mist of time with his arresting eyes glowing to the last.

"*Remember me.*" His voice cracked again. "*Forget me.*"

"Never, Zachariah!" I pounded my chest, shouting into the eddying mist that had swallowed him up. I heard no answer. "You live here!" I pounded my chest again.

There was no answer. I stood staring, witless, into the dusk. Giving myself a shake, I painfully refocused on my dear familiar things, *willing* myself to move.

To take one step. *Away from Zak.*

I must plan for a future that had none.

I laughed bitterly. "Pack? Pack for what? Prison?"

But Zak urged me to live. If even for a few weeks. Perhaps I would yet be with him. "With rope burns on my neck." My better angel lectured me not to be so histrionic. Where was the practical, hardheaded Blossom Cherry? The old Beulah of hated name, who hopped on that freight train hiding in empty travel cars, living on crumbs of leftover picnics and hobos?

I removed my most serviceable dresses—precious few. A travel cloak from the back of the wardrobe, some letters, my faded jewel box, a few daguerreotypes, and my derringer, to keep or toss—I was undecided. Watching the yellow turn to scorch, I burned my copies of the damned poster in the fireplace.

Chapter Twenty-Three
The Spector's Wedding

I stood alone on the veranda roof, watching as a sunset spread a bruise over rooftops and snowy tree-studded peaks. I was too numb to sense the chill, though wind whipped the filmy white nightdress I wore before dressing for the last time. I wanted to feel the prick of winter. I wanted to feel *something* besides pain. My heart beat a ragged tom-tom. Frost plumed from my mouth, blurring the scene. This was the end. I would savor these last hours and pray with all my heart that the room's next occupant treated Zachariah not with fear, or abhorrence, but with the companionship he so needed.

But not the love. Please, not the love.

A lone tear wetted my cheek with chill irritation. I stifled a sob, swiping it away.

I turned back inside to my final packing. I would take my carpetbag to the station and catch the next train east or west. It mattered little.

I started. There stood Zachariah, ghostly pale but solid, framed in the bay window. He stepped through, turning me back to the sky fading lavender to indigo.

I felt hands on my shoulder, warming me somehow, hands slipping down, spanning my waist, drawing me back to him.

"Zachariah." I breathed a plume of frost, arching

my neck so my head rested on his chest.

We both traced the hazy Milky Way necklace against the ebony breast of sky with our twined hands.

I felt his strong fingers separating mine, seeking one out.

I felt cold metal encircling my finger and gently eased down.

I held my hand before me, silhouetted white against the pearl of luminous night clouds. I stared at the wide gold ring. A tiny cabochon ruby winked from the center like a blood drop. It now seemed the only color in the sapphire dusk.

My heart was breaking. My heart bounded with joy.

I whipped my head round with wonder, lips open, eyes questioning.

He bent his dear, rugged, battered face to mine, kissing me deeply. My body flooded with heat. I felt not the cold. I twined arms tight about his neck, making my body one with his.

"*My darling, my dearest one.*" A cry threatened his deep umber voice as he held me, resting his great head against mine.

"*Will you wed me, my dear love?*" I heard the murmur as a vibration through my head.

"Marry!?"

"*Even if you meet some worthless* cabrón *not near good enough for you, I want to be the secret in your heart. The husband who might have been.*" Passion timbred his voice. "*Your lodestone, if ever I am able.*"

"Oh, yes!" I twisted in his arms, clutching him till my bones ached, and kissed him with all the fervor I owned as for the last time, as I kenned it had to be.

"Even if we can never…"

I could not continue. My voice shook with an earthquake of pain.

"*Then let's make this right,*" I heard him say huskily. A whisper.

"With all my heart, but how—"

I felt myself lighten.

My feet slipped off the roof.

For a dizzying spell, I hung suspended in his arms over the street below. Swooping higher, we floated… wafted, *soared!* Wylder, a tiny doll's house display of roofs and snowy roads, chimneys perfuming the night with woodsmoke feathers, corrals with tiny horses in winter coats, mercantiles…the Longhorn distanced now behind me, to the silent church, still green with pine and cedar shingles littering the ground. One brave stained-glass window hauled at great price from San Francisco framed in a place of pride below the cross topping the tiny spire.

As we drifted through the unfinished doorway, a new moon pasted jewels of light through that window, decorating the walls. In place of flowers, the sweet sharp scent of the forest perfumed the interior, in place of song, the whispering, rustling pine needles sighing clear high notes as wind played tunes through the rafters.

We floated down the moonlit aisle to the silent church's tiny nave.

The stained glass played jeweled rainbows over our faces. *But how?* I wanted to ask, then caught the effort it took for him to be here, the struggle in his face and form, as he literally snatched his wavering self back, nailing it in place.

My wispy white nighty wafted in a slight breeze. Zachariah placed a caplet of flowers on my head from the vase of dried Queen Anne's lace decorating the altar, a smile so loving on his rugged face it brought me to tears, yet I cannot weep at my wedding, only tears of gladness. Smiling radiantly back, I fancied a stray moonbeam trailed the aisle as my veil, when I looked behind me.

"I thought you might like this."

I nodded, too full of swirling thoughts to speak. "You?" I asked. His fierce bronze face and blazing, luminescent green eyes said it all.

Then my heart overfilled as I turned to face the altar and noticed wispy forms drifting from the shadows, growing more robust, floating closer as if for invitation. One in particular I saw clearly—a graceful, gravely beautiful woman in a lovely beaded chamois-skin dress reaching her feet, feet clad in doeskin moccasins that I noted did not touch the pine boards. *Kimani.* With a bemused smile on her lips, she gazed with a mother's pride at Zachariah *Tonaioza* Cortez Quinn.

Other shadowy forms appeared as guests at a wedding…some in antique clothes of another century, some in buckskin, some with rough cloth caps and kerchiefs, one in a Union uniform, another with a simple apron over a homespun dress. They hovered around Zachariah and me, giving witness before the rough wooden cross as they surrounded us in a protective circle, rising, falling, wafting, and dimming.

I felt their well wishes, a touch on my cheek from Zachariah's mother like the brush of a rose petal as we took our vows before a fatherly Irish-looking soul, garbed in a cassock, vaguely European. At his right hand, an elderly Shaman, sternly handsome with a regal bearing, nodded his approval, holding his hand and arm aloft as we pledged to each other fealty and love in as holy a ceremony as any, as if we stood in one of the hallowed cathedrals of Europe. I fancied angels as my bridesmaids, with perhaps the devil's minion his best man, sensing a whiff of sulphur.

But Zak gripped my hand, and it was fine.

"*I will never forsake you. I will never let you wander alone in the dark of your soul.*"

I hear the words now.

"*You are the rose I would have picked. The dream I never hoped to own. The sun in my days of darkness and the moon lighting my nights. I will always be your strong arm, your comfort as long as...*" He choked. "*As long as I have breath...and am able.*"

At a nod from the kindly ghostly priest, with my eyes only for Zachariah, I pledged, "You will be my lodestar, my anchor, my safety, my secret love forever. My heart."

We were one.

****

I sat, with my pathetically small amount of baggage about me, on the platform of the Wylder stop, striving to keep in the shadows of bulky freight—wood crates and barrels. The space barely big enough for me and a drummer from Cincinnati who kept ogling, striving to strike up an acquaintance. It was the early train, the one that usually sailed right through unless flagged.

Still kindled by my new estate, no matter how poignant, I was strengthened, though already detecting creepers of melancholy twining my thoughts like poison oak.

I kenned the future might be deadly bleak and each day a battle unless I girded myself. My ferocious look put the drummer off-stride. He about-turned, stalking to the farthest point of the platform and muttering imprecations, I was certain, about the entire unworthy, ungrateful female race.

From the corner of my eyes, I detected a tall, straight-as-an-arrow figure.

I glanced over, resigned.

Another interloper.

My eyes grew to the size of saucers.

I fell lifeless. I could feel myself falling, helpless to save myself until thudding on the rough, splintery platform beside a freight-handling wagon.

I felt lifted. Arms under my back and knees. The drummer looked on from a safe distance. I peered through lashes, afraid of what I might *not* see.

"Zachariah!" I cried.

The drummer looked sourly at us. "Is this *man*," he sneered at Zak's usual mix-match, part-Shoshoni, part-Mexican, part-outlaw garb, "*bothering* you?"

I scrambled up awkwardly, clutching Zak's hand, smiling goofily. I clung to Zak, shaking my head, speechless except for—"No."

"*My darling, I am back. Did you wait long?*" Zachariah's grave face twinkled as he winked.

"Lover's tiff." The drummer sniffed, looking sullen, and stalked off again, muttering something about "female taste in men."

"Too long!" I breathed. "Oh, Zak, what are you— *how* are you—? Can it last? Oh, please! This time?" I touched his face, his chest, holding his arms. I looked over at the Longhorn's menacing presence, expecting to see the actual force of the room clawing to jealously claim him.

"*Don't fuss so! Wifey dear.*" The deep cleft in his jaw winked again. He shrugged. "*Something happened, little one. I felt myself become...*real. *A tug. Something in me—a spirit, or devil, waged a battle to the death ever since our*"—he looked down at me endearingly—"*our wedding.*"

I looked so happy he immediately killed that thought. "*No, my darling. There is little time! The effort it took—I lost, let's say, a few favors. I cannot stay.*"

I drew him around the corner by the baggage, amidst barrels, boxes, trunks, and crates of live chickens, *buck-bucking* away. "You must!" I twisted my hands, fingering my new gold band. "Come with me."

"*Not yet! Not now.*" Frustration pinched his face like a vise. "*Let's not waste time, my dear wife,*" he growled. "*I can't tell if this is... God! How can it be permanent? A miracle I came at all.*" His face rippled with the pain of effort it caused, to be so far from the place where he died. He must feel ripped in twain.

"*Listen to me! You must take the money! I can't draw a map, but this way...*"

He spilled wheat from a one-hundred-pound sack on the trolley, tracing a crude map among the chaff on the splintered boards.

I scattered it with my toe.

"No, Zak." I shook my head, screwing my face in the effort to not cry.

He watched with despair, lifting my chin. "*Think of*

the good it will do. Buy a future I cannot—"

Odd, Dear Reader…

Suddenly reality hit me with the force of a blacksmith's mallet. I was being a stubborn, self-righteous prig. I could do more good with a fortune than let it molder in the ground. I have to say, however, a bit of greed entered in through the devil's doorway as I felt my lips curl up at the corners, in anticipation.

"Wait! I could maybe—*buy* the Longhorn."

He smiled bitterly and shook his head. *"The winds of the gods, yours and mine, blow against us. Your Madame announced last evening—I heard it through the grill—she marries Levi. She is closing down her business."*

I was stunned to stillness. I thought of Flora, Big Bertha, and Little Mae. Even wondered about Mirabella, but she would always land jam side up, I was certain.

Chapter Twenty-Four
The Skeleton Sentry

The moon gleamed off old bones.

Half an enormous, basket-shaped ribcage, polished and yellowed, lay half-sunken in this desolate spot off the trail, rough as it was, ten miles southeast of Wylder as the crow flies. Zak was correct in the distance, although the skeletal remains were concealed beneath scrub invading a gnarled, lightning-blasted cedar, through which wind blew a mournful tune, and hard to spy.

The horse's long skull grinning toothily at me gleamed like old ivory under the yellow moon. Shuddering, I peered close into the night as I dismounted. Too nearby, a pack of coyotes yodeled like organ pipes up and down a chaotic scale. A desolate spot. No one outside of Zachariah had any notion I was here. Anything could happen. I had morbid thoughts of my own bones, bleached, turning yellow, companion to this dead horse. I shivered again.

"Soonest begun, soonest done," I muttered.

Hefting the shovel, I searched the dark, windy wilderness once more. Nothing but scrub casting moon shadows. No red eyes. I fancied, with a gravedigger's mockery, I could see Zachariah quirking his mouth, bemused. *Tree was alive…then, so was I.* I imagined Zak easily dismounting in a graceful fluid way and striding over, toeing the rocky soil by the horse's head. Lord kenned what memories would have been loosed by his dead mount keeping lonely watch over his purloined treasure. "It's here, Zak. It's just as you left it," I whispered.

"Falcon stumbled 'bout a mile back, with a gunshot skinning across his withers," Zak had related. *"Had to bring my friend down at last. I picked out a cedar. Can't miss it. Seemed a noble monument at the time. It's a lone one. No others, at least then..."*

Small comfort, until near the end of ten miles, as I figured, I spied the bent, broken thing sticking up like a crooked finger. The only tree, even though lifeless, among brush after how many years of unforgiving winters. Scraping earth, I kept busy, ignoring the coyotes the best I could. He had knelt, stroking the rough mane and looking to the hills beyond. *"End of the road for both of us,"* he recounted. I shook myself, not from cold. The coyote pack's shrill yipping was closer now. Time to end this foolishment. I dug faster, flinging earth over my shoulder, distress washing my face with cold sweat, seeing again black bullet burns and bloodstains drenching Zak's side, and the suffering that twisted his handsome face.

"How'd you ever make it as far as Wylder, Zak?"

I heard the coyotes howling a dirge. All business now, I plucked a pickax from my mount "borrowed" from the stable, and rammed first the pickax and then the shovel deep beside the bones, grunting, and hearing Zak's instructions. *"Figured poor old Falcon could guard an outlaw's loot as well as any luck charm."* With my shawl wrapped tight against wind keening across frosted brush, I tossed gouts of Wyoming soil while the horse's skull remained sentinel.

I don't ken what I expected.

A chest the size of a steamer trunk? Not if Zak intended me toting it on horseback. My shovel hit a resistance two feet down, feeling rather than hearing a dull *thump*, expecting it to be a dead root. A harsh *rattle-clink* followed the thud, and my shovel sank deeper, more giving. Flinging it aside, I tugged, scraped, and finally hauled two worn, stained saddle bags, straining at rotting straps holding them fast. I worked rusty hasps. One broke like used tinfoil. The other snapped handily. Glitter spilled out, littering the scrubland, winking dully under the wan moon along with rotted boxes and canvas bundles. I panicked, regretting my impulse. *How would I get all this back?*

"Oh, Zak!" I breathed unhappily, sitting on my haunches amid hoar-frosted prickle grass. "You have been a very busy outlaw." I'd expected a few rings, a watch fob or two, and tidy bundles of bank notes in a rusting tin box, easily transportable. I looked askance at my mount. Plenty of reasons for a hanging in Wyoming, not the least being theft of a horse! How would I ever get away with this? It had taken longer to ride out on my uncertain way, and with dawn approaching, the horse would surely be missed. I hadn't thought this out.

I pondered if Zak would have the grace to look discomfited over the excess of ladies' and gents' jewelry—dozens of rings, bracelets, lavaliers, an amethyst necklace, pocket watches, probably ruined, spilling out over frosty weeds and stony soil. I rapidly fingered it, some tumbling back into the hole on more bags of clinking, gleaming wealth after I pried a disintegrating wooden box with the shovel tip.

Palm-sized gold plates gleamed gray. I hauled musty canvas sacks with bank insignias, most I'd never heard of, seeming as sturdy as the day they were stitched. I sucked in a breath as I spied one stamped US Treasury. "In for a penny, in for a pound, Zachariah. That could get you hanged alongside me." At least a prison sentence in some bleak federal penitentiary.

There was nothing for it. I must put all this back. I disbanded bricks of worn Confederate bills tossing them to the wind, where they skittered across prickle grass. A few coyotes stalked after them. My first instinct was to toss it all back into the hole, yet I could hardly bear burying the lovely jewelry and paper money already leathery and dampish, with mold starting to coat the outer stacks. I grabbed the bundles of good notes, the amethyst necklace, and one gold bar. The rest would keep until I could figure out my return.

I looked up at sudden movement, light against dark. Red eyes, I thought I imagined, had manifested into two pairs, until a chorus of eyes and high-pitched *yipping* calls suddenly surrounded me as if they had waited for reinforcements. The coyotes steadily watched, hungrily slavering, drool hanging from chops, licking their muzzles in anticipation, crouched to spring, or slither, shifting between me and my still-living horse, judging distance, making up their wild minds which to tackle, which the danger, as they circled, spreading out on stiff springy legs.

I shoved Zak's and his gang's ill-gotten gains into the rotting bags without taking scrutiny off the waiting beasts for even a hair. Dragged dirt over the hole with my forearm. Just 'cause it was stolen didn't mean I'd turn tail and leave it to the varmints. The last second, I plucked out a pearl brooch the size of a baby's fist to make up for the one Little Mae had relieved me of. Slowly backing, yelling, I made it to the skittery horse, landing on my tummy crossways of the saddle. Time enough to straighten myself as I gave the scared horse a swat. It did not take two swats, and I was fulsome glad it did not bolt and leave me to the coyotes' pleasure.

****

I made good time. Time to catch the early train after successfully returning the horse with a pat on the nose and a bucket of oats. Let the owner wonder. Tried not to think beyond the next stop in whichever direction the train took me.

Zachariah was not on the platform. I kenned it was not to be. The strain of being away from his dying place showed even in the few moments we'd had before. I scrutinized the Longhorn, feeling a lump the size of the pearl brooch. A shadowy figure passed one of the bays, I hugged my knees behind a large bale on the loading dock, feeling very alone indeed.

Suddenly I felt the craving to return, just for a few hours. A last time. Madame need not know. *Zak would be there.*

****

My room was empty. I stood in the middle, waiting, hoping. It was near dawn. Soon I must go. I timidly answered the unidentified knock. In my distraction, I supposed it was Zak, for one frantic second. Just two sharp raps.

There he stood as I swung open the door and found it blocked by a broad black-and-white tweed-clad figure. Derby, handlebar mustache, blocky chin and forehead, the flash of the badge, the hand presumably on the gun belt.

I took it all in, my smile dying on my face like a faded bloom..

"Oh!" Not very original. Just—"Oh!" I kenned my flight was too good to be true. All my fears, hopes, and past was in that fatal "Oh!"

"Yes. I think so," the Pinkerton said enigmatically. "May I come in, or shall I do it here? In the hall, Miss Creighton?"

"Miss Creighton?" I tried. "Sir you must have…"

"Let's not beat the Devil around the stump." He smiled, not meanly. "Not sure the law much cares what you call yourself now, Miss Cherry."

How silly that sounded now. A play on cherry blossom. How childish, I thought.

"Out here?"

He held up an ugly set of manacles. "Wasn't sure it was you, at first."

He pawed out the hated yellow poster with his other hand. He scanned it. "Don't do you justice, does it? Not exactly an oil painting. Still, a good likeness, if you're trained for such. I watched you scurry across from the train station. I've been waiting."

"It was you I saw."

"Hmm? Oh, yes. Me."

"I didn't do anything," I said weakly—then firmer. My back was up. "I am wronged here. I did not do *anything*!"

His sympathy faded as gray eyes changed to silver. "You've been 'among the willows' a long while, Miss Cherry, or should I say, Creighton." With a sick sense, I kenned he meant hiding. On the run. "Might even believe that yourself…may not. However, you will have your day in court."

I kenned even Zak could do no more than delay and confuse. The Pinkerton whipped me about. Weary of running and after my night of digging, I found it useless to struggle. Our wedding seemed a fantasy now. Indeed, I was Miss Creighton once more, feeling the chill metal I had fantasized, the crude welded joints chafing my wrists as he, conferring with his pocket watch, unceremoniously led me downstairs. "Morning train should do it…taking you back to Indiana, where you can stand trial. They may be more sympathetic and not prone to lynching there, though I'm not up on Indiana law."

I watched Little Mae goggling from her room, and Bertha with a dull frown on her face. The thunderous face of Madame Solange in a night dress as we neared the bottom of the steps. "Miss Cherry! How dare you…"

"This is not about you, for once," I snapped. She fell back clutching her throat.

As time crawled like cold molasses, we made it to the Longhorn's swing doors. Pinkerton led me through, holding on to my wrists bound in front, and abruptly halted. I bumped into his back, getting a mouth full of tweed.

He let go.

I waited, head down, my brain spinning like a broken whirligig. Then I heard an irritated grunt.

"Really, ladies!"

I peeked over his shoulder. There stood Little Mae and Big Bertha, arms linked, making a wall of muscle, stoutness and breadth, cat-eyed and indignant, and if you ever witnessed Big Bertha appear indignant, you would ken why my goaler grunted.

They must have gone out the back kitchen door and skirted the Longhorn, to nip here that fast.

"You, madams, are impeding the law."

"We ken that! What I wanta know is why you're a messin' with our friend?"

I bit my lip to keep from crying out. *Oh, Bertha...thank you!* Even if it was a gesture. I thought with sour wryness about the small bit of loot secured in my pocket. Another rope to hang me with.

"Back your wagon up a mite. I don't comprehend what your relationship is with this prisoner, nor do I wish to own that knowledge, but if you don't let me pass, I will have you in the hoosegow, so you can jaw with your friend till the cows come home!" Growing red, he made to go through them, then around them.

Big Bertha folded meaty arms and shoved out her bosom. Mae followed suit. I was smushed between them. "Suits us jes' fine."

Oh, Little Mae!

He sighed, not certain he could take them both on, I calculated. It would only delay the inevitable.

"This female is wanted for foul murder and absconding. Petersen, the victim, was a fine gentleman with a family." He glanced coldly at me. Mysteriously, at the time, he muttered that I was... "a side bet that paid off handsomely." I didn't ponder that then.

"Shoot," Little Mae scorned. "We ken all about that."

"In that case, allow me to do my duty. I don't wish to harm you two *ladies*." He touched his hat and sneered. "But if you don't stop hindering my arrest..."

He lifted his hand to strike Mae.

"Your *duty* is to apprehend murderers, thieving skunks, and card sharks, not her," Mae scorned, blocking his hand with one plump elbow.

He sighed and once more began to bluster past. He got to the boardwalk, harried by both girls, who kept poking and pulling at his suit. He checked his watch. "Tarnation, train's due in two minutes flat!" Bertha swung around him, blocking him once more as they performed a side-to-side dance.

"B'sides, he ain't dead." Bertha had fists on her hips and her double chin out. Even I looked at her, defeated.

He bulled on past in a feint, dragging me with him. The cuffs pinched in the awkwardness of my sideways position, as I crab-crawled along beside him. He halted, whipping me about again.

"*Who* ain't?" His frustration was present in his bull-like stance and blood in the eye. He shook the manacles. "This says he is!"

"But he *ain't*, mister!" Mae this time.

"*Who* ain't?" he bellered. "Who, pray tell, ain't dead? Custer? Judas!"

"*He* ain't!" Bertha poked the Pinkerton's chest. He had to look up at her. "That feller yer all a palavering about. That Petersen rat! He ain't dead."

He groaned. "And how do you ken that? Do enlighten me. Us all!" He waved one hand with a feverish gleam, giving me another shake. My hands were numb.

He narrowed eyes to deadly slits. "That *Petersen*…? What do you ken about it? Were you in on it?"

"Shoot! He ain't dead, I tell ya. I seen them yeller posters! He ain't dead—twice." Big Bertha growled threateningly. "You callin' us liars?"

He studied them equally. "Outta my way, you backwoods hicks! Don't know what con you're playin', but I ain't time for this."

A low animal grumble spread through the early crowd, as the Pinkerton agent barged through the folks of Wylder without caring if he trod toes or thrust people to the ground, shoving me ahead to the rail platform amid the very barrels I hid behind—was it only hours ago?

"Now!" He squinted at all three of us. "You have one minute, by my watch, to tell me *why* Petersen ain't dead."

"Hunh!" Bertha cried, victorious. " 'Cause I seed him crawling outta the pig lot, smelling like a three-day dead skunk in high August! That's why!"

I whipped my head about. "Not—*dead*?"

"Shoot. Thought you knew that, not that I thought yewed care none. Guess it slipped my mind." She winked.

"The pig lots!" Pinkerton held himself together with baling wire. "Okay. Let's get this straight."

And they did. Both telling it between fits of laughter at the telling. Each embroidering the story some, I suspected.

"Hell's bells! That salesman was causing Miss Blossom here all kinds of mischief. I just hauled him out to the hawgs, to cool him off some and scare the be-jeebers outta him. Sputtering mad as a wet hen in a hailstorm! Never seed a man so fearsome mad. Hollering, splashing around in pig shit and muck.

Something about his good suit, and where the Hades is his case, an' he's gonna kill that bitch, *all* the bitches, meaning, you, I 'spect, Blossom. I gave him a kick in the rear as he was tryin' to climb out, and he landed *kerplash*, face first, in… Well, he rolled around in pig muck some, I reckon, 'cause I wouldn't let him out, but he managed to hightail it anyway, afraid they'd make a meal of him." Bertha paused. "Reckon they woulda. All caked in muck, he jumped on the next train out."

"You'd swear?" He rummaged his pocket and dragged out a tintype.

They both nodded at the same time.

" 'Course we swear! What do you think we are?"

The Pinkerton didn't answer to that. He looked deflated. "What the hell?" he muttered. "We'll hear no more of this." His face turned red as he uncuffed me. "I just want to get back to Chicago," he muttered darkly.

I looked at him queerly.

"If it wasn't me, or him…you said—*side bet.*"

He snorted. "Yeah, that's right. You were just a side bet. It's your young dove, miss butter-wouldn't-melt, Flora. Also known as Flossie Broadbent. An embezzler and safe cracker to you."

****

After another trip to a certain lonely dead cedar, I built an enormous log-and-stone ranch house. I like turrets, cupolas, bay windows, gingerbread, and big white columns like the White House in Washington, and broad verandas all around. Other than that, it is pretty simple, with twenty-six rooms, each with a fireplace, an enormous great room, with one on each end, with real indoor plumbing, and a stable for twenty fine horses which I raise on a thousand acres, south of

Wylder, on land a young couple sold me when they decided the West was not for them, and they headed back to the shelter of Massachusetts and wealthy parents.

Much comment was made over the sinful wages of an ex-soiled dove…

****

Zak grew strong enough to meet me. We didn't question *why,* for fear of breaking the chain, the spell, or whatever enchanted turn had caused this to happen. Each dusk we sat, his brawny arm about my shoulders, drinking wild blackberry wine on our wide, pillared veranda, gazing out at empurpled hills, or up at the sky whisking the dusk away with a sweep of the moon.

It was two months, shy a day, before Zachariah made an appearance, an occurrence that lasted only a few moments before his essence was ripped asunder by the pull of the room above the Longhorn. His power to escape the room strengthened with practice and, I would like to say, the supremacy of love and passion, and I think our bond of marriage helped bridge the gap.

I don't speculate. It is enough. I try not to worry that one day he will be gone with no explanation.

In time, with enough affection, Zachariah manifested himself strong enough to venture to town. No worrisome comment was made about the striking, rugged stranger with the quaint clothes, who set up housekeeping with me. Speculation over ranch hands, or lovers from back East, or even renegade soldiers was rife, until they grew used to this able addition to Wylder.

He fools the occasional stranger who tarries for our bounteous suppers, to our hidden delight, with wild tales of his past and the compadres left far behind in some nether world that neither of us wish to dwell upon too long. We take each day as a blessing, each hot-blooded, ecstasy-filled night as a benediction.

Epilogue

Wylder's raw, half-built church mysteriously gained a new bell, with copper intaglios, stamped "Wylder." They had to build a bigger cupola. The bell came clear from some San Francisco foundry and marked our days by sonorous knells harkening Sunday services, fire alarms, and holidays.

Moreover, money was anonymously donated for a school for Wylder's kinder. Previously, classes had been held in the schoolmarm's parlor and front porch.

Zachariah is here most of the time, as I mentioned, solid, warm as any man under the quilts, in the corral breaking our fine imported horses, or fixing fences, and the times he is not here grow ever shorter.

I wish he could make a cradle, but that would be asking for the stars, and tempting fate.

****

Big Bertha ran off with the miniscule ginger-haired actor. They had corresponded all that time. She sent a letter in care of the Longhorn, but I couldn't read where it was from. When I went to fetch it, Madame Solange, now Mrs. Levi Gruenvald and blushingly *enceinte,* as they say in Paris, France, handed it to me. We both read it aloud. They closed down the brothel upstairs as not appropriate for a respectable married lady.

Little Mae is still there, queen of the front boudoir…what she does with it is her business.

Flora. Now Flora was a different skillet of hash.

Seems the Pinkerton was chasing *her* down, not me, at first. I was a bonus. The poster he had shown about lastly? Turns out t'was of her, and they tracked her as far as Wylder. Flora had worked as a private secretary. It seems that's the latest thing in big cities, with females even learning the typewriting machine, and a gadget called a telephone you could hear folks talk on from far away, and shorthand and all, that being in Chicago.

She learned the safe combination in her office, too, embezzling a sizable amount. Never kenned what wind blew her into Wyoming, unless it was an ill wind, or puzzled what she did with the money.

It was "too close to home" as they say.

Flora was carted back to Chicago. We heard through the tom-toms she ended up marrying the boss's son and didn't have to spend a spit in the wind's worth of jail-time and has a fine big house on something called Lake Shore Drive. Imagine that.

****

From time to time, Zachariah and I grow restless, though, and rob Wells Fargo stagecoaches.

They owe me.

Once an outlaw, always an outlaw, I guess.

A simple rancher's life wasn't for me or for Zak, my handsome ghostly lover, and after Wells Fargo stiffed me on my nest egg, I saw no problem with taking back my own, plus interest, from time to time. Though I am getting a reputation as the female *bandido.* Sometimes, I'm pulling off the daring raids on my stony lonesome, whenever Zachariah is feeling fractious and won't show himself.

I even netted an article in *The Gazette*—
   Audacious female outlaw, scourge of the West…
We don't hold up anything or anyone else, though.
At least not widow women.
   Mostly.
   Or trains. Or banks.
   Promise.

Thank you for purchasing
this publication of The Wild Rose Press, Inc.

For questions or more information
contact us at
info@thewildrosepress.com.

The Wild Rose Press, Inc.
www.thewildrosepress.com